PING-PONG
HEART

Books by Martin Limón

Jade Lady Burning
Slicky Boys
Buddha's Money
The Door to Bitterness
The Wandering Ghost
G.I. Bones
Mr. Kill
The Joy Brigade
The Iron Sickle
The Ville Rat
Ping-Pong Heart
The Nine-Tailed Fox

Nightmare Range

PING-PONG
HEART

Martin Limón

Published by
Soho Press, Inc.
853 Broadway
New York, NY 10003

Library of Congress Cataloging-in-Publication Data

Limón, Martin.
Ping-pong heart / Martin Limón.

ISBN 978-1-61695-809-1
eISBN 978-1-61695-714-8

1. Sueño, George (Fictitious character)—Fiction. 2. Bascom, Ernie
(Fictitious character)—Fiction. 3. United States Army Criminal
Investigation Command—Fiction. 4. Americans—Korea—Fiction.
5. Korea (South)—History—1960–1988—Fiction. I. Title.
PS3562.I465 P56 2016 PS3562.I465
DDC 813.54—dc23   2015049369

Interior design by Janine Agro, Soho Press, Inc.

Printed in the United States of America

10 9 8 7 6 5 4 3 2 1

To Gabriel

Major Frederick Manfield Schultz appeared at the 8th Army Provost Marshal's office red-faced and enraged.

"She robbed me," he said.

I took the report, typing patiently as he explained.

"I met her at the UN Club. We started talking, I bought her a drink. Then we went back to her hooch."

"What's her name?" I asked.

"Miss Jo."

"Did you check her VD card?"

"I didn't think to."

"It's a good idea. If she's a freelancer without one, we might have trouble finding her."

This made him even angrier. "She stole my money, dammit. I want it back."

Miss Kim, the statuesque Admin secretary, pulled a tissue from the box in front of her, held it to her nose, rose from her chair, and walked out of the office. We listened as her high heels clicked down the hallway.

My name is George Sueño. I'm an agent for the 8th United States Army Criminal Investigation Division in Seoul, Republic of Korea. Reports of theft were routinely taken at the Yongsan Compound MP Station. But Major Schultz knew Colonel Brace, the Provost Marshal, and had gone to him directly with his complaint. Since he was a field grade officer, it was felt that allowing word of this incident to leak out to the hoi polloi of the Military Police would be detrimental to good order and discipline. So my partner Ernie Bascom and I—CID agents, not MP investigators—were given the job.

Schultz told me that he'd left the UN Club with Miss Jo and they'd walked back to her hooch near the old oak tree behind the Itaewon open-air market. In her room, he handed her fifty dollars' worth of crisp MPC, military payment certificates. She'd taken the bills, helped him off with his clothes and sat him down on the edge of the bed. Then she excused herself to use the outdoor *byonso*.

"I waited and waited," he told me, "until finally I got tired of waiting. So I slid open the door and looked out. Nothing. No light on in the *byonso*. I put on my clothes and went looking for her. She was gone. I pounded on the doors in the neighbors' hooches, but they just pretended not to speak English."

"Maybe they don't," I said.

This made him angry again. Full cheeks flushed red. Even beneath his blond crew cut, freckled skin burned crimson. "They live next door to a GI whore and they don't speak English?"

I shrugged. "So what'd you do?"

He knotted his fists. "I was tempted to tear the place down, rip up her clothes, smash the windows, throw the freaking radio and electric fan out into the mud. But I figured if I did, she might slap a SOFA charge on me."

SOFA. The Status of Forces Agreement between the United States and the Republic of Korea. One of its provisions is to adjudicate claims made by Korean civilians against US military personnel for damages suffered at their hands.

"It was almost midnight curfew," he said, "so I just put on my clothes and left."

"Smart move," I said.

He nodded. "I tell you, though, if I'd gotten my hands on her . . ."

We let the thought trail off.

"Are you on an accompanied tour?" I asked.

Unconsciously, he fondled the gold wedding band on his left hand. "No. The wife's back at Fort Hood." I continued to stare at him. "The kids are in school. We thought it was best not to move them."

I finished my typing, looked up at him and said, "Can you describe Miss Jo?"

He did. But it amounted to the same bargirl description we heard from most GIs: brunette, petite, cute foreign accent. Ernie looked at me and rolled his eyes. I stopped typing and asked Major Schultz to accompany us to the Itaewon Police Station. He agreed, and the three of us walked outside to Ernie's jeep.

Once there, I conferred with the on-duty Desk Sergeant. After a few minutes, he ushered us into a back room, pulled out a huge three-ring binder and plopped it on a wooden table. The book contained information gathered by the Yongsan District Public Health Service and was accompanied with snapshots of every waitress and barmaid and hostess who was authorized to work in the Itaewon nightclub district.

The girls are issued a wallet-sized card and are required to be checked monthly for communicable diseases. If they prove to be disease-free, the card is stamped in red ink. If they're sick, they are locked up in a Health Service Quarantine Center and forced to take whatever drugs the doctor prescribes. GIs call the wallet-sized folds of cardboard "VD cards." In official military training, soldiers are instructed to check that the card is up-to-date before having sexual relations. As you might imagine, few bother.

After the Desk Sergeant left, Major Schultz flipped through a few dozen pages of the book until he found the section marked *UN Club*. He stopped and pointed.

"That's her."

I studied the picture. She wasn't hard to look at. A face that could've belonged to a classic Korean heroine: a perfectly shaped oval with almond eyes and a clear complexion, and framed by straight black hair that fell to narrow shoulders. And maybe it was my imagination, but I thought she looked wistful, slightly ashamed at being photographed for a VD Card but resigned nevertheless to her fate. Next to the photo, written in *hangul*, were her name, date of birth, and National ID card number. I jotted down the info.

Major Schultz rose from his wooden chair. "When do you expect to catch her?"

"If she hasn't left town, it won't take long," I replied.

"It better not."

He turned and stalked out of the police station.

Ernie and I drove back to the CID office. Staff Sergeant Riley, the Admin Non-Commissioned Officer, sat behind a stack of neatly clipped paperwork.

"Where's Miss Kim?" I asked.

"Why?" Riley replied. "She doesn't work for you."

That was him. All charm.

"She seemed shaken up listening to Major Schultz."

Riley shrugged and returned to his paperwork. Ernie ignored our conversation, picked up the morning edition of the *Pacific Stars and Stripes*, sat down, and snapped it open to the sports page. Tissue was still wadded atop Miss Kim's desk and her full cup of green tea had grown cold.

I went to look for her.

I found her sitting on a wooden bench beside a small pagoda containing a bronze statue of the Maitreya Buddha. It had been set up years ago for the use of 8th Army's Korean employees, of which there were hundreds on this compound alone. A small grassy area in front of the shrine was well worn from spirited games of badminton that were held every day during lunch hour.

I sat down next to Miss Kim. "I'm sorry Major Schultz upset you," I told her.

She twisted her handkerchief, rolling pink embroidery around the edges. "It's not him," she said.

"Then what is it?"

She didn't answer. About a year ago, she and Ernie had been an item. She'd taken the relationship seriously. Ernie hadn't. He was tall, about six-foot-one, and had a pointed nose with green eyes that sat behind round-lensed glasses. Why women found him fascinating, I wasn't sure. Maybe it was his complete I-don't-give-a-damn attitude. Ernie'd served two tours in Vietnam, and having survived that, he figured every day was money won in a poker game; he spent them as such, taking any pleasure that came his way. When Miss Kim found out that he had other paramours, she dropped him flat. As far as I knew, she hadn't spoken to him since.

"If it's not Major Schultz that's bothering you," I asked, "then what is it?"

She shook her head, staring at the dirt in front of us. "Cruelty," she said. "So much of it."

I patted her hand. She dabbed her eyes with the handkerchief. I'd known her for well over a year now. I occasionally bought her gifts from the PX: a flower, small bottles of hand lotion, the type of breath mints I knew she liked. I suppose I was trying to make amends for the sins of my investigative partner. When she didn't continue, I said, "There's something else bothering you."

She laughed but stopped abruptly. "You notice things, don't you, Geogie?"

"I try to."

"There is something," she said.

"What?"

"It's nothing, really." She waved her hand in a dismissive gesture. "It's just that when I walk home, after the cannon goes off, somebody keeps staring at me."

Miss Kim was tall and slender and dressed well, which attracted a lot of attention on a compound full of horny GIs.

"Did he do anything?" I asked.

"Not exactly. While I'm heading toward the Main Gate, he follows me. And lately he's been walking up right beside me and when no one else is listening, he says things. Rude things. I ignore him, but he keeps doing it."

"How long has this been going on?"

"Maybe two or three weeks now."

"Describe him to me."

She shook her head vehemently. "No. I don't want trouble."

The Korean War had ended some twenty years ago. Seoul had been completely crushed, and only now was the Korean economy beginning to recover. A job on the American Army compound was considered an excellent employment opportunity, with good pay and job security. Miss Kim was afraid to jeopardize that in any way.

Then she turned on the bench and stared at me. "Don't do anything, Geogie. I can take care of it."

"Has this guy followed you off compound?"

"No. He always stops just before we reach the Pedestrian Exit."

"At Gate Five?" I asked.

"Yes."

"Where there are more people."

She nodded, then reached out and squeezed my hand. "Thank you, though," she said. Then she pointed at her nose. "I will take care of it."

We walked back to the CID office. Before we entered, she stopped and faced me again. "Promise you won't do anything?"

I nodded.

She smiled and trotted up the steps.

Before the cannon went off, Ernie and I found a hiding place amidst a grove of evergreen trees about twenty yards in front of the Pedestrian Exit at Gate Five. While we waited, just to pass the time, I needled him.

"You sure screwed up your chances with Miss Kim," I said.

He shrugged. "There's more fish in the Yellow Sea. Whole boatloads of them."

"Not many like her."

He peeked around his tree, grinning. "You sweet on her, Sueño?"

"Sure, I'm sweet on her. Who wouldn't be? So are you, or you wouldn't be standing here in the cold, waiting to punch the sonofabitch who's been bothering her."

Ernie unwrapped a stick of ginseng gum and popped it in his mouth. "Just out for a little fun," he said.

Which was probably true. Ernie loved conflict. The only time I saw him grin from ear to ear was when people were butting heads or, better yet, swinging big roundhouse rights at one another.

At what the military likes to call close-of-business, exactly seventeen hundred hours—5 P.M. to civilians—the cannon went off. In front of the headquarters building, the Honor Guard was lowering the Korean, American, and United Nations flags. We both looked around. What we were supposed to do, what every soldier was supposed to do, was stand at the position of attention and salute the flag, even if it was so far away you couldn't see it. Which was silly, but that's the Army for you. In the distance, we heard the retreat bugle blasting out of tinny speakers. Since no one was watching, we didn't bother to salute but remained slouched behind the pine trees. In less than a minute, the last notes of the electronic bugle subsided, and down the long row of brick buildings, doors opened and the first early-bird workers trotted down stone steps.

"Free at last," Ernie said.

Within minutes, a line of mostly Korean employees formed at the Pedestrian Exit. We watched down the walkway that led toward the CID office. After three or four more minutes, Miss Kim appeared in the distance. Just two feet behind her right shoulder walked an American in civilian clothes.

"There's the son of a biscuit," Ernie said. Like a hunting dog, his nose was pointed toward his prey.

I studied the guy. He was young, like a GI, but he wore a cheap plaid suit, his face was narrow and pasty and his hair, reddish-blond and curly, was too long for Army regulation.

"Is he a civilian?" Ernie asked.

"Maybe."

To get a better look, Ernie stepped out from behind his tree.

"Don't let her see you," I reminded him.

He waved me off. "Don't worry, Sueño. I got it." He ducked back into hiding.

Miss Kim was walking fast, clutching her handbag; her cloth coat buttoned tightly, her arms crossed in front of her chest. Her head was down, her face grim. The guy stared straight ahead, as if he weren't talking to her directly but his mouth was moving, rapidly. His eyes were wide and glassy.

"He's getting his rocks off," Ernie said.

We were too far away to hear what he was saying, but gauging by Miss Kim's reaction, it wasn't good. The crowd surrounding them was of other Korean workers, and the guy appeared to be speaking softly enough that they couldn't hear what he was saying. Only his intended audience, Miss Kim, was receiving the full benefit of his blather.

Just before crossing the road that led to the Pedestrian Exit, the guy peeled off. As I'd hoped, he headed away from Gate 5, toward Main Post, using the sidewalk that passed the Moyer Recreation Center and the Main PX. Miss Kim disappeared into the flow of employees heading into the single-file line at the Pedestrian Exit.

Ernie smiled broadly. The guy was heading toward us, still mumbling to himself. Ernie reached into his jacket pocket and pulled out a set of brass knuckles.

"All mine," Ernie said, grinning from ear to ear.

"Not out in the open," I said. "Too many eyeballs."

We let the guy walk a few yards past us, and then we both scurried out of the trees and hustled close behind him.

"You drop this?" Ernie said.

The guy stopped and turned, a confused look on his face. "Drop what?"

"This," Ernie said, and stepped close and slammed an uppercut into his gut. Air erupted from his mouth. As he bent over, I grabbed his shoulders and straightened him out, then shoved him toward the shadows among the pine trees. Once safely behind lumber, Ernie slugged him again.

"Let's see some ID," Ernie said.

As the guy continued to grimace and clutch his stomach, I reached into his back pocket and pulled out his wallet. Ernie grabbed it from me and slid out our victim's military identification card, handing it to me. Quickly, I used my notebook to jot down his name, rank, and service number. *Fenton, Wilfred R., Specialist Four.* Next, Ernie handed me the guy's US Forces Korea Weapons Card. I read off the unit. "Five Oh First Military Intelligence Battalion. Headquarters Company."

"The Five Oh Worst," Ernie corrected and slugged the guy again. "Civilian clothes, hippie haircut. What are you, some kind of spook?"

"Counter-intel," the guy said. Counterintelligence.

"Caught any North Korean spies lately?"

"A few."

"Bull." Ernie slugged him again. "All you've caught is the clap."

When he recovered, Specialist Four Fenton pulled himself together enough to ask, "What's this all about?"

"It's about you harassing innocent women," Ernie told him.

"I'm not harassing anyone."

"What'd you just say to that woman you were walking next to?"

"What woman?"

Ernie slugged him again.

Fenton pressed his forearm against his rib. "I didn't say anything to her." Ernie pulled his fist back and Fenton flinched and said, "Nothing bad anyway."

Ernie let loose the punch.

"What the hell do you *want*?" Fenton said.

Ernie straightened him out and turned him toward me. I was six inches taller than him but leaned down close to his face, letting hot breath blast into his eyes. "We want you to stop pestering women who don't want anything to do with you. Maybe that's how you get your kicks, Fenton, but you're through doing it on this compound. No more," I said, pointing my forefinger at his nose. "You got that?"

He turned away.

Ernie shoved him against a tree. "Answer the man."

"I got it," Fenton replied sullenly.

"You better."

Ernie slugged him again, then took Fenton's wallet, turned it upside down, and pulled open the flaps. Calling cards and Military Payment Certificates and photographs fluttered toward the mud. Fenton leaned against a tree, arms folded firmly across his stomach. I tossed his military ID and weapons card into the mud with the rest of his documents.

Before we walked away, Ernie slapped him across the right cheek, gently. As we left, we heard Fenton spitting up something, maybe blood. When we were almost out of earshot he started to curse. Softly at first, then more loudly.

"I'll get you for this," he said.

"Like I'm worried about that, twerp," Ernie muttered.

"I'm with the Five Oh First MI!" Fenton ranted. "We're not called the Five Oh *Worst* for nothing."

Ernie rolled his eyes again. As we rounded the corner, leaving Fenton behind, Ernie waggled his forearms, pretending to shake. "I'm petrified," he said.

"We *never* lose!" Fenton shouted from the distance.

-3-

Black hair cascaded to bare shoulders, partially covering the smooth contours of a face whitened by powder. The voice was husky, inviting; laced, I imagined, with the sweet scent of booze. She made him laugh. Then she leaned in closer and said, "You slicky my ping-pong heart."

In GI slang, "slicky" means to steal.

Ernie and I were hunkered in the shadows of the UN Club in the nightclub district of Itaewon, nursing our beers, peering through swirling clouds of smoke, admiring the line of bull being laid down by this gorgeous woman sitting on a barstool about twenty feet from us. Her mark was a young GI—half looped—with a pocketful of cash from yesterday's end-of-month payday.

The band clanged back to life. Ernie shoved aside his beer and spoke through the din. "The only thing she wants to slicky," he said, "is this guy's wallet."

The guy and the gal were deep in conversation now, their noses almost touching. It was negotiation time; her revealing how much an all-nighter would set him back, him asking how close her place was. She called him Johnny. His hand slipped to her knee. Apparently, they'd come to an agreement. Standing, they both put on their winter coats; she grabbed her spangled handbag, and together they paraded out the front door of the UN Club.

Seeing her face in the glare of the overhead floodlight left no doubt in my mind. The woman was Miss Jo Kyong-ja, whom Major Schultz had identified in the District Health records at the Itaewon Police Station. Johnny was a GI. I could tell from his short haircut and his evident youth, but also, out here in the red light district of Itaewon, there was little else he could be.

The Korean government had designated this area as open to "tourists" only. That is, Korean civilians were not allowed in, unless they worked in one of the bars or nightclubs. I suppose the idea was to protect their morals. Foreigners other than those in the US military were almost nonexistent. The tourism industry was anemic, and the few who did jet into the formerly war-torn country of Korea stayed wisely in downtown Seoul, taking air-conditioned tourist buses to visit the restored palaces and ancient Buddhist temples. Visiting businessmen, other than the Japanese, were still rare, and in either case they stayed in the hotels in Seoul that catered to their specific needs. Besides, it was dangerous down here. Muggings and knife fights weren't uncommon, although both the Korean government and the US military tried to pretend that American GIs would never participate in such naughtiness.

The Koreans catered to the Americans because they were still terrified of the North Korean Communist threat. They'd lost over two million people during the Korean War and were hoping US military would keep them safe from such a thing ever happening again.

After the double doors swung shut, Ernie and I waited about half a heartbeat. Then we followed. Our job was to get a statement from her, and get a statement we would. Outside, business girls lined the road, peering through beaded curtains, cooing for GIs to join them. Neon pulsed. Rock music blared from every bar and nightclub.

Miss Jo Kyong-ja was a shapely woman, wearing high heels with a tight black dress hemmed to about two inches above the knee, covered by an even shorter faux-fur coat. I couldn't see in the dim light, but her flesh must've been goosebumped. Snow from last week's storm still crusted the edges of upturned tile roofs.

"Nice legs," Ernie said.

Johnny was taller than her by about two inches, and once she took off her heels, he'd be taller still. She was about five-four, I figured, maybe -five, and didn't top one-twenty. He would be about one-forty-five. Mentally, I was writing the report I knew I'd have to turn in tomorrow. I pulled my collar up. Not so much to look like a gumshoe, but to keep the frost from biting at my neck.

The joyous couple passed the Lucky Lady Club and were briefly illuminated by flashing red neon. Before my eyes could adjust, they disappeared into a side alley.

"Itaewon Market," Ernie said. "I'll go around the long way."

I nodded and he took off at a jog.

I followed them, away from the brightly lit nightclub district and into the province of night. Brick and cement-block walls lined a narrow pedestrian lane. In the homes behind, single bulbs burned, pots clanged, women pulled dried clothing off laundry lines, old men hacked phlegm. Waste water ran through a narrow channel, blasting my nostrils with the sting of ammonia. I hopped deftly from side to side, crossing the flow.

Around a bend, I spotted Miss Jo and the young GI again, moving faster now, maybe aware that we were following. The pathway twisted and turned and finally let out into an open area surrounding a venerable oak. They passed wooden benches, climbed a flight of stone steps and stopped. Miss Jo pounded on a wooden gate.

"*Na ya!*" she said. It's me.

A few seconds later, a small door in the large wooden gate opened. The two lovers ducked through. Ernie appeared out of a side alley.

"Is this the place Major Schultz described?"

"Yes," I said, double-checking the notepad I carried in my pocket. "He didn't have the exact address, but he said it was just off the circle with the old oak."

"So we have our woman," Ernie said.

"Yep," I replied, staring at the closed gate. "How are we going to get in?"

"Knock," Ernie said.

I shrugged. "That's one way."

We walked to the gate and Ernie slammed his fist onto the top of the splintered surface.

"*Kyongchal!*" he shouted. Police! One of the few Korean words he knew. That and "*Meikju olma-yo?*" How much for a beer?

We heard footsteps and muffled voices behind the gate, but no one came to open it. Ernie pounded again. Doors shut, and the noise faded into silence. He turned to me.

"Hoist," he said.

We'd done this before. I was bigger than Ernie, about three inches taller and easily twenty pounds heavier, so I pulled the hoisting duties. I crouched and cupped my hands in front of my crotch. Ernie stepped up with his right foot, and as he did so, I lifted in one sweeping motion as he reached for the top of the stone wall. Shards of glass were embedded in the mortar, a low-budget security system used all over Seoul. Ernie found a handhold between the razor-like protuberances and I pushed him up higher until his left foot was planted firmly atop the wall. He boosted himself up, rose to his full height and leapt gracefully over the fence. Inside, I heard feet slam on cement, a grunt and then a roll.

The gate creaked open. Slapping dirt off his jacket, Ernie waved me in.

I hesitated a moment, letting my eyes adjust. A flagstone walkway led into an open courtyard. In the center, a rusted iron pump dripped resolutely into a huge plastic pan. A soot-smeared floodlight weakly illuminated a row of earthen kimchi jars along one side of the courtyard. On the other side, an L-shaped wooden porch fronted a half-dozen oil-papered doors.

A couple of the doors rattled and slid open. Faces peered out, sitting or kneeling on vinyl-covered floors. None of them were Miss Jo's. Ernie pointed. The only closed door was the one on the far right. The light was off.

Ernie cocked his head. "*Coitus interruptus*," he said.

He found nothing more enjoyable than breaking and entering, especially if he might catch someone in a partial state of undress. We stepped up on the porch. Ernie grabbed a handhold and ripped the door open.

As Ernie peered in, the young GI Miss Jo called Johnny leapt out of the dark. He was wielding a short-bladed knife, and before Ernie could react, he'd grabbed Ernie by the back of the neck and shoved the blade point at his throat. Ernie held his hands out to his side and froze.

The GI was sweating, nostrils flared. "Why are you *following* me?" he shouted.

Ernie didn't speak.

"Easy, Johnny," I told him. "We're not following you." I

suddenly wished I'd brought my .45. But I seldom checked out a weapon from the arms room, mainly because I didn't want to be tempted to use it. Better to use my wits to solve problems than take the easy way out and settle every dispute with a spray of hot lead. Less paperwork, too.

I cleared my throat and continued. "This has nothing to do with you, Johnny. It's all about the young lady."

Johnny glared at Ernie, then turned and caught a glimpse of me. I stood with my hands out to my side, showing him, I hoped, that he was in no danger. He pressed the tip of the blade a little harder into Ernie's skin. A red drop formed and a miniscule trickle of blood started to flow.

"Easy, pal," I told him. "No need to do something you'll regret."

"This isn't about the motor pool?" Johnny asked.

"No," I replied. "Nothing about the motor pool. We just want to talk to the young lady. Ask her a few questions."

A lot of pilfering went on at the 21st Transportation Company (Car) motor pool, also known as "Twenty-One T Car." GIs sold gasoline to illegal Korean vendors, cases of motor oil disappeared, tires rolled their way into resale warehouses; occasionally, entire vehicles went missing. But we weren't here to fix that.

An interior bulb switched on and Miss Jo Kyong-ja stepped out from her hooch. She was still fully clothed. Instead of berating Johnny for holding a knife to Ernie's neck, she turned toward me.

"Whatsamatta you!" she shrieked. "No have education?"

I flashed my badge. "CID," I said. "We have a few questions for you. And you, Johnny, will need to put that knife down."

"Will I be able to leave?"

"Yes. We don't have a beef with you, but put down the knife. *Now.*"

Johnny glanced back and forth between Ernie and me. I held the badge out toward him and took a step forward so he could see it more easily. As he studied it, Ernie made his move. With one deft motion, he twisted his entire body, pulling his neck away from the knife, and simultaneously snapped a vicious left hook into Johnny's ribs. Hot breath and saliva exploded from Johnny's mouth as Ernie grabbed the young soldier by his collar. Then he flung him around in a broad circle and slammed him up against the dirty stone wall.

The knife clattered on flagstone.

Ernie held him, pushing him hard up against the exterior wall, his breath coming fast.

"You said I could *leave*," Johnny shrieked.

"Oh, yeah," Ernie replied. "You can leave." He slapped Johnny once, twice, hard across the back of his head and then he held out his open palm.

"The blade," he said.

Ernie loosened his grip just enough to allow Johnny to bend down and pick it up, pausing just a second to give Johnny a chance to use it again, if he dared. He didn't. Ernie snatched the knife out of his hand, then slapped Johnny a couple of more times. He stepped back and tilted the open blade on the ground against a brick. Then he stomped on it. The metal snapped. Leaving it there, Ernie returned to Johnny.

He snarled, "You run your sorry ass back to Twenty-One T Car, and don't let me see you out here in the village again. Ever! You got that? Itaewon is off limits to you."

"On whose authority?" Johnny asked.

"On *my* authority," Ernie replied, jamming his thumb into his chest.

Johnny studied him for a minute, turned his head away and nodded. Then he stood up and straightened his jacket. As if he couldn't resist the temptation, Ernie slapped him again. Johnny grabbed the side of his face and, with a resentful pout, walked toward the gate, keeping his eye on Ernie. Ernie hopped forward and planted a roundhouse kick on Johnny's butt. Ernie shouted, "Move!"

Johnny did, hustling toward the gate and ducking quickly out the front door.

Miss Jo groaned.

Ernie dabbed at the blood on his neck, stared at his moist fingertips for a moment, and then wiped the gore on the side of his blue jeans. He repeated the process a couple of times until the tiny cut was pretty well stanched. Then he reached in his pocket and pulled out a fresh stick of ginseng gum. Looking completely relaxed, he took a seat on the porch.

I turned to Miss Jo. "Can we go in?" I asked, nodding toward her hooch.

"Hell no. You takey my money go, now you wanna come in my hooch? Never *hachi*." Slang for never happen.

I stood in front of the three-foot-wide porch; she stood resolutely in her doorway, arms crossed.

"Last night," I said, "you brought a GI here."

She rolled her eyes. "*Him*."

"Yes, him. He says you took his money. Fifty dollars."

"Took his *money*? You *dingy dingy*?" She twirled her forefinger in a circle around her ear. "He pay me money, I do for him. Supposed to."

"What'd you do for him?" Ernie asked.

She placed her right hand on her waist and canted her hip. "What you think I do, GI?"

"He says you took his money and ran away."

"He tell you that? Never *hachi*. I do anything for him. But he got, how you say, *gochangi nasso-yo*."

"Broken."

"Yeah. Broken. His *jaji* no work. It broken."

Jaji refers to an infant's penis. She wasn't being too generous to Major Schultz.

"So it wouldn't work," Ernie said, enjoying himself now. "What happened then?"

"He *taaksan* angry. Say *I* do something wrong." She pointed at her nose. "But I no do nothing wrong. It don't work, that his problem. Not mine. So he say he want his

money back. I say 'never *hachi*.' He *taaksan kullasso-yo*."
Very angry.

"Did he hit you?" I asked.

"No. But he break this."

She stepped back into the hooch, rummaged in a plastic wardrobe, and returned with a radio. It was smashed beyond repair.

"So you kept his money," I said, "and he broke your radio."

Miss Jo nodded grimly.

I asked her to write out a statement.

"In English?" she asked, surprised.

"No, in Korean."

"You can read?"

I nodded. "I can read. Write carefully, though."

She hesitated.

"If you don't," I told her, "we'll take you to the Itaewon Police Station. You can write it there."

Most Koreans steered resolutely away from any contact with the Korean National Police. They were an efficient organization, paramilitary, with the mission of not only stopping crime but also protecting the country from North Korean Communist infiltrators. Things were tough in Korea economically, so it wasn't unusual for a KNP officer to take money on the side. But if you didn't have money to give, heaven help you.

Miss Jo found a piece of paper and a pen and sat down

on the floor to write. When she was done, she handed it to me and I made sure it was signed and dated. I asked her a few more questions, challenging her story, but she stuck with the jaded, simple narrative she'd originally given. I wrote the follow-up questions down, and one by one she wrote her answers. When we were done, I had her sign and date the statement a final time.

As we were about to leave, she said, "What about Johnny?"

"What about him?" I asked.

"He gone. How I pay rent?"

Ernie and I glanced at one another and shrugged. As we walked across the courtyard, she called after us.

"You have money," she said. "You have food. Some people no have. You take Johnny away, how I pay rent?"

I turned. Her face looked small, sad, almost regretful. I guess I could've walked back and handed her some money, but that isn't what a cop is supposed to do. Besides, Ernie was watching, and in the Army, an act of kindness is seen as something to be mocked, not applauded. Instead of doing what I wanted to do, I turned and the two of us crouched through the small door in the gate.

On our way back to the jeep, we didn't talk.

-4-

The next morning in the Office of the 8th United States Army Provost Marshal, Colonel Brace asked me, "Who translated this?"

"I did, sir."

"Did Miss Kim check it?"

"Yes. She made a couple of changes." She hadn't, but I wanted to make sure she received credit.

Colonel Brace nodded and placed the statement on his desk. "That'll be all."

In the Admin Office, Ernie sat in front of Staff Sergeant Riley's desk reading this morning's *Pacific Stars and Stripes*.

"How'd it go?" he asked.

"He's not happy."

"How could he be? A field grade officer lying to him, sending his agents on a wild goose chase. You'd think he'd show the Provost Marshal of the Eighth United States Army a little more respect."

"How come you never show him any respect?" I asked.

"I work for him," Ernie replied. "That's different."

Staff Sergeant Riley stuck a pencil behind his ear and leaned forward. "Maybe you two ought to get off your butts, move out smartly, and make your way over to the commissary and start doing your job."

The words came out as a growl. Even though he had the physique of Tweety Bird in khaki, Sergeant Riley always tried to sound like he was the toughest guy south of the Demilitarized Zone. Still, he was a hard worker. A two-foot-high pile of reports teetered on one side of his desk, completed memos stacked on the other.

"We worked late last night," Ernie told him, "until almost curfew. Don't we get any consideration for that?"

"A soldier's on duty twenty-four hours a day," Riley replied.

"Unless you're not," Ernie said.

"What's that supposed to mean?"

"It means that some guys have cushy office jobs and don't have to go running around Itaewon at night until all hours."

Riley puffed out his chest, but his uniform still hung off him like a starched shirt on a hanger. "I work overtime here."

"You work overtime all right. You and your bottle of Old Overwart."

"That's Overholt!" Riley said. "Premium rye."

"The cheapest rotgut in the Class VI store."

"At least I don't drink soju."

Miss Kim snatched another tissue from the box in front of her, stood, and sashayed out the door. As she left, we all watched her shapely posterior. When she was out of sight, I said, "There you go. You two have upset her again."

Riley grumbled. Ernie snapped the newspaper and pretended to be reading. The intercom buzzed. Riley pressed a button and said, "Sir."

"Contact Major Schultz. I want him here in my office immediately if not sooner."

"Yes, sir." Riley buzzed off.

As he was dialing, Ernie and I glanced at one another. He slipped the newspaper into his jacket pocket and we walked out of the building to the jeep.

Attempting to obstruct the illicit flow of duty-free goods from the PX and commissary was a fetish within the command structure of the 8th United States Army. Groceries, clothing, stereo equipment and American consumer goods of all kinds were shipped to Korea at US taxpayer expense for exclusive use by servicemen and their dependents. However, there was an acute demand for these items in the Korean economy. Twenty years ago, at the end of the Korean War, the country's industrial capacity had been totally destroyed. Even now it was still recovering, and exotic items like freeze-dried coffee, granulated sugar, imported bananas and jars of maraschino cherries still commanded a high price on the black market. GIs could buy a cartload of groceries at the commissary and sell them to Korean black market honchos for twice what they paid for them. Certain items, like Johnny Walker Black Scotch and Kent cigarettes, had an even bigger markup. Under the Status of Forces Agreement, 8th Army is tasked with stopping this illegal flow of goods. The rationale was that if fledgling Korean industries had to compete with a flood of cheap US consumables, they'd never get off the ground.

The real reason 8th Army was so obsessed with the black market was pure and simple: racism. Most of the purchasers of these goods were the Korean wives of American GIs—derisively called *yobo*s. They flooded both the PX and the commissary, especially after payday, and made it hard for "real Americans" to shop. Also, most of these Korean women were married to enlisted men, not higher-ranking officers. So race *and* class came into the disdain with which the command treated them.

Our main job, more important than investigating murder, mayhem, robbery, and rape, was to arrest as many *yobo*s as possible for trafficking on the black market.

"Tools of the power structure," Ernie said.

"That's us," I replied.

We were sitting in his jeep, parked in the last row of the lot in front of the Yongsan Commissary, watching *yobo*s exit with cartload after cartload of duty-free US goods.

"Who should we bust?" he asked me.

"Take your pick."

"Riley said we had to make at least four arrests today."

"Four? He can forget it. Give 'em two and they get spoiled."

"So what excuse do we use for just making one?"

"I'll think of something."

"That's what I like about you, Sueño. You're creative."

A Korean woman exited the Commissary. She wore a long green dress that clung to the higher-altitude points of her figure. Loose flesh jiggled beneath. Behind her, a Korean man wearing the smock and pinned-on identification badge of a bagger pushed a cart fully laden with groceries. He loaded them into the trunk of a Ford Granada PX taxi and accepted a two-dollar tip from the fancy lady.

"Two bucks," Ernie said. "A high-class *yobo*. I think we should bust her."

The drill was that we'd follow the cab to the ville, where she'd unload part of her haul in front of one of the many black market operations, and when she accepted her payment we'd swoop in for the arrest. We'd done it so many times it had become routine. Usually, we escorted the woman to the MP Station, wrote the report, and waited for her husband to show up and sign for her release. According to Army regulation, a soldier is responsible for the actions of his dependents, even to the point of court-martial if he doesn't control their errant behavior.

"Might as well get it over with," I said.

Ernie reached for the ignition, but stopped when we heard the roar of an engine approaching. A jeep rolled in front of us. The MP in the passenger seat hopped out and walked toward us, hoisting his web belt as he did so.

"You Bascom?" he asked.

"Yeah," Ernie replied, "what's it to ya?"

"Not a goddamn thing, except I have to relay a message."

"So relay."

"Colonel Brace wants to talk to you. ASAP!"

"Okay, Charlie," Ernie said, tossing the MP a mock salute.

"The name's Wilkins," he said, but Ernie had already fired up the jeep and we were rolling away.

"Why do you have to aggravate people like that?" I asked.

"Like what?" Ernie said.

"You treated him like he was your servant."

"I did?"

"Yes, which is maybe why Miss Kim won't talk to you anymore."

"What's she got to do with this?"

"It's your attitude, Ernie. She's a catch. You ought to treat her better."

Ernie seemed puzzled by this. "I treated her as good as I've ever treated any woman."

That, of course, was the crux of the problem.

■ ■ ■

Colonel Brace kept us standing at attention. He shoved the translated statement across his desk.

"He says it's a lie," he told us.

"Of course he says that," Ernie replied. "He's not gonna admit that he can't get it up."

"He can't get it up, *sir*," Colonel Brace replied.

"Yes, sir."

Flustered, Colonel Brace continued. "It's not about not getting it up. Major Schultz still claims that she took off with his money. He wants to make it official. He wants to file a complaint with the KNP Liaison Office."

"He'll be laughed out of Itaewon," Ernie said.

"He'll be laughed out of Itaewon, *sir*." Colonel Brace was reaching the limit of his patience.

"Yes, sir!" Ernie replied again.

"I know," the Colonel said, "it doesn't make sense. This will destroy his reputation."

Yongsan Compound had about 5,000 soldiers. Since it housed 8th Army headquarters, its personnel roster was top-heavy with brass, with almost half of those soldiers being officers. Gossip swirled fast, not only here, but throughout the military community. Even all the way back at Fort Hood, Texas, it seemed almost certain that if Major Schultz pressed this case, his wife would eventually catch wind of it.

We were all thinking the same thing. Major Schultz was having an emotional meltdown. He was destroying his military career, maybe his marriage. I'd seen it before: the vagaries of military life, the separation from home and family, the intense peer pressure not only to conform, but to paradoxically be in constant competition for promotion with the people you lived and worked with. Sometimes it was all too much for even experienced soldiers. Many of them turned to drink, a few to drugs, and occasionally some acted out by breaking the law.

"Can someone talk sense to him, sir?" I said. "Even if he's telling the truth, all he's out is fifty dollars."

"I've tried. But he just left on his way to the Liaison Office. Do you have a contact over there?"

"Yes, sir. Lieutenant Pong, the officer in charge."

"Speak to him. See what can be worked out."

"You want us to quash the report?" I asked.

"Maybe. Let's talk it over with them. See if they have any ideas."

We did. And the KNPs were more than happy to set Major Schultz's report aside and take no action. A few days went by and we expected him to calm down and forget the whole thing. Unfortunately, he didn't.

Three days later, Ernie and I were making our customary rounds of the Itaewon gin joints when Captain Kim, the commander of the Itaewon Police station, sent a runner.

The young cop found us at the bar of the Seven Club and escorted us to the hooch near the old oak tree. Miss Jo had been beaten, and badly. Blood smeared the vinyl floor. The neighbors said they thought they had heard someone speaking English, probably American soldiers. Two attackers, that's the one thing they all agreed on. But the night had been dark and no one had seen them clearly. And as soon as they could, they all shut their doors firmly, hiding from the unwanted presence of the Korean National Police.

Miss Jo had already been taken to the hospital. The deed had almost certainly been done by American GIs. It would be up to us, Agents George Sueño and Ernie Bascom, to find the perps and bring them to justice, or at least what passed for justice in these parts.

-5-

The next morning, Doctor Park was gruff with us. "She pay nothing. Who is going to pay for her?"

He was a middle-aged man with grey streaks running through his hair. His white coat was so fresh, I figured he'd put on a new one just to talk to us.

"She'll be filing a Status of Forces charge," I told him. "She should make enough to pay her hospital bills and more."

"How long will that take?"

I shrugged. "Maybe a couple of months."

He sighed. "And once she gets the money, she'll run away."

I handed him my card. "I'll put you in touch with a SOFA Liaison Officer. Maybe he can arrange for her bill to be paid directly."

He gazed at me skeptically but stuck the card in his shirt pocket. The three of us walked to her ward. Down the long cement corridors, Ernie kept swiveling his head, checking out the nurses.

Miss Jo was in a dimly lit room with about a half-dozen other patients, asleep, a tube down her nose and a hanging bottle feeding liquid into her arm.

"When will we be able to question her?" I asked.

"If you want, we'll wake her now."

I glanced at Ernie. He nodded. "No time like the present."

The doctor called for a nurse and one scurried in. She must've been hovering just outside the door. He barked an order that I couldn't understand, and in less than a minute she came back with a syringe and a bottle of fluid. Doctor Park administered the shot himself. Within seconds, Miss Jo Kyong-ja's eyelids fluttered and then popped fully open.

The doctor checked her pulse once again and left us alone.

I patted her forearm. "Hello, Miss Jo."

She nodded weakly.

"We're here to help you. Tell us who did this to you."

There seemed to be little understanding in her eyes. "Miss Jo, last night, who came to your hooch? Who hit you? Who beat you up?"

Her lips moved and it was as if she were trying to coax long-rusted machinery to crank over. Finally, she spoke. "You know who."

"Was it Major Schultz?"

"Who?"

"Fred Schultz."

"Freddy? Yes, Freddy."

"A big blond guy," I said. "Red face. Fat cheeks."

She nodded. "Yes, him."

"Did he say why he was doing this to you?"

"He wanted me to say not true."

"Not true what?"

"What I told you."

"About him not being able to do it?"

She nodded.

"Did he ask for his money back?"

"He say no, keep money. He just want me change story."

"And you told him no."

"I told him never *hachi*." She gazed around, as if examining the ward for the first time. "How much this cost?"

"I don't know."

"Who pay?"

It wasn't our job to advise her about filing a SOFA charge. Ernie and I glanced at one another.

"He pay," she said. "Right?"

"Maybe," I replied, "if you file a SOFA charge."

She knew what it was. As a business girl in Itaewon, it was one of the first things you learned.

"Okay," she said, satisfied. "I sleep now."

"One more question."

She reopened her eyes.

"Was Freddy alone?"

"No, one other man with him."

"Did he hit you also?"

"He hit. Freddy no hit."

"He didn't?"

"No. Other man do everything."

"Do you know who this other man was?"

She shook her head. "*Molla-yo*," she said. I don't know. "I sleep now."

"But he was a GI?"

She nodded drowsily. "Yeah. Big GI." Her eyes closed and her breathing became slow and steady.

The written report of our findings was signed by both me and Ernie. It created somewhat of a furor at the Provost Marshal's office, since it directly accused a field grade officer of being party to a felonious assault, which the 8th Army honchos weren't happy with.

One of the first consequences, other than placing both me and Ernie firmly back in the doghouse, was that Major Frederick Manfield Schultz withdrew his complaint with the KNPs for the missing fifty dollars. He also denied in writing that he had been in Itaewon or anywhere near the home of Miss Jo Kyong-ja on the night on which she was assaulted. Ernie and I were not allowed to interrogate him. As a field grade officer, Colonel Brace allowed him the courtesy of responding to the accusation through a written statement, vetted by a lawyer from the 8th Army Judge Advocate General's Office. The statement went on to say that Miss Jo had probably accused him of the assault in order to qualify for a larger SOFA settlement. If she had been assaulted by a Korean, as the statement speculated, she would receive nothing. Even if she'd been assaulted by an American GI of lesser rank, it would not be as embarrassing to 8th Army and she would probably end up with a smaller settlement.

Ernie and I reviewed the evidence gathered by the KNPs at the scene, but there wasn't much. Nobody called out the forensic investigative team when an Itaewon business girl was beaten up. In fact, the KNPs had allowed the landlady to clean up the blood while they were still at the scene. She'd also washed the bedsheets and tidied up the room, hoping to sign a new tenant up soon if Miss Jo didn't make rent.

The statements from the neighbors were pretty much uniform. When the commotion started, they'd been frightened and just stayed in their rooms. When asked what exactly they had heard said during the melee, they all said they weren't sure.

So that's where it stood. A classic he-said, she-said case.

Still, Miss Jo might make some money out of it if she hired a Korean attorney familiar with SOFA claims procedures. Keeping the incident quiet, even if it meant paying out a little money, would be 8th Army's main goal.

And that was where it stood for almost three weeks. Miss Jo, I found out later, was released from the hospital two days after we'd seen her. I also found out that she hadn't yet filed a SOFA charge, though she had six months to do so.

Ernie pestered me with questions about my conversations with Miss Kim. I told him what I could—our talks hadn't been confidential—and he kept asking me how I thought she was holding up. It seemed that the sight of Specialist Fenton following her, touching her elbow and whispering rude comments in her ear had upset him more than he'd originally let on. In the office, he started being nice to her: making sure she got a cookie whenever somebody received a care package from the States and walking Riley out into the hallway when he let loose with too much profanity.

She noticed. Of course, she'd always noticed what Ernie did, casting furtive glances at him even during the frostiest days of their busted relationship. The tension in the 8th Army CID Admin Office started to ease. Finally, what I thought was going to happen happened.

Ernie asked Miss Kim out on a date. She hesitated, but Ernie kept after her. Ignoring her unspoken cues, he forced her into giving him an answer. She stood up from her desk, looked him straight in the eye, and turned him down flat. Never, she said, would she go out with him again. Red-faced, she walked out of the Admin Office and marched down to the ladies' room, where she stayed for almost half an hour.

"Will you quit harassing my secretary?" Riley said. "We have work to do in this office."

"Paper," Ernie said. "Nothing but paper." But he disappeared too, for the rest of the afternoon. After the cannon went off at close of business, I wandered casually down the walkway toward Gate Five. I watched Miss Kim leave, along with hundreds of other Korean employees, and then outside I saw someone following her at a distance. This time, it wasn't Specialist Fenton. If it had been, I would've busted his chops. Instead, it was who I'd expected it to be: Agent Ernie Bascom. I wasn't sure if I'd ever seen him so determined, not when it came to a woman anyway.

On the main road outside of Gate Five, Miss Kim climbed onto a packed Seoul metropolitan bus. After about a dozen other customers clambered aboard, Ernie pulled himself up the narrow steps and wedged his way into the teeming mass of humanity. The bus pulled off in a cloud of exhaust.

I met Captain Leah Prevault at Hanil-guan, a restaurant in downtown Seoul that specialized in noodles. It was a large place with two floors and probably more than sixty tables, vastly popular with young Koreans. What Leah and I liked about it was that it was miles from the compound and, other than us, we'd never seen any foreigners there.

"You're getting better with chopsticks," I told her. Only about half the noodles were sliding back into the broth. She dabbed her lips with a folded napkin.

"I bet you say that to all the girls."

"Only you."

We'd been seeing each other since we'd first worked on a case together some six months ago. Captain Prevault was a psychiatrist, and I often picked her brain about the cases I dealt with.

"Major Schultz has everything going for him," I told her. "A wife, a family back at Fort Hood, a solid military career. Even after losing that fifty bucks to that business girl, he should've kept his mouth shut. Instead, he makes it worse."

She'd heard about the beating Miss Jo had received.

Leah Prevault picked up the flat metal spoon and ladled broth into her mouth.

"Male pride," she said. "Can't admit that he can't get it up." She grinned devilishly.

"You think that's it?"

"Yup. And when he can't get it up, he has to blame somebody. Unfortunately, it's usually the woman."

"You've seen cases like this before?"

She nodded her head. "Often."

"You think his wife has heard about it?"

"No question. So has his boss, the J-2."

The J-2 was the staff officer in charge of military intelligence, who reported directly to the Commanding Officer of the 8th United States Army. The "J" stood for joint command—of both the ROK and US—and the "2" was the standard designation for military intelligence operations.

"Has the J-2 relieved him of his regular duties?" I asked.

"That's not what I hear at the O Club." She was referring to the 8th Army Officers Club. "In fact the J-2 is backing him up, keeping him on some important investigation he was in the middle of."

"About what?"

She shrugged. "I'm just a lowly MD. You'll have to talk to the honchos about that."

When we finished our dinner, I took her hand. "Thanks for coming out here with me."

She stared straight into my eyes. "Wouldn't miss it."

Leah Prevault wasn't the most beautiful woman in the world, but she had brains and an outgoing personality that made most people relaxed enough to confess their innermost secrets to her. By Ernie's standards she was plain: She wore no makeup, her long brown hair was usually knotted in the back of her head, and her horn-rimmed glasses often slipped halfway down her nose. But her full-lipped smile was generous, her complexion smooth, and I'd probably fallen for her the first time I met her.

"You like the brainy ones," Ernie told me, without a tone of approval. "They just land you in trouble."

"Trouble in what way?"

"They make you want to settle down."

"What's wrong with that?"

Ernie looked at me like I was mad. "There's a whole

world of women out there." He waved his arm. "How can you settle for just one?"

"How many do you need?" I asked.

"More than I'm getting," he said.

Captain Prevault and I didn't return to the compound that night. Fraternization between the ranks is a court-martial offense. We stayed at a Korean inn, away from the prying eyes of the 8th US Army.

Two days later, the word came down. Riley hoisted the phone to his ear, listened, and barked, "Roger that!" He slammed down the receiver. "You guys remember that Major Schultz?" he asked.

"What do you mean, 'remember'?" I asked.

"He's history."

"What are you talking about, Riley?"

"That was the KNP Liaison. They found Schultz dead, at some dive out in Itaewon." He jotted something on a slip of paper and handed it to me. "Captain Kim's at the scene right now."

I looked at the paper. The Dragon King Nightclub.

"Dead?" Ernie asked.

"Deader than a ping-pong ball in a minefield," Riley replied. "Better get your asses in gear."

We did. Ernie grabbed his coat and I grabbed mine. Within seconds, we were in his jeep and speeding out Gate 7, waving at the MPs, swerving toward Itaewon. Ernie honked his horn and zoomed past a three-wheeled truck loaded with a small mountain of garlic. He held his nose.

"I'll never get used to this country," he said.

"Oh, bull, you love every minute of it," I told him. "I've seen you pop down three orders of roasted garlic in one sitting."

"That's after a bottle of soju."

"You like the smell of garlic better after a bottle of soju?"

"I like *anything* better after a bottle of soju."

6

Captain Kim, Commander of the Itaewon Police Station, stood waiting for us. He was a lugubrious-faced man with sagging jowls and eyes that sloped downward at the edges, as if weighed down by years of misery. He opened his palm and waved us through the door of the Dragon King Night-club.

It was a small joint off the main drag of Itaewon, along the main supply route. One of the boutique barrooms that had sprung up not only to cater to GIs, but also to the growing class of young Koreans from wealthy families who could afford to spend ten or twenty thousand *won* per night—twenty to forty US dollars—on beer or liquor and an evening of cabareting. These youthful elites found it particularly exciting because these nightclubs were near the notorious red-light district of Itaewon, restricted to foreign guests only. Nothing is more titillating than that which is forbidden.

The place was modern compared to the old joints in the

heart of Itaewon. The floor was tiled, the bar lit with a wedge of neon, and the stools made of stainless steel. We followed Captain Kim to the hallway in the back that led past the bathrooms and through a swinging door and into a neatly kept storage room. The back door was open. Sunlight filtered through a heavy overcast. We stepped into the alley.

"Here," Captain Kim said, pointing, "next to those."

Four wooden crates, all full of empty crystalline soju bottles, were piled on top of one another. But beyond that were more crates, some of them smashed, bottles shattered, and the strong rice liquor long since seeped into the ground. I knelt and watched the dim sunlight play off the jagged edges of the glass, stained with tiny spots of reddish-brown. The spray droplets grew larger as they consolidated into a pool of something sticky and black, looking as if they had been tossed from a large pan.

I stood slowly. "The technicians?" I asked.

"They come soon," Captain Kim said. "Truck come."

"And the body?"

"Already take to Seoul. They gonna check. Everything."

He meant the morgue in downtown Seoul. Ernie and I had been there many times before.

"Why didn't you wait for the Eighth Army Coroner?" Ernie asked.

"First, we don't know he GI. No wallet, no nothing."

"We're right next to Itaewon," Ernie replied. "You must've known he was a GI."

"Maybe," Captain Kim said, shrugging. "But honcho say take Seoul."

"Which honcho?" I asked.

"You know."

I stared at him. "No, I don't know."

He shrugged, resigned to the fact that we'd find out soon enough. "Gil Kwon-up," he said.

This was indeed a man we knew well. The brilliant chief homicide detective of the Korean National Police, whom American GIs called "Mr. Kill."

"Why's he interested in this?" Ernie asked.

Captain Kim shrugged again. "You ask him."

"When we took the call, we were told that the victim was Major Schultz. If you had no wallet and weren't even sure he was a GI, how'd you know his name?"

"Maybe they find wallet later. I don't know. You ask chief inspector."

The KNPs were just making excuses for having transported his body to the downtown morgue. Routinely, if the victim was an American, they were more than happy to turn it over to us; less trouble for them, less scrutiny from their superiors. In this case, there had to be a reason they'd wanted to examine the corpse on their own.

"How was he killed?" I asked.

"A lot of blood, you see. Body cut bad. Maybe twenty, thirty times."

"What type of blade?"

"Maybe more than one type."

"A knife?"

"You look at body. You see."

"Did he fight?"

Captain Kim spread his arms and turned slightly. "Look."

What surrounded us were neatly stacked wooden crates filled with glass bottles, beyond the stack that had been turned over and smashed. Not one of the others had been knocked over.

"Did somebody clean up?"

"No, still same."

That meant that if a fight had taken place, it had been short and sweet, and Major Schultz had gone down quickly.

"What time was the body found?"

"This morning, old lady come. Her job, clean up."

"She has a key?"

"Yes. Always come in back door. First she see body, then she see blood. She run away, go KNP station."

"Did she see anybody else around here?"

"No, just body."

"And last night, was there a fight?"

"Owner at station now. We go talk."

We did. The owner claimed to know nothing about the big American who'd ended up dead behind the Dragon King Nightclub. As a matter of fact, no Americans at all had entered his club last night. Just before the midnight curfew, he had personally locked the place up tight and left through the back door. He hadn't noticed anyone lurking in the alley at that time.

When we were through talking to him, I asked Captain Kim, "Has he already been interrogated by Gil Kwon-up?"

Captain Kim nodded. "Already."

Ernie and I returned to the jeep. As we climbed in, Ernie started the engine and said, "Looks like we're sucking hind tit."

"Mr. Kill wants to get a handle on this crime," I said. "An American officer stabbed to death on the edge of Itaewon. His bosses will want a report every five minutes."

The Republic of Korea was receiving hundreds of millions of dollars in economic and military assistance from the United States government. There were more than 50,000 American military personnel stationed in country with the mission of helping to protect the ROK from another invasion by the Communist regime to the north. Incidents involving the murder of American soldiers generated bad publicity back in the States, put pressure on politicians, and directly threatened the flow of military and financial aid. The Korean government leaders refused to tolerate such a risk. As such, as soon as it was out that an American field grade officer had been murdered, they'd put their best man, Mr. Kill on it, and so far he'd taken full control of the case and full control of the evidence.

"Before we go to the morgue," Ernie said, "maybe we should check on Miss Jo."

"Maybe we should," I said.

Ernie parked the jeep on the edge of the Itaewon Market and we hoofed it into the narrow pedestrian alleys. But the landlady told us that Miss Jo had already moved out. With her hospital bills, she hadn't been able to make the rent.

"Where's her stuff," Ernie asked, "the bed and her clothes?"

I translated and the landlady led us to a wooden storeroom. She pulled a keychain out of the deep folds of her house dress and popped open the padlock. Inside, stacked upright were the bed, the now dismantled plastic wardrobe, and cardboard boxes full of clothes.

"Is she coming back for them?" I asked in Korean.

The landlady shrugged. "That's what she said. If she doesn't, I'll sell everything."

I asked the landlady for a forwarding address, but of course she didn't have one. She did believe that Miss Jo would be staying nearby, here in Itaewon, so she could earn enough money to pay her back rent and reclaim her clothes.

"Clothes are very important to a young woman like her," she said.

The City Morgue in downtown Seoul is a giant stone building one major street over from KNP headquarters. There was no place to park, so after I hopped out, Ernie cruised around the block. Wisps of cold rain splattered against my face as I made my way up the steps and through the big glass double doors. Inside, the clerk was less than helpful. Even my 8th Army CID badge didn't impress her. She did, however, pick up the phone, press a button, and was soon chattering away with someone who I believed was at KNP headquarters. She hung up and said, "You wait."

Ernie showed up.

"Where'd you park?"

"I paid a mama-san to move her cart."

Pushcarts serving bean curd soup or roast corn-on-the-cob or *pindaedok*, mung bean pancakes, roam the crowded streets of Seoul, mainly at night but some to service the lunch crowd during the day. They guard their territory with their life, but room can be made for a jeep if the price is right.

I was about to question the clerk again when a man accompanied by a young woman wearing the neat blue uniform of the Korean National Police pushed through the front door. Chief Inspector Gil Kwon-up, aka Mr. Kill, with his female assistant, Officer Oh.

He was dapper as usual, with grey hair swept back from his forehead and a neatly pressed suit that, for all I knew, was imported straight from Europe. They walked briskly toward us, then swerved to the right. "Come," he said.

We did. Officer Oh lagged behind, making sure we followed her boss. She looked crisp and efficient in her knee-length dark-blue skirt with a sky-blue blouse buttoned to the collar. A flat, upturned brim cap sat atop a cascade of curly black hair. When I caught her eye, I nodded to her and she nodded back, smiling politely. We'd worked with her and her boss before; sometimes cooperatively, sometimes not so much. The four of us trotted down two flights of broad cement steps. At the bottom, we entered a low-roofed hallway illuminated by yellowing fluorescents. The bulbs grew dimmer as we rounded a corner until we finally pushed through a pair of swinging doors and entered a refrigerated room bathed in reddish light. A technician with a white smock stood at attention.

Mr. Kill barked an order.

The tech retreated to an inner room and within seconds, he rolled out a long table and shoved it in front of us. Then he pushed over a lamp on wheels and switched it on. When the lumpy object in front of us was fully illuminated, Mr. Kill whipped off the sheet.

Major Frederick Manfield Schultz, lifeless eyes staring straight ahead, looking, now, a little worse for wear. His cheeks weren't puffed out anymore; they were sunken, and they certainly weren't red, but a sickly grey. A stench wafted off the corpse. I knew the body had been washed, but the odor of two hundred pounds of dead meat still reminds one of the undiscerning darkness that will one day embrace us all.

Mr. Kill pointed toward the wounds. "Two knives," he said. "Maybe one a small axe?" He made a chopping motion.

"A hatchet," I said.

"Yes. A hatchet." He seemed satisfied with the word.

Inspector Gil Kwon-up was a highly educated man, both in formal Western education and in the classical curriculum of the Far East. After receiving a four-year degree in Korea, he'd gone on to graduate work at an Ivy League school in the States. He was also versed in the Four Books and the Five Classics of the Confucian cannon, and was such an expert on Chinese calligraphy that he often lectured on the subject at local universities. Still, he was a man of the streets. He'd been working at this job for over twenty years, since the end of the Korean War, and he'd put away more killers and psychopaths than Ernie and I were ever likely to see.

I studied the wounds. "Two different blades," I said.

"Yes. Here are the measurements."

Officer Oh handed me a sheet of paper written in both *hangul* and English. The measurements were in centimeters. I thanked her and pocketed it.

"What was the cause of death?" I asked.

Mr. Kill nodded toward the technician, stepped forward and, with Officer Oh's assistance, rolled Major Frederick Manfield Schultz onto his side. As they did so, his right arm flopped forward lifelessly, as if waving for us to join him in the endless depths.

While Officer Oh held the corpse in place, the technician hurriedly repositioned the lamp, aiming it at the back of Major Schultz's head.

"Christ," Ernie said.

I let out a gasp too.

It was a neat chop, slicing the flesh and then the skull, like a tomahawk blow to a tree.

"Hatchet," Mr. Kill said once again.

"Hatchet," Officer Oh repeated.

Then he turned to us. "Tell me what you know," he said.

The KNPs put out an all-points bulletin for Miss Jo Kyong-ja. After her recent trouble with Major Schultz, she was a prime suspect in this murder. It was physically unlikely that she could've pulled off the attack herself, unless she'd caught him completely unawares, but it *was* possible that she put somebody up to it. In fact, Mr. Kill thought it likely.

The tentacles of the Korean National Police spread down every back alley of Seoul and into every village and hamlet in the still-pristine countryside of South Korea. If she was out there, they'd find her eventually. But sometimes, when people are well hidden, that can take years. It was agreed that for the first foray into Itaewon, Ernie and I would take the lead.

"She's a GI business girl," Mr. Kill told us. "You're GIs. You go."

When the KNPs are on a search mission in Itaewon, word spreads fast and people hide like scattering rats. Ernie and I could, if we played it right, draw less attention.

■ ■ ■

We returned to Yongsan Compound. At the barracks, we changed into our running-the-ville outfits: sneakers, blue jeans, button-down collared sports shirts, and nylon jackets with fire-breathing dragons hand-embroidered on the back; sinuous creatures, with gaping mouths and wicked claws. The caption beneath mine said: *Republic of Korea, 1972 through 1975.* Ernie's not only had a dragon on the back, but a voluptuous lady locked in a less-than-subtle embrace. He'd added an additional epitaph, *I've served my time in hell.* Overstated, but most GIs not only weren't into subtlety, but didn't know what the word meant. An assignment in Korea was officially termed a "hardship tour," but it was hardly a sojourn in hell. Still, I didn't quibble. Our object, after all, was to fit in.

I used the military phone in the barracks lobby to dial the CID office. Staff Sergeant Riley answered on the first ring.

"You're gonna do what?" he said.

"We're gonna run the ville."

"You've got a damn murder to solve."

"And this is how we're going to do it."

"The Provost Marshal wants you back here, in uniform, giving him a full report."

"No time now." I explained the urgency to find Miss Jo before she decided to run.

Riley still didn't like it. "Do you have any idea about what kind of pressure the Chief of Staff is putting on Colonel Brace? They're livid up at the head shed. A field grade officer hasn't been murdered in this country since the Korean freaking War."

"Been that long, huh?"

To me, the premature taking of life was a sin against humanity no matter the rank of the victim.

"Colonel Brace is the Provost Marshal," Riley continued. "It's his job to *protect* people."

"It's our job too."

When he continued to cuss, I hung up on him. Ernie and I trotted out to the jeep.

"They took it well?" he asked.

"They're delighted with our plan," I told him.

He hopped behind the wheel of the jeep and started the engine. "I knew they would be."

7

Delicate flakes of snow drifted in the gentle breeze until they slapped haphazardly onto the grease-stained pavement of the main drag of the Itaewon nightclub district. The afternoon was so dark and overcast that most of the joints had already switched on their neon. Beneath a red glow, we entered the King Club.

The first thing we did was sit at the bar. We ordered two beers; the young bartender wearing a white shirt and black bowtie popped the bottle caps off for us as the middle-aged female cashier took our money.

"You early."

It was Miss Peik, the senior waitress at the King Club. Koreans often form a family structure in business, even if everyone involved is not related. The King Club's "parents" were the owners, the aunt was the cashier, the grandson was the young bartender, and the sisters were the cocktail waitresses. Miss Peik, as the oldest cocktail waitress, was uniformly called *onni*, older sister, by the other girls.

She had "CQ" today, the daytime shift. They'd stolen the term from the US Army. The CQ, or Charge of Quarters, was the GI who was hit with the unfortunate duty of staying up all night in the barracks, forced to be alert and answer the phone in case there were any fires or other emergencies. During the work week, daytime business at the King Club was so slow that they only needed one "CQ" waitress. On weekends, two or three. At night, of course, all the waitresses were on duty, about a dozen of them in a busy joint like the King Club. Holidays were not observed, and each girl was granted only one day off a month.

Miss Peik wrapped her arms around Ernie's neck. She was a tall, thin woman wearing the bright red smock that was the uniform for the King Club. I pegged her at pushing forty.

"You *rabu* me?" Ernie asked.

"I *rabu* you too muchey. You buy me drink?"

"*Ijo jo!*" Ernie said. Forget it!

Another phrase I'd taught him. He'd worked hard at memorizing it because it came in so handy.

Miss Peik backed away. "You no *rabu* me?"

"I *rabu* you too muchey." Ernie pulled her back toward him.

While Miss Peik and Ernie horsed around, I asked the bartender where the other waitresses were. The club was empty. None of the two or three dozen cocktail tables held any customers, and the stage where the rock band usually performed was dark. Not unusual for a mid-afternoon on a work day, but I had paid for the beer with a 10,000 *won* note—about twenty bucks—so they'd know I wasn't short on cash. By my impatience, I made it clear that if there were no girl for me, I'd pick up my change and suggest to my friend that we try another bar.

The bartender whispered to the cashier. She nodded her approval and he trotted out back. Ten minutes later two more cocktail waitresses joined us. It cost management nothing to bring them on duty. The girls were paid by the month, the equivalent of about forty dollars. Any other money they made was from tips, which were few and far between from their frugal clientele, and from direct payments from any boyfriends they were able to land. Many of them had steady *yobo*s, GIs who lived in their hooch and paid their rent and, more often than not, bought black market items out of the PX or commissary that the girls then resold for a tidy profit. It was a way of life in Itaewon that had lasted, as far as I could tell, since the end of the Korean War. It had been over twenty years now, and I saw no indication that this method of employing the excess Korean female labor force was about to change.

The two waitresses glommed onto me. I did my best to act interested, but these girls were experts at reading men—that's how they made their living—and they soon realized I was faking it. One of them stood back and placed her manicured fingernails on her hip. "You have steady *yobo*?"

"Not steady," I said, "not yet."

"Why not?"

I sipped on my beer. "I met her at the UN Club, about a month ago," I told them. I described her and then told them her name. "Miss Jo," I said. "I went to her hooch but the mama-san said she doesn't live there anymore."

They pulled Miss Peik away from Ernie. As I suspected, they loved nothing better than a soap opera situation to add spice to their boring days. They conferred amongst themselves, speaking rapid Korean. I pretended not to understand. In fact, much of it I couldn't understand because they were speaking so quickly and in shorthand bursts. But I did get the gist of it. They had decided that she was the Miss Jo who'd been beaten up by GIs and had to go to the hospital, and they were wondering how much they should tell me.

Finally, Miss Peik stepped toward me. "You likey Miss Jo?"

I sipped on my beer and set it on the bar. "She's okay."

"You wanna talk to her?"

"You know where she is?"

"You wait," Miss Peik told me.

The three women conferred again and one of them left through the back door.

Ernie pulled Miss Peik back toward him and reached out for the other remaining waitress. Both women laughed and pretended to resist, but finally gave in as Ernie Bascom, agent for the 8th United States Army CID, nuzzled their necks and tried to paw at their bodies, especially the round parts.

The building had long been notorious as a brothel in the heart of the Itaewon catacombs. The waitress who led us there had us follow her through twisting pedestrian lanes until finally we reached a crossroads and she pointed and said, "That gate."

Then she ran back to the King Club.

"Aren't you going to tip her?" Ernie asked.

"She didn't give me the chance."

He nodded, agreeing with me. "They don't think like Americans."

The small door in the large wooden gate was open. We pushed through into a narrow courtyard. To the right stood a low wooden porch that ran the length of the building, lined with sliding oil-papered doors that led into one-room hooches. The *byonso*, with the letters w.c. etched into the wooden door, stood alone along the back wall. Ernie and I strode down the row. Many of the doors were padlocked shut.

"Probably at the bathhouse," Ernie said.

"Or the temple," I replied. Many of the girls who worked as prostitutes in Itaewon were surprisingly religious. Mostly Buddhist. They routinely made pilgrimages to temples here in the city or monasteries in the surrounding countryside.

A few of the rooms were occupied and unfamiliar faces stared out at us.

A wooden flight of stairs led upstairs to another long row of hooches. We walked along it, planks creaking beneath our shod feet, until finally we found her at the end. Miss Jo Kyong-ja. She stood and approached the door and peered at us as if she'd expected us.

"You," she said.

"Yes, us."

With her right hand, she brushed back her hair. "Okay," she said, as if resigned to some tedious task. "Come in."

She switched on the overhead bulb and tossed two flat cushions on the floor. Ernie and I slipped off our shoes and entered.

"Sit," she said.

We did. She squatted in front of us, shoving a glass ashtray in the center of our cozy circle. She pulled out a pack of Turtle Boat cigarettes and offered one to each of us. We both declined. She slid a box of wooden matches out from beneath the Western-style bed, pulled one out, struck it, and lit up. After a couple of puffs, she lowered the cigarette and said, "You find me."

"Yes," I said. "We found you."

"Why you come here? You wanna catchey girl?"

"No," I said. "No girl."

I noticed a flimsy plastic armoire, unzipped and bereft of clothes. The same spangled handbag I'd seen in the UN Club lay at the far end of the bed.

"Why'd you move here?" I asked.

"You know," she said, suddenly angry. "Mama-san keep all my clothes. She say, pay rent first, then get back. I come here to make money." She puffed on her cigarette, blew the smoke out long and slow. "But no can make money. Too many GI *kokcheingi*. How you say? *Stingy*."

"So what are you going to do?" Ernie asked.

"I don't know," she said, stubbing out the half-smoked cigarette.

"Where were you last night?"

She frowned. "Where you think? Where can I go? No money. I stay here. Work."

"There's a place called the Dragon King Nightclub," I said, "on the MSR, across from the Crown Hotel. Have you ever been there?"

She stared at me blankly.

"Your friend," Ernie said, "Major Schultz, he went there last night."

"I know," she said softly. "I hear."

"He's dead," Ernie continued. "Stabbed to death in the alley behind the Dragon King. Maybe ten knife wounds. Some people think you did it."

She looked at us calmly, first at Ernie then at me.

"He big man," she said. "How I do?"

Ernie continued. "Maybe you had some help from your friends."

"My friends," she said, laughing, her gaze fixed on the ground. "My friends."

"Tell us what happened," I said. "Otherwise, we have to turn you over to the KNPs."

She laughed again. "Anyway, you turn me over to KNPs. They ask me anything. I have to answer what they want. If I answer they no like, they knuckle sandwich me."

She clenched her small fist and held it out to us.

Based on her reaction, I immediately felt that she was innocent. I knew it was unprofessional of me, but none of it made sense. Of course she'd held a grudge against Major Schultz, and with good reason. He and his pal, whoever he was, had beaten the hell out of her. But this was a woman with no power, with no money and, as far as I could see, no friends. Who would agree to attack a burly American officer for her? Who would agree to commit murder for her? It made no sense. But what she said about the KNPs did make sense. They would be under tremendous pressure to solve this murder quickly. Miss Jo Kyong-ja had a motive for that murder, and even if the facts didn't fit the crime, the KNPs would make them fit. She had no leverage. She was a convenient—and obvious—scapegoat.

"Do you have witnesses who saw you here last night?"

She waved her left arm. "Many business girls."

"Any GIs?"

Briefly, she looked ashamed, then she tilted her face up, defiant. "Three."

"Do you know their names?" Ernie asked.

"Timmy, one is called. I think."

This wasn't good. The 8th Army Judge Advocate General didn't give much credence to the testimony of Korean business girls. The Korean judicial system, even less. And whether or not we'd be able to find the three GIs was problematic to say the least. Miss Jo's three customers had no reason to admit they'd been out here. Paying for sex is embarrassing to most men, both professionally and personally. This despite the fact, that from my experience, when given the opportunity, most are more than willing to cough up the cash, as long as they believe the transaction can be kept secret.

"Okay," Ernie said, standing up. "You're going to have to come with us."

Miss Jo stared at the floor for a moment, but after the pause she rose to her feet. She was already prepared, wearing the one black dress she still owned. She reached for her jacket on the bed as I grabbed her handbag and lifted it up for her. Unexpectedly, the contents shifted in the flimsy material and tumbled to the floor: makeup, a mirror, brass coins, a small brush, her national ID card, and a thin fold of Korean and US bills. What caught my eye, though, was a card with a young girl kneeling in prayer, staring up at a golden light.

Many Korean Christians carry these cards, with pictures of an angel or a saint or, more often, a sweet-faced young girl praying to the sky. On them was usually imprinted the name and address of their church, and sometimes the name of their pastor. I was surprised that Miss Jo was a Christian.

Statistically, Christianity was the second most prominent religion in Korea, but ever since the days of Western missionaries, it had been associated with the upper-class educated elites. Not with business girls.

Without a word, Miss Jo knelt and shoved everything back into her purse. Straightening her dress, she walked serenely out onto the porch and slipped on a pair of low-heeled shoes. I led the way. Ernie took the rear. Some of the other business girls stood at their doorways, watching us as we escorted her out.

When we reached the mama-san's hooch, Miss Jo stopped to talk to her. In Korean, she told her she'd be back when she could to collect the money she'd earned last night. Apparently, she thought it would be safer here than it would be at the KNP headquarters. The old woman nodded, face impassive, but with a slight hint of amusement in her eyes. She probably thought Miss Jo would never return.

They talked through what the total would be, mentioning how long she'd spent with each GI and how much she'd made from each one, then deducting the old woman's percentage. After listing off the men and the times, it seemed as if Miss Jo was a little confused and then she paused and said "*Koshigi . . .*" I'd never heard the word before and wanted to ask what it meant, but figured this was neither the time nor the place.

As we left, the business girls continued to stand and stare. None of them said goodbye.

We pushed through the small door in the gate and marched our little parade, single file, through the dark passageways of the back alleys of Itaewon. Occasionally, we could see the flickering neon of the nightclub district above the high brick and cement block walls. As we rounded a bend and dodged a trash cart, I thought of how the interrogation should go. Mr. Kill would want first crack at her, and we'd probably defer to that wish since Miss Jo Kyong-ja was a Korean National. I'd insist on observing through one of the two-way mirrors at KNP headquarters to be sure they didn't abuse her, but I couldn't guarantee her safety twenty-four hours a day.

I should've been more alert. Instead, those were the thoughts I was mulling through when something that seemed like a giant bat zoomed toward us. I ducked, and heard a grunt and a thud behind me. Miss Jo started running. Before I could turn to stop her, a dark figure enveloped Ernie. He was down. I ran toward him and momentarily sensed something behind me, whistling through the night. The air around its path seemed to vibrate, and then like a resonant wave it touched me, ever so gently. I lost my balance, my head exploded in pain, and light wavered in front of me. I struggled to maintain consciousness.

Ernie shouted.

Someone cursed. My eyes popped open to feet shuffling around me. Apparently, I'd fallen down. Without thinking, I reached out and grabbed one of the feet and then I was on my knees and somebody was pounding on my back. I grabbed someone else's arms and pulled myself upright. Two Korean men. Ernie tried to wrestle himself away from the one who was hitting him and the one in back of me turned to grab Miss Jo. He dragged her into a run through the dark alley. I tried to follow them but was still so groggy from what seemed like the ton of cement that had fallen on me that I reached instead for the guy who was punching Ernie.

They'd gotten the drop on us. Literally. From the roof, they'd leapt down upon us. We'd both been surprised, but fought back gamely. The guy punching Ernie saw me coming and planted a final roundhouse kick onto Ernie's ribs, then swiveled and took off running. Holding his side, Ernie staggered after him, as did I.

The alleys were narrow and the stone and brick walls hovered over us. We had to run single-file. The guy ahead of us was moving at top speed. He'd planned his escape route and knew exactly where he was going. We managed to stay close enough, however, to hear his heavy breathing and footsteps as he raced through the dark catacombs of Itaewon.

Finally, we burst out onto the neon-lit pavement of the main drag. Ernie pointed. "There!" He was running toward the Lucky Seven Club.

We took off at full tilt.

He could've continued on to the MSR—the Main

Supply Route—which was the busiest road that traveled through this part of the city. But Ernie and I had recovered our senses now and were on him like a pair of hound dogs. Maybe he thought he couldn't escape, or maybe he thought he could throw us off by darting into the Lucky Seven Club. Whatever his logic, he scurried up the big stone steps beneath the club's neon-lit awning, but instead of entering through the padded double doors, he snuck up the side steps to the Victory Hotel, which occupied the three floors above the Lucky Seven.

Ernie hit the stairwell first, taking the steps three at a time. He was fully recovered from the initial surprise and angry as hell. I followed, trying to figure where this guy was going. As far as I knew, this stairwell was the only way in or out of the Victory Hotel, and we were so close now I could hear his huffing and puffing.

Where had Miss Jo gotten off to? No way of knowing, but if we caught this guy, I was furious enough to beat the information out of him.

We finally hit the top floor, and when we burst into the hallway we saw him at the end of a line of tightly closed doors. He hesitated for a moment, as if deciding what to do next. There, in the yellow overhead light, I could see that he was definitely Korean, with a square-jawed face, wearing sneakers, a pair of faded blue jeans and a cloth jacket with dark-blue streaks on it. Above him was a glowing red sign that said *chulgu*, exit. He opened the door and disappeared.

We charged down the hallway just as a middle-aged Korean woman peeked out of her doorway. Her eyes just about popped out of her head at the two sweaty Caucasians barreling through the narrow passageway. Her head ducked back into her room and she slammed the door shut. Ernie hit the exit first, pushed through, and a short flight of steps led up and outside into the open air on the roof of the Victory Hotel.

The panorama of Itaewon spread before us. In the distance loomed the dark edifice of Namsan Mountain, with an enormous radio tower blinking red above it. Storm clouds had gathered, and the afternoon was so dark it seemed almost like night. At the edge of the roof, standing on the stone parapet, stood our attacker. I propped the door open so light flooded out. He had his back to the edge and was staring right at us. His face was somber, eyelids sagging.

I spoke to him in Korean. "Step away from the ledge. We won't hit you any more."

The side of his mouth turned up in a knowing smile.

"*Ssibaloma*," he said, a particularly vile insult which translates roughly to "born of afterbirth." Smiling even more broadly, he stepped backward into nothingness and fell off into space.

-8-

The narrow face of Staff Sergeant Riley stared down at me.

"Sueño, can you hear me?"

He waved his open palm back and forth in front of my eyes, shielding me sporadically from the twisted snarl of his lips.

"He's awake," Riley said, turning to someone behind him. A blue-smocked medic replaced him in my line of sight. A hand reached toward my nose and the sharp tang of ammonia jerked me alert. I started to sit up. Gently, the medic pushed me back down. "I'll call the doctor," he said.

In a few minutes, a harassed-looking MD appeared at my side. Heavy jowls sagged as he shone a light into my eyes and told me to sit up and swing my legs over the side of the bed. "Do you know where you are?" he asked.

"No, sir," I said.

"In the One Two One Evac Hospital," he told me. "Do you know where that is?"

"Yes, on Yongsan Compound."

"Do you know what happened to you last night?"

"I think I passed out."

"Yes, after you were hit on the head and ran through half of Itaewon."

It had also been the shock of seeing our attacker leap off that roof. When Ernie and I sprinted to the ledge, we realized that he hadn't leapt to his death. What he'd done was grab hold of the fire escape and slide down like an expert climber, hitting the edge of the building every few yards with his feet as if rappelling down a mountain. By the time we clambered over the edge and lowered ourselves rung by rung, he was long gone. A few feet from the ground I became dizzy, probably from the blow I'd taken when the first guy jumped me, and I'd lost my footing and fallen. Apparently my head clunked on the pavement, and that was the last thing I remembered.

"How's Ernie?" I asked.

"Never mind that now."

The doctor continued his examination, checking my heart and breathing and waving his finger in front of me, telling me to follow it and asking me questions. Finally, his interrogation was over. Apparently, I passed. He scribbled something on a sheet of paper with the 121 Evac logo imprinted on it and handed it to Staff Sergeant Riley.

"Forty-eight hours quarters," he said. I would be restricted to the barracks and unable to work for two days. Then the doctor wagged his finger at Riley. "And don't let me hear about your commander putting this man back to work before the two days are up. I won't hear of it. Understood?"

Riley nodded.

"Good." The doctor patted me on the shoulder and said, "And when the two days are over, go on sick call so they can check you once more." He peered at me, and when I didn't answer, he said, "Repeat that back to me." I did. He patted me on the shoulder one more time, said, "Keep your head down," and walked briskly out of the ward.

"Your clothes are behind that curtain," the medic told me before he left the room too.

Riley tapped the paper in his hand. "What a get-over."

"I'm not getting over on anybody," I told him. "The doctor says I should rest, so I'll rest."

"The Provost Marshal wants you to report to his office, immediately if not sooner."

I groaned. "Let me get dressed."

I did. Slowly and painfully, my head still throbbing, but soon I was back in my running-the-ville outfit, which was soiled where I'd fallen but not much worse for wear.

Riley had parked a green Army sedan out front. I hopped into the passenger seat. He drove.

"Where's Ernie?"

"Already back at work, on black market detail."

"Alone?"

"They assigned an MP to him."

"Who?"

"A female type. I forget her name."

"How long was I out?"

"Just overnight."

I stared down at my clothes. "Don't you think I should change?"

"Naw. The Colonel said bring you in as is."

So I went into the office of the Provost Marshal of the 8th United States Army "as is."

"What is *this*," Colonel Brace asked, "an insult?"

He put his pipe down and stared up at me from his chair behind his desk. He was referring to my slovenly attire. I held my salute.

"No, sir. Sergeant Riley told me I was to report to you immediately."

"Don't blame other people for your shortcomings, Sueño."

That's the Army. You receive conflicting orders, try to follow them—which is impossible—and no matter what, it's always your fault.

"I'll return to the barracks and change, sir. Then I'll be right back."

"No time for that." Instead of returning my salute, he waved me toward one of the chairs in front of his desk. "Sit."

I sat.

He tapped burnt pipe tobacco into an ashtray. "I

understand," he said, "from the KNP Liaison officer that you and Bascom had taken our prime suspect in the murder of Major Schultz into custody."

"Yes, sir."

"And then you lost her." He glared at me from across his mahogany desk.

"We were attacked, sir."

"By whom?"

"We don't know. It was a narrow alley. One of them, at least, was on a building overhead. They jumped down and landed on us."

"Your friend Bascom was pretty successful in fighting them off. At least *he* didn't end up in the hospital."

"Good for him."

"Not so good," Colonel Brace said, his tone guarded. "The suspect still escaped. Bascom pursued, he says, but lost them in the narrow alleys."

I nodded, wondering where this was going. That wasn't *exactly* what happened, but Ernie had a policy of providing officers as little information as possible. In keeping with that policy, I kept my mouth shut.

Colonel Brace paused while he stuffed fresh tobacco into his pipe and then, using a stainless steel lighter emblazoned with the red and white 8th Army cloverleaf patch, he lit the concoction and puffed heartily. A cloud floated across the desk and rolled into my face. It smelled like cherry wood. I resisted the urge to wave it away. He lowered the pipe.

"Do you always dress like that when you go to the ville?"

"This is how most GIs dress, sir. We want to blend in."

"I'll bet you do."

He seemed disgusted by the mere thought of going to the ville. More smoke billowed as he continued to puff away. Everything with him was an accusation, as if we'd done something wrong. But I was used to that. It seemed to be the strategy most military officers used to maintain discipline—by keeping their subordinates worried and off-balance. Straight out of the handbook; it was probably a seminar subject at the Reserve Officer Training Corps.

"That homicide detective," Colonel Brace said, "Mr. Kill, he called about you."

I immediately understood why he was being so condescending. He knew that Chief Inspector Gil Kwon-up had connections to officials at the highest levels of the Korean government, who in turn had connections with those at the highest levels of the 8th United States Army. Even higher, if they wanted to push it; as high as the US Ambassador to South Korea. Colonel Brace wanted to impress upon me that even though I might be consulting temporarily with someone who had power over him, in the end I was just a GI, just an enlisted man. And once my sojourn in the halls of power was over, the 8th United States Army could eat me for lunch, if they deigned to choose that particular blue-plate special on that particular day. Still, for the moment, I had power. I exercised some of it.

"What did Mr. Kill say, sir?"

"He asked about your health. I told him the doctor thought there was no serious concussion. You'd recover soon."

I waited. There had to be more. Colonel Brace wanted me to beg for it. I wouldn't.

"He also asked that you and Bascom be assigned to him for the duration of the investigation."

"The investigation into Major Schultz's death?"

"Are we talking about another one?"

I didn't answer. After staring me down, Colonel Brace began fiddling with a stack of paperwork on his desk. That was the signal that this interview was just about over. Without looking at me, he said, "You and Bascom are to report to the KNP headquarters immediately. He'll probably want you to make up for what you've already screwed up." He became very interested in the contents of one of his plastic binders for about half a minute, then he looked up at me, as if surprised that I was still there. "That'll be all."

I rose to my feet, assumed the position of attention, and saluted.

While I held my salute, Colonel Brace said, "And one more thing, Sueño. While on this detail with the KNPs, you are to report to Staff Sergeant Riley every morning at zero eight hundred. Is that understood?"

"Yes, sir."

He flicked his wrist and waved me away.

I dropped my salute, did an about face, and marched out of his office.

Before I left, I stopped by the Admin Office and asked Miss Kim if I could borrow her Korean-English Dictionary. She studied me with a worried look on her face. "You need to rest, Geogie."

"Maybe later," I told her.

She motioned for me to sit down. I did. She grabbed her dictionary and said, "What's the word?"

"*Koshigi.*"

She set the dictionary down. "Where'd you hear that?"

"The woman we took into custody last night, the one who escaped. She used it."

Miss Kim nodded and sipped cold tea. "Would you like something to drink?"

I shook my head.

She knew I was growing impatient so she said, "*Koshigi* is a word used by people in the south. Usually Cholla Namdo." South Cholla Province. She noticed that I leaned back slightly. "What's wrong?"

"Nothing. Go ahead, please."

"It's what someone says when they can't think of the right word."

I nodded slowly. "Like whatchamacallit."

"Yes, something like that."

Which made sense. Miss Jo had rattled off a list of

customers and how much money she'd made and then shaken her head slightly, as if she couldn't concentrate.

Miss Kim thumbed through the dictionary, found the word and turned the thick onion-skinned book around and pointed with her neatly manicured forefinger to *koshigi*. There were a number of translations, all of them vague, all meaning something like "thingamajig."

"But it's used only by people from the south?" I asked.

"Almost always. It makes Seoul people smile."

I knew that in ancient times, Korea had been broken into three countries. Paekche was the kingdom that ruled the southwest corner of the peninsula, where Cholla Province was now located. Over the centuries, distinct dialects of the Korean language had evolved. Nowadays, the Seoul dialect was considered standard, but people still had little trouble discerning which part of the country someone came from by listening to their *saturi*; their pronunciation and word choice.

"You need rest, Geogie," Miss Kim told me again.

"Yes, I'll rest. Soon." I figured now was as good a time as any to ask her. "Ernie followed you," I said, "on the bus. Was everything okay?"

Her face turned beet red, and I immediately regretted asking.

"Okay," she said but she held her head down and I knew she didn't want to talk about it.

"I hope he didn't bother you," I said.

"No. He didn't bother me." After a long silence, she looked up at me. "What is it about Cholla Province that bothers you?"

"It's a long story," I said.

"It's about her, isn't it?"

By *her*, she meant Doctor Yong In-ja, my former girlfriend. Someone I'd lost.

"I can't fool you at all," I told her.

She nodded. "We both have long stories. And secret stories."

I didn't disagree with her.

Ernie was at the MP Station, writing an arrest report for a Korean woman with a giant diamond on her left hand. She was sniffling and wiping her eyes with a pink handkerchief, occasionally blowing her nose.

"My husband *taaksan kullasso-yo*," she said. Very angry.

Ernie continued writing. "You sold ten cans of Spam, one jar of soluble creamer, a pound and a half of frozen oxtail, and thirty-two ounces of Folgers freeze-dried coffee out in the ville. Of course he'll be mad. Not because you sold them, but because you got caught."

He turned the report around and showed the woman where to sign. She reluctantly obliged.

A female MP stood behind Ernie, watching everything he did. She wore a polished black helmet with a white-stenciled MP on the front and highly spit-shined jump boots, and her fatigues were tailored to show off her figure. A web belt was cinched tightly around her waist, the holstered pistol looking large on her hip. Her nametag said Muencher.

Ernie tore off the yellow copy of the arrest report and handed it to the Korean woman. "Your husband is on the way," he said. "He'll escort you over to the Ration Control Office to apply for a new plate."

There would be a much smaller limit on her new Ration Control Plate. The woman knew this and she started to sniffle again.

Ernie stood up from the rickety wooden field desk and walked toward me. "Have you met Muencher?"

"Not yet," I said.

He made the introductions. She had a long face with a smattering of freckles across the nose. I could tell by the way that her helmet sat too high on her head that plenty of reddish-blonde hair was knotted up and hidden under there. Pinned to her lapel was the rank insignia of corporal. She held out her hand.

I shook it. The flesh was cool and smooth.

"Sergeant Sueño," she said. "I've heard of you." I nodded. "You speak Korean, they tell me."

"A little."

"More than that."

"When I have to."

"And you work with Mr. Kill."

"Also, when I have to." I smiled. Some of the MPs were

jealous of the special details Ernie and I were assigned to. She didn't seem to be. I turned to Ernie. "We gotta go."

"Where?"

"Downtown."

He nodded, knowing that meant the KNP headquarters. "What about the black market detail?"

"Looks like Corporal Muencher has it all to herself."

She pointed to her chest. "Just me?"

"You can handle it. In any given situation, just do what Ernie would've done."

"What's that?"

"Whatever is most likely to piss off Eighth Army," I told her.

-9-

After shaving in the barracks and changing into my jacket and tie, I jumped into Ernie's jeep and he drove us to the KNP headquarters in downtown Seoul. Traffic swirled around us, honking loudly, until we reached the inner city, where it went silent because there was a serious fine for using your horn there. We parked next to the same *pindae-dok* vendor Ernie had used before. She was happy to see us. Her round face shone as Ernie slipped her a thousand-*won* note, about two bucks. After jostling our way through a heavy flow of pedestrians, we entered the KNP headquarters.

"Another ass-chewing?" Ernie asked.

"I don't think Kill works that way."

"How does he work?"

"I haven't figured that out yet."

Despite the hiss of warm air in the temperature-controlled building, every foyer and hallway was permeated with the pungent smells of cigarette smoke and kimchi. We climbed two flights of stairs and followed the signs written in *hangul* down a long hallway. At the end, Officer Oh was waiting for us. With an open palm, she ushered us into the office of Chief Homicide Inspector Gil Kwon-up.

He sat on the edge of his desk, arms crossed, staring at a map of Korea. We walked up next to him. Without turning around, he said, "I understand you experienced a small mishap yesterday."

"They jumped us from a roof," I told him. "And the guy we chased was an expert at evasion and escape."

Kill glanced at the KNP report. "He slid down the fire escape?"

"'Rappelled' would be the more exact term."

"Who was he?" Ernie asked.

Mr. Kill shook his head. "We're not sure. Not yet."

"Unlikely to be relatives," I said.

"Yes, very unlikely."

Once a woman became a "business girl" in Itaewon, she was most often shunned by her family. It was unfair, because almost all the girls who worked there were forced into prostitution by poverty. There was no social safety net in Korea—no food stamps, no welfare, no unemployment insurance—and jobs were tough to come by, especially for young women who'd only completed *Kukmin Hakkyo*: People's School, the minimum six years of elementary education. There were factories opening up that employed legions of young women in very controlled conditions, reminiscent of the military, but even those jobs were highly sought-after and typically required at least a middle school or even high school education.

Farm families could seldom afford to feed an unmarried daughter. Or if they could, they required her to perform grueling work in the fields. Rice was still the main crop in South Korea. Wading in knee-deep water all day in the blistering sun, bending over to carefully transplant tender rice shoots in vast acres of mud was back-breaking work. Under such pressure, many girls ran away. From there, they too often ended up in the brothels and nightclubs of downtown Seoul, catering to Korean salarymen, or in the red light district of Itaewon, servicing American GIs.

"So who else would help her?" Ernie asked.

"Someone who didn't want her answering questions about Major Schultz," Kill replied.

"Are you saying there might've been a motive for Schultz's murder other than revenge for Miss Jo?"

Mr. Kill shrugged. "We don't know. What we do know is that we have to find her and ask her that question, amongst others." He turned to give us the full benefit of his piercing stare. "And this time, we have to make sure that once she's taken into custody, she stays in custody."

"All right," Ernie said, flopping down in an unused chair. "Now that the ass-chewing is over, how do we find her?"

"She might have stayed in Seoul," Mr. Kill said. "In a city of eight million people, she could be difficult to track down. But we have an all-points bulletin out on her. We'll find her eventually."

"But you don't think she stayed in Seoul," I said.

"Why go to all that trouble just to change neighborhoods? I think she might've gone south," he said.

"But if you have an APB out on her," I said, "it will be dangerous for her anywhere in the country."

He shook his head. "Not so much. Seoul generates more alerts for fugitives than any other part of the country, by far. Local police don't have time to follow up. They just file the alerts and forget them, unless the miscreant happens to fall into their lap."

Kill was always doing that. Using vocabulary like "miscreant" or idioms like "falls into their lap." Most Americans took his expertise in English for granted. After all, wasn't *everybody* supposed to speak English? But I knew how much hard work went into being able to use certain words and idiomatic constructions with ease, and I marveled at his skill. I only wished that someday I would be able to speak Korean half as well as he spoke English.

Kill stood and turned away from the map. He was wearing a charcoal-grey suit, different from the one he'd worn yesterday. His white collared shirt was cut to his exact proportions and sported French cuffs. He cleared his throat. "Officer Oh has been looking into her background." At his nod, she stepped forward in her neatly pressed blue uniform, bowed slightly, and, arms at her side, she began to recite the information like a schoolgirl in front of a class-room.

"Miss Jo Kyong-ja was born in the city of Mokpo in South Cholla Province. After middle school she lived with her family but leave them, not sure when. Her father die now and mother live with younger brother who study at high school."

This was common. The older sister's future had been sacrificed in order to provide an education for the younger brother. But at least she'd been put through middle school.

"Her first District Health Card was issued by Pyong-taek-gun," Officer Oh continued. The county of Pyongtaek. "Nightclub she work at was Yobo Club in Anjong-ri."

Ernie whistled. "Right outside the main gate of Camp Humphries," he said.

We'd both been there. Camp Humphries was the largest Army base in the country, not in population, but in square mileage. Mainly because the compound's mission was the training of attack helicopter crews and plenty of space was required.

"Do we know how long she worked there?" I asked.

Officer Oh shook her head. "One year later, she register health card again at the Yongsan District Health Center in Itaewon. Say job is UN Club but we ask owner. He say she no work there, just come in all the time. Meet Americans." Officer Oh didn't have nearly the same grasp on English as Mr. Kill, but her pronunciation was impressive.

Mr. Kill turned back to the map.

"The hometown of Miss Jo is down here." He pointed to Mokpo on the southwest corner of the Korean peninsula. "Her first job, or at least the first job we know about, was up here in Anjong-ri." That was about two hundred miles north. "Far enough that she was unlikely to see anyone she knew."

"She started a new life," Ernie said.

"Yes," Mr. Kill agreed, "from small-town girl to courtesan. A story too common in my country, I believe."

"Then she left Anjong-ri and came to Seoul," I added, "where it appears she worked independently."

Another common story. Once they learned enough English and the rudiments of the sex trade, they threw off the shackles of anyone they owed money to and struck off on their own. At least, the strong-minded ones did.

"But if she worked alone," Mr. Kill said, "who were these men who attacked you in the night?"

My head throbbed at the thought. I stared at the map, fondling a tender bruise on the back of my head. The bright colors and curved lines started to waver and blur, like a moving collage, until they blended together. I closed my eyes and pinched the bridge of my nose.

In Korean, Mr. Kill barked an order to Officer Oh. Within seconds she returned with a paper cup filled with cold water and two pills.

"Aspirin," she said.

I plucked them out of her palm, popped them in my mouth, and washed them down with the water.

"You need rest," Mr. Kill said.

"No," I said. "We lost her, we have to find her."

He didn't respond.

I leaned back in my chair and studied the map. This time, the contours of the ancient Korean Peninsula held steady.

"She hadn't been in Seoul long," Mr. Kill continued. "She only registered at the County Health Clinic three months ago."

"So those men who helped her," Ernie said, "they could be from Anjong-ri, where she had her first job."

"Yes. The criminal syndicate down there is slippery."

"And the KNPs don't clamp down on them, why?" Ernie asked.

Mr. Kill looked away. Officer Oh shuffled her feet nervously. We all knew the answer. Corruption was endemic in Korea. The KNPs took money from not only people who ran successful businesses, but also from organized crime. The average cop was underpaid and life was expensive, especially tuition if you ever planned to send your children to university. Still, there were lines that even organized crime wouldn't cross. They never used firearms, they never sold hard drugs, and they never, by any means, posed any threat to the stability of the Pak Chung-hee military dictatorship. As long as society ran smoothly and no one was embarrassed, the system worked well; except for now. With Major Schultz dead, the rules had been broken. Slaughtering an American military officer was outside of the range of acceptable behavior and would not be tolerated. Mr. Kill's bosses were nervous. That was why they'd assigned him to the case. To fix it.

"What about Mokpo?" Ernie asked. "Maybe she's gone there."

"So far no sign of her," Kill answered. "The local KNPs are handling that part. They have her mother's house staked out and they'll conduct interviews with people who might've known her; very low-key, so as not to frighten her away if she is nearby."

There were no US military installations anywhere near Mokpo. Two American GIs like Ernie and me would stick out like the proverbial sore digit.

"So what about us?" Ernie asked.

Mr. Kill pointed to the village of Anjong-ri. "As you said, Anjong-ri borders Camp Humphries. There are at least a dozen bars only a few yards from the main gate, including the Yobo Club. If she is there and the KNPs start asking questions, they'll frighten her away. You two can blend in with the other GIs like you did here in Itaewon."

I rubbed the back of my neck. "Not so successfully."

Mr. Kill shrugged. "Things happen. No police operation is perfect."

"What about the autopsy and the forensic evidence? Anything new there?"

"Not completed yet. But so far, nothing new. It looks like Major Schultz was taken by surprise. Hit in the back of the head with a hatchet and then chopped repeatedly with both the original weapon and with a long-bladed knife."

"The same guys who jumped us?" Ernie asked.

"Maybe."

"But if they took out Major Schultz for her," I asked, "why not leave Itaewon then? Why would she bother getting a new job here?"

Mr. Kill shrugged again. "When you find her, we'll ask her those questions."

Officer Oh stepped forward and handed Ernie an envelope. He opened it and riffled through a stack of Korean bills.

"Your expenses," Mr. Kill said, "for—what do you call it?—running the ville."

"The army provides us an expense account of fifty dollars a month," I replied.

"You'll need more than that," he said. "We don't want to lose her."

Ernie signed a chit that Officer Oh had prepared for him, kept a copy, and slipped the envelope into his inner jacket pocket.

As we were leaving, Mr. Kill put up his hand to stop us. "Some of the people who run the rackets down there in Anjong-ri are not nice people. If you get into trouble, see Officer Kwon. He's a good man. I trust him."

He handed each of us one of Officer Kwon's business cards. English was printed on one side, and *hangul* on the other.

"Don't take weapons with you," Mr. Kill continued. "Too

much of a giveaway. Make sure that everyone believes you're just two GIs from out of town, down there to have fun."

"Don't worry," Ernie said, "we won't have to fake that."

As he backed the jeep into the narrow road, Ernie waved to the *pindaedok* dealer. Ernie turned around, honked his horn and made his way into the swirling Seoul traffic. Soon we'd reached the expressway that led to the Namsan Tunnel. In the darkness, Ernie turned to me.

"You're quiet."

"Yes."

"What's wrong?"

I waited, unsure if I should even mention it. Trust between law enforcement units, especially when they're working a dangerous case together, is absolutely vital, even between the US Army and the Korean National Police. And that trust should never be questioned, unless there's no choice. Doubt can poison an investigation. After working with him for months, I had come to trust Mr. Kill, but something was wrong here.

"Go ahead and talk," Ernie said. "I can handle it, whatever it is."

"I know you can."

"Then spill."

Finally, I asked, "What did you think about that crime scene?"

"Schultz's?"

"Yes."

"I've been waiting for you to say something."

"And I've been waiting for you to."

"I didn't say anything," Ernie told me, "because I didn't want to influence your thinking."

"Don't worry," I said, "you never do."

"Never?"

"Well, maybe sometimes. But you first, what did you think?"

"As phony as a new friend on payday. Somebody dumped the body there, then broke a few empty soju bottles and spread the blood around. Schultz was probably dead before he got there. The Good Major was a prime jerk, but if he'd fought for his life, there would've been a lot more splintered crates and smashed glass. And most of those wounds didn't bleed much."

"Which means they happened after he was dead."

"I'm not a doctor, but it didn't look right to me."

"And so far, the KNPs haven't released the body to Eighth Army."

"You mean, Kill hasn't released the body."

"You think he's covering something up?"

"Sure. That's why they put him in charge."

"And they want us to collar Miss Jo Kyong-ja—to make it look like the arrest is Eighth Army's doing, not the KNP's."

Ernie dodged a kimchi cab that swerved into his lane. "So the KNPs will look more objective once they put her on trial in a Korean court."

"And the court will do whatever the ROK government wants them to do."

Ernie honked at the cab driver and flipped him the bird. In response, the man smiled and waved, thinking it a friendly gesture. "And what the government wants to do," Ernie said, "is find Miss Jo guilty and close the file on the murder of Major Schultz."

"Exactly."

"So maybe we shouldn't go find her?"

"They'd court-martial our butts," I said. "Besides, we need to talk to her. But we should talk to someone else first."

"Who?"

"Our favorite pervert."

"Strange?"

I nodded.

Ernie groaned. "You know what he'll want."

"I do."

What Strange always wanted was a story from one of Ernie's recent sexual escapades; long, vivid, and with not the slightest detail left out. In return, he provided us with excellent intel. As the NCO-in-charge of the Classified Documents Distribution Center, he was privy to everything that happened in the hallowed halls of the 8th United States Army headquarters, including the contents of Top Secret communications.

A pervert in charge of military secrets. Who else?

-10-

All the tables in the 8th United States Army Snack Bar were either occupied or covered with dirty plates left by recently departed diners. The lunch hour was almost over. Busy GIs grabbed their caps, civilian workers slipped on their coats, and the few American women who worked on post—mostly the wives of officers and senior NCOs—grabbed their purses. Ernie and I stood just inside the main door and scanned the cafeteria. Ernie elbowed me in the ribs.

"There he is."

We walked toward a table against a side wall of the huge Quonset hut, pulled over two chairs, and sat down opposite a man wearing the long-sleeved khaki uniform of a Sergeant First Class.

"Strange," Ernie said, plopping his elbows on the table. "How's it hanging?"

"The name is Harvey."

He wore dark glasses. His sparse hair was well-oiled and

slicked back, and an empty cigarette holder dangled from thin lips.

"Long time no see," I said, adding "Harvey" only after a pause.

Even though his glasses were entirely opaque, Strange's facial expression broadcast grievance at a world that didn't understand him.

"What do you want?" he asked.

"Nothing," Ernie replied, "just the usual."

"Information?"

In response, Ernie stared at him, a half-smile on his face.

Strange glanced around the rapidly emptying snack bar, making sure that no one was listening. Then he leaned forward and asked Ernie, "Had any *strange* lately?"

"Does a general fart through silk? Of course I have."

Strange waited, twisting his head slightly so his right ear was placed at a more advantageous angle.

"But you're not going to hear about it," Ernie continued, "not until you spill a little information of your own."

"What information?"

Ernie looked at me. Strange turned in my direction, cigarette holder waggling.

"Major Schultz," I said.

Strange stared at me like an overweight, wanton grasshopper. "What about him?"

"What's his story? How'd he get himself dead?"

"You're the cops. You're supposed to know that."

"We want to know more about his personal life."

Strange nodded, getting it now. "You want to know if he had any *strange* lately?"

"Exactly. And if there were any problems he had. Any enemies. Anybody who would want him dead."

"Wait a minute." Strange sat back. "This could be dangerous."

"Maybe."

"It'll cost you."

"Cost me what?"

"*He* always tells me stories." Strange jammed his thumb in Ernie's direction. "You want this information, now it's *your* turn."

"Maybe I haven't had any *strange* lately."

Strange crossed his arms. "Maybe you'd better find some."

Ernie was grinning ear to ear. "Right, Harvey. That's telling him. It's his turn."

Strange nodded.

I was stuck, but we needed the information. "Okay," I said, "you win. I'll get some *strange*. ASAP. But we'll be out of town and we need everything you can dig up on Major Schultz. I'll call you."

"*No!*" Strange said. "No phones."

"Why not?"

"They're tapped. Every line in the Yongsan Telephone Exchange is recorded and listened to daily."

Panic rose in me for a moment as I thought of my calls with Leah Prevault. But we'd spoken in code and never said anything incriminating. "By who?"

"I ain't saying."

"Okay, Strange," I said. He frowned. "I mean Harvey. We'll be back in a couple of days. I'll call you and we'll set up a meeting."

"Say it's about the football bet I won."

"Gambling's against Army regulation. If somebody's listening . . ."

"They don't care about football betting," he explained. "That's all-American."

"And so are you, right?"

"To the core."

And the damn thing was, he was right.

We stopped briefly at the CID Admin office to let Sergeant Riley know where we were going.

"Anjong-ri?" he asked. "Why the hell you going down there?"

"None of your beeswax," I said.

"You and that Mr. Kill," he replied. "You think you're hot shit now, but you'll be back on regular duty soon."

I asked him to check with his sources at personnel to find out what he could about Major Schultz.

"Why? He was offed by that business girl. What do you need to go poking into his background for?"

"Just find out, will you?"

"You'll owe me."

I glanced at Miss Kim's desk. It was bare except for her teacup, which was empty.

"Where'd she go?" I asked Riley.

"Hell if I know. She's been leaving the office a lot lately, and her work's been backing up. She'd better get on the stick."

Her in-box was empty as far as I could tell, but that was Riley for you. Always put the worst face on any given situation. On the way out, when Riley wasn't looking, Ernie grabbed Riley's copy of today's *Stars and Stripes* and stuck it in his back pocket.

Ernie and I returned to the barracks and changed back into our running-the-ville outfits. Mr. Yim, the houseboy, had already washed and pressed my blue jeans and my button-down shirt. My previously dirty nylon jacket he handed me on a hanger. We were still more than a week out from mid-month payday, but since Ernie had given me part of the KNP expense money, I decided to pay Mr. Yim now. I handed him three ten-thousand-*won* notes, almost sixty bucks.

"Too much," he said.

"Forty for the month," I said, "and I won't have time to buy soap or shoe polish."

"No sweat," he said. He'd ask another GI to purchase extra from the PX.

He was a middle-aged man, probably in his fifties. Before dawn, when he made his way to work, he—like the other houseboys—wore a suit and tie. Face was everything to him, and he didn't want other Koreans to know that his job on the compound involved menial labor. Once Mr. Yim reached the barracks, he locked his suit in a wall locker and changed into the baggy shorts, T-shirt and flip-flops that he wore now. Some of the GIs lorded their status over the houseboys, barking orders at them. This wasn't smart. They found minor ways to take their revenge; refusing to take combat boots off compound for repair or not bothering to carry their uniforms to the base laundry to have new patches sewn on. I was always respectful of Mr. Yim. Not only was he older than me—and Confucian propriety dictated that I be respectful to my elders—but I knew he'd lived through a lot. More than twenty years ago, as a young man, he'd been conscripted into the North Korean army. During one particularly horrific battle, he'd managed to slip away from his unit and escape to the south. Unfortunately, once he arrived in Seoul, a big army deuce-and-a-half rattled by, full of armed soldiers, and he was once again conscripted, this time into the South Korean Army. He'd survived the war, but just barely. After I'd gained his trust, he showed me the shrapnel wounds he'd suffered on his back and his upper thigh.

"American doctor save my life," he told me. "I always like America."

I supposed that was as good a reason as any.

He'd landed a job on compound washing GI laundry, shining GI boots and making GI bunks, and had been here ever since. Somewhere along the line, he'd married and he now had two kids, both recent high school graduates. He was proud that he'd gotten them such a high-level education. Still, they were both looking for work, and so he continued to put up with abuse from obnoxious American soldiers.

Once I made the mistake of asking him about his family in North Korea. When the war ended and the heavily fortified Demilitarized Zone was set up, it became almost impossible to escape from the Communist-controlled north. Hundreds of thousands of families were divided. Mr. Yim stopped shining shoes and looked at the ground. It was almost two minutes until I realized that a puddle of tears had formed on the cold cement.

I never asked him again.

-11-

We gassed up the jeep at the 8th Army POL point (petroleum, oil, and lubricants) and crossed the Chamsu Bridge, leaving the Han River and the City of Seoul behind. We cruised south on the Seoul-to-Pusan Expressway, admiring the new road that had been completed little more than a year ago.

"Korea's going to hell," Ernie said.

He was alluding to the road. It looked almost like a Stateside freeway: two lanes in either direction with a ten-yard-wide divider in the middle. Much of it had been carved into the countryside, and the ridges on either side were lined with newly planted birch trees.

"Can't even see the rice paddies," I said.

Ernie nodded.

We preferred the old roads. Two-lane affairs that wound through pear orchards and passed craggy peaks and narrowed when entering farming villages, with ramshackle wooden buildings and homes covered with straw thatch and old men sitting on stone porches puffing serenely on long-stemmed pipes. Of course, this new expressway from Seoul to Pusan did cut the driving time by more than half.

"Look!" I pointed at a billboard with a giant picture of a pretty young girl about to chomp into a Choco Pie. Such advertisements were never allowed before.

"I told you," Ernie said. "The road to perdition."

About sixty kilometers south of Seoul we turned off the expressway, heading for the city of Pyongtaek. Before we reached it we turned west toward our destination. After passing a busy bus station and bouncing over a double row of railroad tracks, we entered the small village of Anjong-ri. As far as I knew, it hadn't even existed before the Korean War. If it had, it was probably just a country intersection that wasn't on maps. But after the war, it was settled that the US military would be using the flat plains in the surrounding area to construct a large helicopter base, and the town had sprung up like wet rice shoots reaching toward sunlight. First had been the bars, then the chophouses, and finally the shops: tailor shops, brassware souvenir emporiums, photography studios, sporting goods stores. And from there, the place had continued to grow. Rat-infested *yoguans*—Korean inns—and endless catacomb-like alleys where the business girls plied their trade.

One thing Anjong-ri did have was a brand-new white cement-block building housing the local office of the

Korean National Police. We cruised past it, the flag of the Republic of Korea—its red and blue yin-yang symbol on a pure white background—fluttering in the cold morning breeze. I thought of the card Mr. Kill had given me for Lieutenant Kwon. I hoped I wouldn't need it.

As we neared the front gate, pedestrian traffic increased: young women scantily clad, wearing just shorts and T-shirts with a sweater thrown on to protect them from the cold, plastic pans canted against their hips, on their way to the bathhouse; old men pushing carts laden with produce or hay or old pieces of junk metal that were somehow valuable to them; the occasional GI in civvies, rubbing his eyes and making his way back toward base.

At the big front gate of Camp Humphries, we were waved to a halt by an MP. Without a word, Ernie handed him our dispatch.

"CID," the MP said.

"No," Ernie snapped, "just Eighth Army Provost Marshal's office. Nothing to be gabbing about."

The MP handed the clipboard back to Ernie, who in turn handed it to me.

"ID," the MP said.

We both showed him our military identification. Grim-faced, he waved us through.

Ernie gunned the engine. "In five minutes, every MP on base will know that two CID agents from Seoul have come to poke into their business."

"Forget 'em, Ernie," I told him. "We'll be operating off base. They won't bother us."

"They better not."

Ernie turned left into a row of angled parking spots. He switched off the ignition, lifted the chain welded to the floorboard, and wound it through the steering wheel. When it was knotted securely, he clicked home the padlock. We hopped out of the jeep and strode toward the pedestrian exit. The same MP glanced at our identification again and stared at us suspiciously, but waved us through.

The dirty neon of Anjong-ri flickered in the overcast afternoon, the village greeting us without emotion, like a sullen victim of domestic abuse.

It wasn't difficult to find the Yobo Club. We wound around the narrow alleys past the Kisaeng Bar, China Doll Nightclub and Mini Skirt Scotch Corner until we found it. As we pushed through the single wooden door, a bell rang above us. A girl who had been dozing behind the bar sat upright.

The joints in Anjong-ri were much smaller than the spacious nightclubs of Itaewon, which made sense because they were catering to fewer GIs. Only a few hundred soldiers were stationed full-time at Camp Humphries. And Anjong-ri didn't draw anyone other than GIs. No English language teachers, no tourists, no foreign businessmen, no Peace Corps workers on a Friday night out. What it had was GIs. GIs and business girls. And that was it.

"I love this place," Ernie said.

Other than the girl behind the bar, the Yobo Club was empty. "You love the Yobo Club," I asked, "or the whole village?"

"The whole village," Ernie said, spreading his arms. "It's so beaten up, so run-down, so depraved."

"Like you," I said.

"Like my ping-pong heart."

We took a seat at a table against the wall. The girl came out from behind the bar. No sense beating around the bush. I asked her if she knew Miss Jo Kyong-ja. She shook her head no. I explained that Miss Jo had left Anjong-ri a few months ago, and the girl said that she'd only been working here a few weeks. She seemed pleased to be speaking Korean to an American, a new experience for her. She told me how difficult it was to understand the English the GIs spoke, so different from what she'd studied in middle school, but apparently the more experienced employees of the Yobo Club had told her she'd pick it up soon enough. She hoped that was true.

Ernie waited patiently while we talked and finally said, "Can a guy get a beer around here?"

The girl didn't understand, so I translated.

She brought two brown bottles sporting the Oriental Brewery label. When I ordered a glass to go with mine she seemed surprised, but brought it back quickly. It was smudged and dusty, but I'd used worse.

Ernie paid her out of the envelope Mr. Kill had given us.

I asked to talk to the mama-san. The girl seemed surprised and explained that she wouldn't be in until five, when the cannon on compound went off.

"Tell her we need to talk to her now." I showed her my badge. She couldn't read it or understand it, but just knowing we were some sort of government officials was enough to frighten her. Without hesitation she took off through a door in back. Ernie and I sat alone, quaffing our cold beer.

"You gotta stop being so friendly to these girls, Sueño."

"Why?"

"They lose respect for you."

"What makes you say that?"

"You make it too easy for them. Speak their language and all that. You gotta make them work for it."

"Being mutually unintelligible helps interpersonal relationships?"

"Lets them know who's boss."

I was formulating a response when someone burst through the back door. A small woman with a round face and a grey bouffant hairdo, wearing black slacks and a red Chinese blouse. Without slowing down, she barreled around the far edge of the bar.

"Who wanna talk mama-san?" she asked, peering around the small barroom like a bull who'd just entered the ring. Surprised, Ernie turned and studied her. Slowly, he raised his right hand and pointed at me.

She pounded across the wood-planked floor. "What you want?" Her voice was like the scrape of a razor along leather.

"Have a seat," I said, motioning to an open chair.

"You talk first," she said. "Then I sit. Maybe."

Before I could say anything, the cannon went off. In a few minutes, off-duty GIs would be filtering out of the front gate of Camp Humphries and into the village of Anjong-ri.

"You talk," she said. "Pretty soon I busy."

I asked her again to sit, this time in Korean. She thought it over, stepped forward, and keeping her butt toward the front edge of the chair, sat down. "You speaky Korean pretty good," she said. "Who teach you?"

"I study it," I said. "On compound."

"They teach Korean on compound?"

"In Seoul, yes."

She shook her head. "Number *hucking* ten." No good. There's no "f" sound in the Korean alphabet so often it's replaced with "h." And in GI slang, number one—or *hana*—is best and, reasonably enough, number ten is worst.

"Why number ten?" I asked.

"GI speak Korean, all girl lose respect for GI."

Ernie grinned and sipped on his beer.

I took the bait. "Why lose respect?"

Her eyes widened. "Talk like baby. All girl laugh at them."

Ernie glugged even more of his beer down, trying to keep from bursting into laughter.

"Okay," I said. "No more Korean. Only English."

"That smart," she said, reasonably.

Then I asked her about Jo Kyong-ja.

Her eyes squinted but she answered. "She long time go."

"Go where?"

"Seoul. She owe me money. Why you look for her?"

I showed her my badge.

"You MP?"

"No, CID."

I explained the difference. We handle mostly capital crimes as opposed to misdemeanors and lesser felonies and we're trained in the latest techniques of forensic science. When I was done, she waved her hand. "MP same same."

Ernie was thoroughly enjoying himself.

"You want 'nother beer?" she asked, turning to him. When he didn't answer right away, she shouted to the girl behind the bar to bring two more beers. For a moment I thought she was going to pay for them, but when she demanded money, I realized she wasn't impressed with our law enforcement status. Ernie pulled out the wad of Korean bills again and the mama-san eyed them knowingly.

"You not GI," she said.

"What makes you say that?"

"Too much Korean money."

I was about to steer her back toward the subject of Jo Kyong-ja when a half-dozen GIs pushed through the door. They wore dirty fatigues and the shoulder patch of the local aviation unit, and every one of them, it seemed, had fingers darkened with grease. They marched resolutely toward the bar and the girl pulled out cold OB and set them up all around. One of them kept turning his head toward me and Ernie and the mama-san sitting at the table.

She ignored them, keeping all her attention on Ernie's envelope of *won*.

I asked her when she'd last seen Jo Kyong-ja, and she said months ago and that the girl owed her money for the last month's rent; all the girls who worked in the Yobo Club also lived out back.

"Why didn't she pay?" I asked.

"She wanna go to Seoul. So she pack her bag, leave at night time, everybody sleep."

"Did she go with a boyfriend?"

"No. By herself. Probably she take taxi to Pyongtaek. From there take train."

"Did you try to find her?"

"No." The old woman pulled out a pack of Kent cigarettes and lit one up. "Too hard find. Anyway, I make money. She gone."

Ernie leaned toward her. "If she came back to Anjong-ri, would you know it?"

"Course I know. Anybody know Yobo Club mama-san. Anybody tell me."

The GI at the bar kept swiveling his head, eyeing us suspiciously, clearly jealous that we were involved in such an intimate conversation with the mama-san of the Yobo Club. He chugged down a huge swig of beer, set the bottle down, and rose to his feet.

"Here he comes," I told Ernie.

We were used to this. In these little GI villages, everyone knows everyone else, and they're suspicious—and resentful—of strangers. The guy walked up behind the mama-san. I saw that his rank was staff sergeant, and his nametag said Torrelli. He leaned down and put his arm around her shoulder.

"Are these guys bothering you, Mama?"

"No. Okay," she said, waving her cigarette.

"If they bother you," he continued, "you let me know, okay, Mama?"

"Yeah. Yeah. I let you know."

Then he stood to his full height. "Nobody," he said, pointing a grease-stained forefinger at us, "and I mean nobody, messes with our Mama-san. You got that?"

Ernie rolled his eyes. I was hoping he'd ignore the guy, but instead he said, "What're you? Her daddy?"

Torrelli stared at him for a while, letting his eyes go lifeless. "Where I come from," he said, "we eat guys like you for lunch."

"Well then," Ernie said, "you can bite me right now."

Torrelli stepped toward Ernie and Ernie—never one to de-escalate a confrontation—lifted the cocktail table and threw it at him.

Mama-san started screeching about the broken glassware. Torrelli backed up, wide-eyed now, wondering what the hell he'd gotten into.

Maybe it was the pressure of the Schultz investigation, or maybe it was the humiliation we suffered when we'd taken Miss Jo into custody and then lost her. Whatever the reason, Ernie'd just about reached the end of his rope. He stepped around the tilted table and over flooding beer and started for Torrelli. I jumped up from my chair and reached for Ernie, grabbed him by the shoulders and held him back. The guys at the bar were up now, all of them gathered around Torrelli.

The Yobo Club mama-san had handled incidents like this before. "Whatsamatta you?" she screamed at Ernie. "You breakey all glass." Turning to Torrelli she said, "Why you bother mama-san? We talk about something important! We talk about Miss Jo." Torrelli looked stricken. "You know now," the mama-san said, wagging her forefinger in Torrelli's face. "Your old *yobo*."

"Is she all right?" Torrelli asked.

"Maybe all right. Maybe no." The mama-san pointed to the bar. "You sit down, mind own *business*."

"Okay, Mama," Torrelli said, chastened now. Grumbling, he and the other GIs returned to the bar. I helped the mama-san set the table back upright. The first girl we'd encountered hustled out from the behind the bar with a damp cloth and a dustpan, and soon everything was mostly dry, the broken shards were collected and the Yobo Club was once again shipshape.

We were pretty much done here. The mama-san had no more useful information for us, but we ordered another round of beer simply to save face. We didn't want to run off too soon. Still, Torrelli kept glaring at us. Ernie glared back.

Finally, Torrelli came over again. "I just want to show you something."

I nodded. He reached into the breast pocket of his fatigue shirt and pulled out a folded envelope wrapped in a thick rubber band. He unwrapped the package and pulled out a short stack of Polaroid snapshots. Leaning over mama-san's shoulder, he spread them on the table.

"That's her," he said. "And me. I took them last summer."

"I go now," the mama-san said and rose abruptly and left.

I studied the photos. They were mostly of Miss Jo. She had a different look then. Shorter hair, heavily permed; more makeup, making her look older and more severe.

In the photos of her inside the Yobo Club, she crossed her shapely legs and smoked a lot. But there were other photos of Torrelli and his buddies having a barbecue, probably on base. Miss Jo and a few other Korean women were there, dressed more demurely for an outdoor outing. Torrelli was proudest of the photos he had taken by the shores of Namyang Bay. Miss Jo wore a two-piece bathing suit and looked like a knockout, although she spent most of her time in the water, trying to avoid Torrelli's omnipresent camera lens.

"Have a seat, Torrelli," I said.

He sat. Looking sheepish, he said, "Sorry for interrupting you guys earlier."

"That's okay," I replied.

Ernie sipped on his beer.

Nervous, Torrelli said, "Do you know where she is?"

"No," I replied. "Not too long ago she was in Itaewon, but now she's gone. We were hoping someone down here could tell us how to locate her."

Torrelli shook his head sadly. "I wish I could."

"She didn't say goodbye?" I asked.

"Not a word."

Ernie sneered and gurgled some beer between his teeth. Torrelli glanced at him, but I brought the conversation back to the subject at hand.

"Have you ever gone to Seoul to look for her?"

"No. She used to talk about it all the time, the big city

and all that. But I've never really spent time there, and I wouldn't know where to start looking."

"What would you do if you found her?" Ernie asked.

Torrelli studied Ernie for a moment; deciding, I believe, whether or not to take offense.

"I don't know," he answered. Then he lowered his head. "Maybe that's why I didn't go looking for her."

"How long did you steady her?" I asked.

"Almost six months."

That was six months of paying her rent and providing her a stipend upon which to live. Many GIs did this. The advantage was that it was safer, from a disease standpoint, to stick with one woman. Also, much of the expense could be defrayed by simply spending all your PX ration on easily black-marketed items and bringing them out to your *yobo*. The problem was feelings. GIs often fell in love, sometimes to the point of matrimony.

"Six months," I said. "Unless you extended your tour, it was too late to put in the marriage paperwork."

"Yeah," Torrelli replied.

A GI's tour in Korea is one year. If you decide to put in the paperwork to get permission to marry a Korean woman, it takes anywhere from nine to ten months. Both the 8th United States Army and the Korean government have to sign off on it. To keep the number of marriages down, the paperwork is purposely cumbersome and very slow.

"Have you put in an extension?" I asked.

Torrelli nodded. "Yeah."

So he had another year in country. Enough time to find her and put in the marriage paperwork. Also enough time to do something else, like maybe track her down and beat the crap out of her.

"When were you last in Seoul?" Ernie asked.

"I told you. I've never been there. Only during in-processing."

"If you hear from her," I said, "or find out she's contacted anybody, give me a call." I slipped him one of my cards.

Torrelli studied it. "Eighth Army CID," he said.

I was hoping Ernie wouldn't say, "Hey, he can read." Luckily, he didn't.

"Is she in trouble?" Torrelli asked.

"I'm afraid she is."

"For what?"

"Some people think she murdered someone."

"Murder?" he said. "She wouldn't do that."

"I don't think so either. But unless we talk to her, I won't be able to get her off the hook."

Torrelli policed up the photographs like a stack of cards, rewrapped them, and stuck them carefully back in his pocket. He slid my card in there, too.

"There's no way she could murder somebody," he said. And with that he rose and stalked back to the bar. His buddies were talking but mostly ignoring him. Even though he stood amongst them, he was the odd man out.

"Talk about carrying a torch," Ernie said.

"Do you think he'd commit murder for her?" I asked.

"I think he'd do anything for her."

We were back in the jeep, speeding on country roads toward Pyongtaek. The sun lowered in a reddish light, casting long shadows. I was driving because Ernie had somehow jammed his finger when he'd flipped over the cocktail table at the Yobo Club. Amidst straw-thatched homes, a pack of small boys played on the edge of the road. I slowed. Suddenly a ball rolled toward the center white line and a small figure darted after it. Without thinking, I slammed on the brakes.

The jeep's front bumper came to a halt just inches from the boy.

Ernie let out a breath.

"Good stop," he said.

The boy hardly noticed us. He retrieved his ball and returned to his comrades. I watched him for a long while, until I knew he was safe. Then I restarted the engine and we proceeded on our way.

Ten minutes later, we passed the city limits of Pyongtaek and approached the on-ramp to the Seoul-Pusan expressway. Seoul, north of us, was the way I was supposed to go. Ernie glanced at me.

"I know what you want to do," he said. "And why you didn't want to stay in Anjong-ri. I have you all figured out, Sueño."

My hands tightened on the oversized steering wheel.

"If you feel it," Ernie said, "do it."

At the last second, I jerked the jeep to the right and sped up the ramp with a sign in both Korean and English: SOUTH, BUSAN. Busan was the new, government-approved English spelling for the ancient port city of Pusan.

Ernie leaned back in his seat, preparing for a long ride. "You really think you can find her?"

"Probably not," I answered.

He leaned on his right shoulder, favoring his jammed finger. "At least you're not delusional," he said.

-13-

I'd met her on a cold case we'd worked: an American soldier who'd been killed right after the end of the Korean War. For almost twenty years, the murder had remained unsolved. Her name was Doctor Yong In-ja, and she was in charge of the Itaewon branch of the Yongsan District Public Health Service. With her help, we'd closed the case.

She wasn't a standout beauty, as Ernie had repeatedly mentioned to me, but she smiled often and radiated warmth. One thing led to another and we'd become close. I later discovered that her parents had been murdered by the right-wing reactionary forces who were fighting for control of Korea immediately after the war. They'd been leaders in a trade-unionist movement that sought true democracy, and were resisting the rule of the Koreans that had collaborated with the Japanese colonizers oppressing the country from 1910 through the end of World War II in 1945. She was committed to the same cause her parents had been devoted to, and it was this commitment that put her in danger. The military dictatorship of Pak Chung-hee saw her, and those of a like mind, as a threat to their iron-fisted control.

She soon escaped to North Korea, but when she ran into problems with the regime there as well, I'd helped her escape. Now she lived as a fugitive in Cholla-Namdo, South Cholla Province, and as far as I knew she lived either in or near the city of Mokpo. We had a son. His name was Il-yong, the First Dragon. I hadn't seen him for almost a year now, and he'd soon be two years old.

Since she'd fled Seoul, she hadn't contacted me. It was too dangerous. The Korean CIA had its tentacles deeply entrenched in all corners of Korean society. I also hadn't attempted to search for her. If I had, the KNPs would almost certainly have followed me. An American in the southwest of Korea was unusual, and my movements would be reported and tracked. I couldn't risk leading the extreme right wing of the Korean government to In-ja and our child. So I waited, hoping she'd reach out to me. She never did.

Ernie told me time and again to forget about her, to move on with my life. For months I couldn't, but finally I realized that he was right. We'd never married and any further relationship between us was doomed by the forces that would just as soon arrest and interrogate her, torture her and dump her mutilated corpse in a shallow grave.

"She knows that," Ernie told me. "That's why she's not in touch. She wants you to move on."

And so I did. Finally. When I met Leah Prevault.

But when you have a woman you once considered to be your partner for life, and a son, maybe you never move on. It might not be possible.

After over an hour of driving we reached a split in the road. The sign to the left said BUSAN, and the one to the right said MOKPO. I veered to the right.

Ernie woke up. "You want me to take over?"

"I'm okay for now."

"All right," he said, crossing his arms and trying to get comfortable in the big canvas seat. We passed another billboard advertising Choco Pie, with the same cute girl smiling brightly.

Ernie knew why I was doing this. It was my chance. Miss Jo Kyong-ja's hometown was Mokpo. Inspector Kill had told us that the KNPs would handle that aspect of the investigation, but he hadn't told us specifically not to go there. Ernie and I could plausibly claim that we felt it was important for the investigation for us to actually visit Jo Kyong-ja's home of record. It was a stretch, and we would almost certainly get our butts chewed for doing it, but nobody could accuse us of directly disobeying orders. And, just as importantly, it gave me a reason to go to Mokpo that the Korean National Police wouldn't flag as suspicious. They wouldn't wonder why an American investigator was prowling around Mokpo. They'd know. Or at least they'd *think* they knew.

How much could I find about the location of Doctor Yong In-ja and my son, Il-yong, under the guise of the Schultz investigation? Probably not much. But I had to try. Something deep down was telling me to go to Mokpo. It wasn't rational. But this might be the only chance I'd ever have to go there, to see the city, to breathe the same air as In-ja and Il-yong. With no US military installations anywhere near Mokpo, the likelihood was vanishingly small that I'd ever have a reason to come here again. I had to take advantage of this opportunity. It would almost certainly be my last.

We finally rolled off the expressway and onto the broad road leading to the port city of Mokpo. Even out here, the sharp salty tang of the ocean bit into my nose, bringing me alert like smelling salts. Ernie rubbed his eyes and sat up. "Where the hell are we?"

"Mokpo," I said.

We'd driven all night. The sun had been up for over an hour.

"Where we going?" Ernie asked.

"To the KNP headquarters," I said. "I don't want anyone to think we're sneaking around."

Ernie nodded.

We were unfamiliar with the city and didn't have a map,

but I stopped at a traffic circle next to a white-gloved cop on a platform directing traffic. In Korean, I asked him where we could find the KNP headquarters building. He waved and described two or three turns and streets. I thanked him and promptly forgot the instructions, but at least we were headed in the right direction. After a mile or so, I asked another cop who gave similar directions, and after a few minutes of wandering we pulled up to the big cement-block two-story building that housed the Mokpo headquarters of the Korean National Police.

We parked the jeep out back, Ernie padlocked the steering wheel, and we climbed out.

To say that we were gawked at like celebrities in the Mokpo police station is an understatement. We attracted so much attention, we were more like aliens who'd just landed in a spaceship. The cops down here, and the city's general Korean population, saw very few foreigners and even fewer in military law enforcement. When we made it clear why we were here and mentioned Inspector Kill's name, a young officer was assigned to us: Lieutenant Taek. He took us to the childhood home of Jo Kyong-ja.

"It is being watched twenty-four hours a day," he said in passable English. "Nobody know." Meaning the stakeout was clandestine.

We climbed into the back of a cramped Korean-made van and were introduced to two surveillance technicians. They let me look through a telescope that peeked through a hole drilled into the side of the van. Midday sunlight illuminated the scene.

"Mother live there and work there," Taek said.

"And her son?"

"Yes. Now he in school."

"High school?" I asked.

"Yes."

It was a shanty in back of a fish cannery. Skinny dogs frolicked in the mud. A couple of toddlers wearing no diapers were being watched over by an old woman who squatted on a splintered wooden porch. Tin roofs spread over what appeared to be four or five hooches.

"How many families live there?" I asked.

"Twelve," Lieutenant Taek replied.

"Twelve?"

He nodded.

Ernie took a look. The chomping on his ginseng gum sped up, but otherwise he showed no reaction.

"So the mom's working in the cannery now?"

"Yes. And daughter not here."

"Do you expect her to show up?"

He shrugged. "We don't know. Seoul say watch, we watch."

"Tell me about her, the mom. Who is she? What is she like?"

"She work in cannery," he said.

"That's it? That's all you know?"

Lieutenant Taek paused, thinking something over. Apparently he decided that cooperating with us was better than facing the wrath of Gil Kwon-up, whose intimidating reputation reached even the very edges of the country. "She's troublemaker," he said.

Ernie sat back from the telescope, listening now.

"In what way?" I asked.

"She union. Not supposed to have union."

The Pak Chung-hee government had banned unions. All except for the FOEU, the Foreign Organizations Employees Union—the one that represented the workers on the US Forces Korea compounds; in other words, the Korean civilians who worked for 8th Army. The workers in other industries, like steel foundries, ship-building docks or mining companies, were prohibited from forming unions on pain of death. The rationale was that the country couldn't afford these unions yet. The rebuilding after the Korean War had to be done in a "cooperative spirit," or the nation wouldn't be able to lift itself out of poverty. This meant, in effect, that workers got the shaft while the *chaebol*, corporate conglomerates, made millions and continued to reinvest and grow larger.

"They have a union in this cannery?" I asked.

"*No*," Lieutenant Taek said. "No can have. But secret, maybe they have."

So the workers were organizing clandestinely. I'd heard about that. Just a few months ago, an illegal union had been formed by coal miners in the Taebaek Mountains. They'd brought production to a halt with a strike and even armed themselves to resist the KNP. Pak Chung-hee didn't mess around. He sent in a battalion of ROK Army infantry, and they ruthlessly eliminated what the president considered to be an armed rebellion. None of this appeared in the Korean press, not even in the *Pacific Stars and Stripes*. I'd read about it in *TIME* magazine.

"So if she's in a union," I asked, "why haven't you arrested her?"

"Maybe we do someday. Right now, we watch."

"You want a bigger catch," I said.

Lieutenant Taek looked at me, puzzled.

"A bigger fish," I said, spreading my arms.

He smiled, understanding now.

"Do you think the North Koreans are helping the union?" I asked.

He shrugged. "Maybe. Maybe no. Anyway, we watch."

I took another look through the telescope. The gigantic cannery loomed over dozens of tin-roofed shanties. What was taking place behind those walls was probably a scene right from an Upton Sinclair novel, and in a way I was glad I couldn't see it. I thought of another question.

"What's it mean, *koshigi*?"

Lieutenant Taek smiled even more broadly. "Who teach you?"

"I heard it. In Seoul."

Taek shook his head. "Seoul people no speak. Only Cholla people."

Of course, I knew that Miss Jo was from here, from Cholla province. "What's it mean?" I asked.

Lieutenant Taek thought about that. "It's like when you forget something or don't know. So you wanna say something, anything."

"So it means nothing," I said.

"Or everything," Taek responded. "But most important thing, *koshigi* means you're Cholla people."

"And Cholla people are troublemakers," Ernie said.

Taek's face darkened. He turned to Ernie. "Seoul people say so. Maybe *they* are troublemakers."

His face flushed red. He'd said more than he intended to. But what he'd shown me was that the ancient animosity between the people of Cholla, who'd once been an independent kingdom, and those who imposed a central government from Seoul, ran very deep indeed.

I thanked Lieutenant Taek for his help and we returned to KNP headquarters.

An hour before noon, Ernie and I drove out to a long wharf near the cannery. It was lined with a promenade along the beach and what appeared to be hundreds of small fish eateries. Live mackerel splashed in green tanks. We climbed out of the jeep and walked.

"Do you suppose they're close?" Ernie asked, meaning In-ja and my son.

"Impossible to say."

"Right," Ernie said. "You don't know where they are, and if you try to find them you put them both in danger."

"You think they'd hurt the boy?"

"Probably not," Ernie replied. "But he'd be left without a mother."

I nodded, knowing from experience how painful that was. My mother died when I was a toddler. My father disappeared into the endless murky sea known as Mexico. I'd been brought up by the Supervisors of the County of Los Angeles, moving from foster home to foster home. When I turned seventeen, I joined the Army.

Ernie stared out to sea. A blue KNP sedan sat parked near the beach, not too far from our jeep.

"They're watching," Ernie said.

"I know."

He sighed. "You need to let it go, Sueño. In-ja and Il-yong have made a life without you. Not because they wanted to, but because they had no choice. Now it's up to you. You can wallow in grief forever or you can suck it up and get on with it."

"Get on with my life?"

"Yeah. With somebody else."

"You mean Leah."

"Whoever. That's up to you. But someone. You're not like me. You're a homebody, a one-woman man."

Beyond the vast bay in front of us, small islands dotted the horizon.

"You want some *haemul-tang*?" I asked. Ernie stared at me blankly. "Fish soup," I translated.

"Before we hit the road?"

"Yes," I said. "Before we hit the road."

"You're on," Ernie said, patting the envelope in his pocket. "I'm buying."

-14-

We drove straight through and made it back to Seoul two hours after close of business. Staff Sergeant Riley was still at his desk.

"I *know*. I *know*," Ernie said. And then, in a nasal voice, "Where in the hell have you two guys *been*?"

"The Provost Marshal is about to bust a gut," Riley told us.

"We were on an investigation," Ernie replied.

Riley stuck his finger into the center of his desk blotter. "You're required to report in at zero eight hundred hours every day, Trooper. No exceptions. No ifs, ands, or buts."

Ernie ignored him and stalked to the counter in back and tilted the stainless steel coffee urn. "What, no java?"

"You're late," Riley said. "By about twelve hours."

Ernie fiddled with the coffee urn for a while, as if to prepare another pot, but finally gave up in disgust.

I sat down in front of Riley's desk. "What'd you find out about Major Schultz?"

"What's to find out?" he said, pulling out a sheaf of papers.

"Been in the army for twelve years. ROTC from some agricultural school in Texas. Pretty good efficiency ratings. Comes to Korea and is assigned to the J-2."

"What'd he do there?"

"His official title was Adjutant. But in reality, he was a gopher. Go for anything Colonel Jameson wanted."

"Isn't Jameson *the* J-2?" This was the full colonel in charge of military intelligence for the Joint Staff of the United Nations Command, US Forces Korea, and 8th United States Army.

"Yeah," Riley said. "Took over about five months ago. They say he's a go-getter."

"So Schultz was, too?"

Riley shrugged. "Hell if I know."

"What was Schultz working on?"

"I don't know that either. What's that have to do with being stabbed by some business girl in Itaewon?"

"Maybe nothing."

"Maybe nothing is right." Riley pointed his forefinger at me, resembling some sort of debauched Uncle Sam. "Don't be poking your nose into things that don't concern you, Sueño. Especially when it deals with those spooks over at J-2."

Ernie walked back from the counter. "Who turned you into an enforcer?"

"Just a word to the wise," Riley said.

"Wise? You're nothing but a paper-pusher."

After all that driving and lack of sleep and a painfully jammed finger, Ernie was in a bad mood. I stood up.

"Come on, Ernie," I told him. "Let's get some chow."

He glared at Riley on the way out, and Riley glared back.

Leah Prevault, at least, was glad to hear from me.

After washing up in the barracks, I called her BOQ—Bachelor Officer Quarters—from the Charge of Quarters phone. Even though the BOQ phone sat on a small table in the hallway, shared by all the female officers who lived there, she picked up after two rings.

"I was hoping it would be you," she said.

"Can I come over?" I asked.

"All clear on the female BOQ front," she said.

Twenty minutes later I was knocking on her door and she let me in, glancing up and down the hallway as she did so.

"Did anybody see you?"

"I don't think so."

"Good," she said, throwing her arms around my neck. "That means you can stay the night."

"Is that an order?" I asked.

"Consider it so."

Later, I told her about Mokpo. She was quiet as she listened, and for a long time after I finished. Finally, she said, "What happens if you find her?"

"I take care of my son, that's first and foremost."

She waited. I knew the unspoken question she was asking. I continued. "Between me and his mother, I'm not sure. It's been a long time." I paused. Captain Prevault was a good shrink. Instead of prompting me with another question, she waited for me to go on. "I believe I'm over her," I said.

She had a sharp intuition, and she also knew me well. The question rushed out of her. "But if you saw her, if she was standing right in front of you . . ."

I swung my legs out of the bed, stood up, and walked toward the small window. I peered outside of the long Quonset hut that had been remodeled into the Female Bachelor Officer Quarters. It was cold outside. Wind whipped through the few remaining leaves on a line of poplar trees. Down the hallway, someone turned on a shower.

I knew what it was like to grow up without a mom, without a dad, to be the child of a broken home. In my case, a completely shattered home. How could I do that to my son? And how would I explain all this to Leah? Maybe I eventually could, but at that moment, standing there in that poorly heated Quonset hut, I was unable to find the words.

"I don't know," I said finally.

This didn't make her happy. She sat up, slipped on her robe and kept her back toward me. I grabbed my clothes, stepped into my pants and buttoned my shirt. I started to leave. I hesitated at the door, hoping she'd ask me to stay. She didn't. She just sat huddled on the edge of the bed, looking small.

"I'll call you," I said, then I opened the door and left.

The next morning, Colonel Emmett S. Jameson sat behind a mother-of-pearl nameplate that was almost as wide as his desk. Behind him, a framed diploma, various photographs, and military awards were hung in three busy rows. Leaning atop a varnished bookshelf, a ceremonial bayonet gleamed against a velvet backdrop, testifying to the great man's martial prowess.

Ernie and I were there early, showered and shaved and wearing newly pressed coats and ties. We wanted this man's cooperation, and from what we'd gleaned from his receptionist, he was a bereaved man.

"He thought of Major Schultz as a son," she told us solemnly.

A slight paunch bulged out from above Colonel Jameson's highly polished belt buckle. Not enough to classify him as a slob, but enough to make it clear that he'd spent many years fighting battles more concerned with memos, reports, and briefings than with bullets and hand grenades.

"I've been waiting for you two," he said. I raised an eyebrow. "Not you specifically," he continued, "but someone from law enforcement."

"Concerning Major Schultz's death?" I asked.

"Yes."

"Why is that, sir?"

He interlaced his fingers. "I knew Major Schultz quite well, and his wife and children. He was assigned to me back at Fort Hood, and when I was appointed to this job, I asked if he'd accompany me. He agreed." Colonel Jameson placed his hands on his desk. "As such, I feel aggrieved not only about his death, but also about the earlier allegations that were made against him."

Ernie sat expressionless and completely still. In formal interactions with the brass, he usually liked to let me take the lead, unless something pissed him off.

"Aggrieved, sir?"

"Yes. About the accusations of infidelity on his part."

Ernie glanced at me. When I didn't speak, he said, "They're not just accusations."

Colonel Jameson shrugged. "There're two sides to every story."

I was worried that Ernie was about to say something rude, so I spoke up quickly.

"What exactly were Major Schultz's duties, sir?"

"Duties?" Colonel Jameson seemed surprised by the question. "He was my adjutant."

"So he did the work you assigned to him?"

"Yes, of course."

"What, for example?"

Colonel Jameson squirmed in his seat. "Well, some of it was administrative, making sure that our personnel system ran smoothly and that the right people were being slotted into the right jobs, things like that."

"But some of it was classified," Ernie said.

"Yes, of course. That's what we do here at J-2."

"What sort of classified work was Major Schultz doing?" I asked.

"Well, if it's classified," Colonel Jameson replied, "then, of course, I can't tell you."

"We have Top Secret clearances," I told him.

"Yes, but do you have a need to know?"

"It could've had to do with Major Schultz's death," Ernie said. "We damn sure do have a need to know."

Colonel Jameson swiveled his chair and stared at Ernie. "I'm not sure I like your attitude."

"I'm not sure Major Schultz liked getting dead," Ernie replied. "Maybe you ought to tell us what the hell he was working on, Colonel."

He squinted at Ernie, as if trying to memorize his face. "What's your name again?"

"Bascom," Ernie said, and then spelled it for him. "First name Ernest."

Colonel Jameson jotted it down. "Your rank?" he asked.

"Classified."

"Oh, that's right. CID." He tossed his pen down.

In theory, the ranks of CID agents was classified because the army didn't want higher ranking officers to be able to put pressure on field agents in order to quash an investigation. In practice, everybody knew we were low-ranking schmoes and pressure could be placed on us through informal channels, such as a conversation over drinks at the Officers Club.

I spoke rapidly, trying to break the tension. "It probably has nothing to do with his death, sir. Even if his duties were of a classified nature. But his killer is still on the loose and we have to cover all the bases. Make sure we're not missing something."

"I heard you missed *her*," he said, "after you took her into custody."

News spread fast at the 8th Army Officers Club.

"Yes, sir. She got away. A mistake we will soon rectify. In the meantime, was Major Schultz working on any special projects? Anything out of the ordinary?"

Colonel Jameson took a deep breath and apparently willed himself to calm down. "There was one thing."

I pulled out my notebook. "What was that, sir?"

He waggled his finger at me. "Don't write anything down."

I stuck my notebook back into my jacket pocket.

"I had him doing a full review of operations," he said. "The J-2 organizational chart is a mess. So many functions have been added over the years, sometimes operated for a while and then forgotten, that it seemed to me there was a lot of dead wood floating around. I wanted to streamline and con-solidate where possible. Fred was looking into that."

"Major Schultz?"

"Yes, Major Schultz."

"Had he found anything in particular that seemed anoma-lous?" Then I remembered that field grade officers sometimes found the use of sophisticated words to be insubordinate, as if you were trying to prove that you were smarter than them. Quickly, I added, "Anything out of line that needed to be fixed?"

"The Five Oh First," Colonel Jameson said without hesitation. "Their TO&E has grown tremendously over the years." Table of Operations and Equipment. "We thought they might've become top-heavy."

"Empire-building," Ernie said.

"It happens," Colonel Jameson replied.

The US Army is fundamentally a bureaucracy. Whenever they have the chance, bureaucrats enhance their authority, which means acquiring new funds, facilities, equipment and, most importantly, personnel.

"So Major Schultz," I said, "was looking into streamlining operations, eliminating redundancies, maybe eliminating a few positions?"

"Yes. But certainly that couldn't have had anything to do with his death. That sort of thing happens every day."

Keeping the giant blob that is the military industrial complex from endlessly expanding is a full-time endeavor.

"Yes, sir," I said. "You're probably right. Probably had nothing to do with his death. Was Major Schultz working on anything else?"

For the first time, Colonel Jameson barked a laugh. "That seemed like a full plate to me."

"Yes, sir," I replied. "I can see that it would be."

I thanked him and started to get up but Ernie said, "Why don't you believe the allegations of infidelity?"

Colonel Jameson studied Ernie as if he were looking for a soft spot to shove in the lethal end of the bayonet above his shelf. "Because I know his wife," he said, in a low firm voice. "She's a fine woman. And I know his children." Blood had flushed up through his neck and quickly spread to his upper cheeks. "And I know Fred Schultz would never be playing around with a business girl out in the ville."

Ernie grinned at him, a wide, toothy grin. "Yes, sir," he said.

Then we both stood up and saluted. Colonel Jameson returned our salute, but he kept his eyes on Ernie until his office door closed behind us.

"Why'd you have to do that?"

"Do what?" Ernie asked.

"Make him angry."

"Christ, Sueño. If we stuck to your style of questioning, all we'd ever get is puréed pabulum."

"'Puréed?'" I said.

"You know. Ground-up mush."

"I know what it means. It's just not a word I would've expected you to use."

"You're not the only intellectual around here," Ernie said.

"Could've fooled me."

We walked straight from the J-2 building to the 8th Army Snack Bar.

-15-

"I'm ready," Strange said.

"Ready for what?" I asked.

"For you to tell me about the *strange* you've been getting."

"What've you done to earn it?" Ernie asked.

"What do you mean?" Strange's eyebrows drooped and once again he looked aggrieved.

"I mean you haven't told us squat. Not about Major Schultz. Not about nothing."

"What do you want to know?"

Strange's cigarette lighter waggled with excitement. Ernie reached out and, with the tip of his thumb and forefinger, held it steady.

"Everything," Ernie said. "Start from the beginning."

Strange kept his hands flat on the table. "Let go of my cigarette holder."

His words were garbled because he was keeping his lips tightened around the holder.

"Why don't you ever put a cigarette into this thing?" Ernie asked.

"I'm trying to quit." This came out as something like, "I dying to kit."

Ernie let go of the holder. "Okay, Strange. Spill."

"The name's Harvey." He grabbed the cigarette holder, pulled it out of his mouth, and tugged a paper napkin from the stainless steel dispenser. Ostentatiously, he used it to scrub the holder thoroughly before shoving it back between his lips.

"Major Schultz," Ernie repeated.

"Mama's boy," Strange told him. "Or more exactly, Daddy's boy. Been working for Colonel Jameson for years, ever since he was a First Looey." First Lieutenant. "The Colonel took care of him, made sure he received top efficiency reports, made sure he got every promotion as soon as he was eligible for it."

"Why?"

"That's the mystery. There's some talk about the Colonel and Schultz's wife."

"People always say shit like that," I said.

Strange smirked at me. "Do they?"

"Sure," I replied. "Gossip, that's all it is."

"Well," Strange said, leaning back in his chair, "if you don't want to hear gossip . . ."

Ernie grabbed the cigarette holder again and pulled Strange back toward the table.

"Keep going," he said, glaring at him.

Strange pulled the holder free, straightened his khaki shirt, and continued to talk.

"So there's that, about the Colonel and Mrs. Schultz. Only a rumor, sure, but it's a fact that Schultz owed his successful military career, as far as it got, to his daddy, Colonel Jameson."

"Okay," I said.

Strange seemed pleased with himself, now that his cigarette holder was free and he had our full attention. He frowned. "Don't I get any hot chocolate?"

"For Christ's sake," Ernie said, exasperated. "Sueño's going to tell you about the strange he's getting. What more do you want?"

"Hot chocolate," Strange repeated.

I rose to walk to the serving line. "With two marshmallows," Strange said.

Next to the big steel coffee urn was a small hot chocolate dispenser. I pulled a steaming cup. Using tongs, I plopped one, then a second marshmallow into the concoction. At the cash register, the middle-aged Korean lady who seemed to always be on duty looked at me curiously.

"Not for me," I said and slapped the money on the counter.

When I returned, Strange frowned and said, "No spoon?"

Ernie was about to strangle him, but I hurried back to

the counter and plucked a small stirring spoon out of the huge array of utensils. When I came back, Strange finally smiled, wiped down the spoon with another napkin, and stirred the marshmallows into his chocolate until they were frothy at the edges. Then, one by one, he pulled them out of the cup and slid them into his gullet. Ernie grimaced. I looked away. I'd seen Strange do this before, but no matter how many times I witnessed it, it was still disgusting. I'm not sure why. He had a talent for these things. He sipped on the chocolate and, finally satisfied, set the cup down.

"The Five Oh Worst," he said. The 501st Military Intelligence Battalion, where our twerp pal Fenton was from.

"What about them?" Ernie asked.

"That's who Schultz was after. Headquarters Company has been running a semi-autonomous operation for years. Previous J-2s haven't given a shit about them, too busy worrying about the daily briefings they have to give to the Chief of Staff Eighth Army. So, year after year, the Five Oh First has been running their own show."

"Until Colonel Jameson arrived."

"Right. He wanted to bring the hammer down on them."

"And Major Schultz was the hammer."

"So they tell me," Strange said. "Of course, all this is just rumor. Gossip, you might say."

"Okay, gossip. We got it, Strange. Just tell us what you know."

"The name's Harvey."

"Right. Harvey. Sorry."

Strange slurped on more hot chocolate, glanced at us to make sure we were still enraptured, and continued to talk.

"The commander of the Five Oh First Headquarters Company is Captain Blood."

"Captain *Blood*?"

"Yeah, cool name, huh? Like Errol Flynn."

"That's his real name?" I asked.

Strange looked slightly offended. "Check the personnel records if you don't believe me. Lance P. Blood, Captain, O-3, US Army."

"What's the 'P' stand for?" Ernie asked.

"Penis. At least, that's what everybody says. Captain Blood is a real dick. And Headquarters Company is the only company in the Battalion that counts. The other companies are on the books but not staffed, only there to be activated in case of war."

"What does the Five Oh First do?"

"Counter-intel. Keeping us safe from those pesky North Koreans."

"Spy hunters."

"Right. And that's how they've been able to expand over the years: keep scaring one Eighth Army Commander after the other as to the extent of North Korean espionage. From what I hear, it's all bull. But if you see a spy under every mattress, you get more money in your budget, more spooks assigned to your command, and new branch offices throughout the country."

"Branch offices?"

"Yeah. Detached subordinate units. Small desks from Munsan to Pusan, all staffed by spooks under the command of Captain Blood."

"How come we haven't heard about them?"

"Because you've been sitting on your ass over at CID." He glugged down the last of his hot chocolate. "Too worried about cute Korean dollies black marketing duty-free goods out of the PX and Commissary. Not worried enough about North Korean spies."

"Has the Five Oh First actually caught any Commie spies?" Ernie asked.

Strange shrugged. "Depends on who you ask. They've railroaded enough guys out of the Army. Some of them even ended up in Leavenworth." The Federal Penitentiary in Leavenworth, Kansas. Serious business. "But real North Korean spies? None that I've heard. They mainly deal in accusation and innuendo."

"But they stay busy?"

"Very. Captain Blood is always on the road, zipping around the country to personally oversee their operations. He's after his next promotion. Once he's a field grade officer, watch out."

"How did he and Major Schultz get along?"

"Screaming matches, they tell me. Both of them with

tempers that exploded about half a dozen times a day. Major Schultz had Colonel Jameson backing him up. Good thing he did, because Lance Blood is as tall as Sueño here, but with muscle on him. They say he bench presses four-twenty."

Four hundred and twenty pounds? I could bench press two-forty and was proud of it.

"Four-twenty ain't shit," Ernie said.

"You try it."

"When I have time," Ernie replied.

"So did Major Schultz conduct a formal inspection of the Five Oh First?" I asked.

Strange grinned. It was a hideous sight to see. His cigarette holder waggled between greasy lips, and his eyes seemed to grow even more opaque behind his thick sunglasses.

"Thought you'd never ask." He unfastened a center button on his khaki shirt and slid out a folded packet of paper. "Right, *here* it is." I reached for it, but he quickly slid it back into his shirt and refastened the button.

"Uh uh *uh*," he said. "First what you promised." I glanced at Ernie. "No, not him. You." Then he leaned closer to me and said, "Had any *strange* lately?"

I was tempted to punch him out right there, rip the copy of Major Schultz's 501st inspection report out of his shirt, forget Strange and continue on with our investigation. The problem was that he was our only source for information directly from the Headquarters Command Staff of 8th Army. Asking for classified information formally was a waste of time. In the Army, it's always safer to disallow a request for information than grant it. You can't get into trouble by saying no.

Ernie patted my arm as if to say, *We can't afford to lose him*. Then he rose from his seat and walked out of the snack bar, leaving me alone with Strange. Strange leaned even closer until I could smell his hot breath. "Well?" he said.

My problem was that I *hadn't* had any strange lately. And even if I had, I'd sure as hell never tell him about anything with Leah Prevault. Even if I left her name out of the story, it would still feel like a betrayal.

"Strange," I said.

"Yes," he replied. "Strange."

I remembered a blue movie I'd seen years ago in high school. My classmate's older brother had a projector and some 16-millimeter film, and he'd shown it to us in his parents' basement. To be honest, I'd been shocked by it at the time, but like the other kids in the room, I pretended that I experienced such things every day. I looked back at Strange, trying to imagine myself back in that formative moment. Stammering, I started to describe what I'd seen.

After a few sentences, Strange interrupted me. "Not the guy in the gorilla suit."

"Huh?"

"That's what you're describing. That old smut film about

a guy in a gorilla suit who breaks into some innocent girl's house and rapes her."

"I didn't say anything about a gorilla suit."

"I know the plot," Strange said, crossing his arms and leaning back. "I want something real. Not made up."

Apparently, Strange was an expert at these things. How did Ernie fake it? Suddenly it occurred to me that maybe he didn't.

I started to talk. But after every sentence or two, Strange interrupted me and told me he didn't believe my story. Finally, after several attempts, I remembered an article I'd read on the Stanislavsky method, something about putting yourself into the story and living it to make your emotions more believable. I remembered what Miss Jo had said to that hapless GI: "You slicky my ping-pong heart." I took a deep breath and tried again, describing an Itaewon bar, a business girl approaching me and whispering those words. My imagination began to move forward on its own: We walked to her hooch, I handed her a folded stack of bills and she began to undo my belt. This time, Strange didn't interrupt me. I envisioned Miss Jo Kyong-ja with her clothes off—it wasn't difficult, especially after seeing Torrelli's Polaroid of her in a two-piece bathing suit. I took her in my arms, feeling her closeness and warmth, hoping upon hope that she was still actually, truly alive.

When I was done, Strange seemed satisfied. He

unbuttoned his khaki blouse, pulled out the paperwork, and set it down in the middle of the table.

"The last report Major Schultz turned in," he told me, "just before he died." He stood up and said, "Thanks for the hot chocolate. But that ping-pong heart bit, you're going to have to work on it."

He waddled his way out of the 8th Army Snack Bar. I sat there for a few moments, feeling soiled. Then I grabbed the report and, holding it with two fingers, walked back to the CID office, wishing I had an evidence bag to drop it in.

16

Ernie and I drove to the 501st headquarters building, which was on Camp Coiner, a small base adjacent to Yongsan Compound. The camp remained off by itself with its own entrance gate, its own small barracks, and even its own flagpole, used to raise the flag at zero eight hundred every morning and lower it at seventeen hundred every evening, seven days a week.

"So what'd it say?" Ernie asked. I'd read Major Schultz's last inspection report. Ernie hadn't.

"The usual," I said. "He saw plenty of duplication of effort and ample opportunity to cut the operating budget and staffing."

"Inspection reports always say that."

"Right. But this one had some added recommendations. Namely, that the Five Oh First had established too many branch offices."

"Like where?"

"All over the damn place. In the Second Infantry

Division along the Demilitarized Zone and at every major logistics and supply point all the way down to the Port of Pusan."

"Did they all put up a sign saying Five Oh First Counter Intelligence?"

"No signs. These places are off base and kept completely covert. Their expense budget has ballooned because of all that civilian rent they have to pay. Usually they set up near the local AmVets Club or Veterans of Foreign Wars."

American veterans associations are chartered by the Korean government to operate legitimately as nonprofit organizations. This gives them permission to run small bars, restaurants, and even gambling halls in addition to granting long-term work visas for the Americans staffing the organizations.

"You mean they set up operations in those little casinos?" Ernie asked.

"Not in the casinos themselves, but they rent office space in the building. They justify it by claiming that they have to be off base so the military community won't be aware that counter-intel is operating in their midst. But mainly it's a way to have an unsupervised office with a desk and a chair, plus a special Eighth Army phone line."

"So they don't have to go through the Korean telephone exchange."

"Right. And with a monthly rent check coming in, the

veterans' organizations are more than happy to share their facilities."

"Meanwhile, the agents of the Five Oh First can range out from there and go pretty much wherever they want."

"Right. And their agents receive a per diem."

"On top of their regular pay?" Ernie was impressed.

"Yes."

"*And* separate rations?" Money paid by the military to servicemen who were not able to use the free military dining facilities—necessary for the 501st guys, since they weren't on base.

"And separate rations," I confirmed.

Ernie whistled. "And here we've been happy with our fifty-dollar-a-month expense account. These counter-intel pukes are pulling down more per month with these extras than we pull down in our regular paycheck. Nice deal. And if they black market on top of that . . ."

"These are dedicated counter-intel agents," I said. "They wouldn't break the law just for a little extra cash in black marketeering."

"Yeah, right," Ernie said. "So a bunch of guys were getting over. Away from the flagpole, pulling down good money. They must worship Captain Blood."

"They do. And he's been here for over three years."

"Steadily building his empire," Ernie said.

"Right. And according to Major Schultz's inspection report, most of these policies were implemented as soon as Captain Blood arrived. The J-2 who ran things before Colonel Jameson thought Blood walked on water."

"Max OERs?" Top ratings on his Officer Efficiency Reports.

"Every one," I said, "until maybe the next one."

"After Colonel Jameson reads that report."

"Which he has. The one Strange gave us is just a copy. The official report was already submitted, just before Schultz's death."

"So the kingdom Blood painstakingly set up over the last three years was about to be dismantled, piece by piece, because of Schultz's inspection." Ernie thought about it. "Happens every day. Not exactly a motive for murder."

"Not usually. But there's something else."

"What?"

"The number of North Korean spies arrested."

"How many?"

"In the last three years, not one."

Ernie guffawed. "That's a lot of money spent for zero results."

"Not zero. Over two dozen GIs were brought up on charges. Mainly for aiding and abetting enemy espionage."

"If they didn't collar the North Korean handler, how'd they prove that the GI was a spy?"

"They did collar the handler. In almost every case, it was the GI's *yobo*."

"Their *yobo*? Their *yobo* is the North Korean spy?" Ernie

was incredulous. "You can coerce a *yobo* into admitting anything! They're poor country girls. Everybody pushes them around."

"I couldn't agree more. They're easily manipulated."

"So that's no kind of credible evidence. How come we never heard about this?"

"The proceedings are conducted *in camera*."

"What's that mean?"

"In secret. Classified. And CID didn't have a need-to-know."

Ernie shook his head. "The court-martial boards went along with this?"

"Not always. Sometimes they let the guy settle short of criminal prosecution. Take a bad discharge, leave the service. Most of them jumped at the chance. A few of them fought it and ended up serving time."

Ernie took a deep breath, his hands clutched on the steering wheel. We stopped at the main gate of Camp Coiner and I handed the MP our dispatch. He glanced at it.

"Destination?" he asked.

"None of your freaking business," Ernie growled.

The MP stared at him, bug-eyed. His right hand slid toward his holstered .45. "*Destination*," he repeated.

I grabbed the dispatch back. "Five Oh Worst MI," I said.

Suspiciously, the MP stepped back and waved us through. Ernie wound through the tree-lined lanes. "What it looks like," he said, "is these counter-intel losers were setting up bogus arrests just to make their stats look good, so they could keep on drawing their per diem and living in the lap of luxury."

"Let's not jump to conclusions."

"But that's where Major Schultz was headed," Ernie said.

"No question about it," I replied, "if the J-2 has the balls to follow up the report."

Ernie gunned the engine and rolled up a ten-foot incline into the small parking lot in front of a long wooden building with a white placard out front that said HEADQUARTERS COMPANY, 501ST MILITARY INTELLIGENCE BATTALION. We climbed out of the jeep and walked toward the double front door. The firelight beneath the awning shone yellow. A man in fatigues and highly spit-shined jump boots opened the door before we could get there. Massive arms were folded across a broad chest.

"Get the fuck off my company street," he said.

The embroidered nametag on his fatigue blouse said Blood, rank insignia Captain. From around the edge of the building, four more GIs appeared. Two of them held M-16 rifles.

Slowly, I pulled out my badge and held it up to what little sunlight filtered through the overcast sky. "Eighth Army CID," I said. "Agents Sueño and Bascom, here on official business."

"I don't give a fuck who you are. Get off my company street."

"You don't seem to understand," Ernie said. "We're here conducting an official investigation."

Captain Blood motioned with his forefinger. All four GIs rushed us. One of them I recognized. Specialist Four Fenton, the guy who'd been harassing Miss Kim, the one who Ernie'd called a twerp. He didn't seem like a twerp now. Reinforced with backup, he took the lead and reached out to shove Ernie, but Ernie sidestepped him and cracked a left hook into the side of his head. His black helmet liner flew off his skull, but then the other three were on top of us; screaming and shouting, trying to overpower us with their sheer weight. It was foolish for two of them to be carrying rifles if they didn't intend to use them. They tried to shove me with the weapons, but I lowered myself and rammed one fist, then another into their unprotected midsections. After a few seconds of cursing and grunting, first Fenton, then two more of them went down. The last one stepped back, unsure of himself, and aimed the M-16 rifle at us. This focused our attention. Ernie and I stepped back and raised our hands. Captain Blood continued to stand on the porch, feet shoulder-width apart, arms crossed. During the entire fracas, he hadn't moved.

"You'd better have him put that rifle down, Captain," I said.

In the dim light, I thought I saw a smile crease his broad cheeks. After a pause, he said, "Stow it, Benson."

Private Benson lowered his rifle.

Two of the men on the ground shoved themselves back to their feet. The twerp, Specialist Fenton, appeared to be out cold.

"Get Fenton out of here," Captain Blood said. The three of them picked him up and carried him over to the back of a three-quarter-ton truck. They tossed him unceremoniously in the back. Once they drove off, Captain Blood said, "If you wanna talk that bad, then we'll talk."

He turned and strode back through the building entrance.

Ernie and I glanced at one another. Captain Blood had known he'd eventually have to talk to us; he'd just wanted to put us through some sort of macho "test" to see if we'd stand our ground and fight, or run back to the head shed for reinforcements.

I wasn't sure if we'd passed or not. But frankly, I didn't give a damn what he thought. We trudged up the steps and pushed through the big double doors.

17

The hallway was floored with cheap brown tile, Army-issue. After passing three or four closed doors, we went through an archway into what appeared to be your typical Orderly Room. Grey desks in the center, even greyer filing cabinets lining the walls, telephones and in-trays scattered around the room. A bulletin board with a white organizational chart and yellow carbon-paper duty roster, bristled with stainless steel thumbtacks. Off to the left, a sealed door with a double-paned glass window in the center was marked SECURE COMMUNICATIONS. It was dark, but the room behind it appeared small, like a phone booth.

"A direct line to DC," I whispered to Ernie. Secure satellite communications with the Pentagon.

Another door was open in the right corner, and Captain Blood flicked on its overhead fluorescent light and strode into the small office. As we caught up with him, he was pulling shut a long curtain over a huge map on the wall. He turned and glared at us.

"Who the hell do you think you are?" he asked.

I told him.

"CID," he said, shaking his head. "Criminal freaking investigation. Whoop-dee-doo."

He was the type of guy who liked to use plenty of obscenities so that no one missed the fact that he was tough. He backed that up with muscles so pumped up from lifting weights that his fatigue blouse could barely contain his shoulders. On his desk, where a photo of the wife and kids would normally be, stood a photo of Captain Blood almost nude, greased down and wearing the silk briefs of a body-builder, facing the camera, every tendon tensed, flexing and smiling with all the wattage he could muster.

Ernie pointed at the photo. "Did you win?"

Captain Blood seemed thrown by the question. "Win what?"

"That body-building contest."

His forehead crinkled over bushy eyebrows. "Came in second. The winner had a fix in with the judges."

I was going to ask him how he knew that, but decided to drop it. Instead, I asked, "When did you last see Major Frederick M. Schultz?"

Blood plopped down in his big leather chair, crouching first, then letting his entire weight fall from a height of three feet, as if his bulk were too much for his knees to bear.

"That asshole," he said. "That's why you're here?"

"That's why," I said.

He grabbed a rubber ball about the size of a grapefruit and started to squeeze, his massive fingers straining, turning white, then red. Before he answered, he switched the ball to the other hand and squeezed again, ten times, as if wringing someone's neck.

"Do you realize what that moron was trying to do?" he asked. His eyes were wide, his face grim. When we didn't answer, he continued squeezing and grimacing. "To save a few dollars," Blood said, "that moron Schultz was planning on eviscerating our hard-won ability to go after Communist agents. *Eviscerating* it! Do you know what that means?"

Again, we didn't answer.

"It means cutting the guts out of our counterintelligence operation. Cutting the guts out of the very thing that is holding the line against those Commie bastards up north." He pointed to the north, waving his forefinger as if he were ordering a hot dog at a crowded ball game. "The GI villages in this country are *crawling* with Communist agents. All these Korean bitches have to do is spread their legs and the dumb-as-bricks American GIs tell the whore anything she wants to know. *Anything*. I've seen them bring reams of classified information out to their *yobo* just because she refused to give head. I mean they're *dumb*, manipulated by every cunt who bats her fake eyelashes."

He paused, studying us, his eyes so wide they were moist.

"You didn't answer my question," I said.

"*What*?"

"When did you last see Major Schultz?"

He stared at me, incredulous, and then slowly, like bubbling magma rising from his chest, his rage grew. "When did I last *see* him?"

"That's the question," I replied.

His eyes widened, and he ponderously lifted his tremendous bulk from his seat. He placed both hands on the edge of his desk and leaned toward us. "You think I did it, don't you?"

"Did what?"

"Don't play innocent with me. You think I killed the poor dumb son of a bitch."

I shrugged. "We've come to no conclusions, Captain. We're just investigating."

"Just *investigating*? No, you're not. You're doing more than that. You're messing with our operations here. You're going to take up my time and take up the time of my counter-intel agents, and all because you think I'm the guy who offed that prissy asshole Schultz. That's what this is all about, isn't it? You think I killed the twerp."

Twerp. The same thing Ernie had called Fenton, now being tossed around as an insult to a dead man.

Ernie took a half step forward. "Hold on there, Captain *Blood*." He dragged out the name, letting him know that it sounded phony. "We're here on an official investigation. A homicide investigation. Now, you can answer our questions here, or you can answer them down at the MP station. It's up to you."

I wished Ernie hadn't said that. The fact of the matter was, we didn't have the authority to take him in. At least not yet, because the Provost Marshal hadn't signed off on this part of the investigation. He was still banking on pinning Schultz's murder on the fugitive Miss Jo. So we had neither the legal authority, nor apparently the manpower to take him in. Especially if those three, still-standing GIs returned any time soon.

Captain Blood realized Ernie's mistake.

"Have I been brought up on charges?"

"The investigation hasn't reached that stage yet."

"Then you have no right to take a commissioned officer into custody. Who do you think you're bluffing?" He waggled his finger at us. "I could eat you two guys for lunch."

I was getting a little tired of these tough-guy clichés. "You make that one up yourself?"

"What?" Blood seemed genuinely befuddled. He was so impressed with his own bluster that he probably wasn't even hearing himself anymore.

"If you don't cooperate," I told him, "it's not going to look good for you or for the Five Oh First."

"What the hell do you know about what looks good? I've been dealing with this Command for the last three years. And dealing with it well. The Eighth Army Chief of Staff understands the importance of our mission, even if you two half-assed gumshoes don't." I was about to reply when he said, "Now get out of my office."

I looked at Ernie, he looked at me. He shrugged. We hadn't really expected any cooperation, but we'd had to stop here and put the 501st Commander on notice. Give him a chance to cooperate. Document that we'd asked him questions and he'd refused to answer. That's the way Colonel Brace, the Provost Marshal, always insisted investigations be conducted. We'd done what we could. If Blood wanted to do things the hard way, that was up to him. We turned to leave.

"And one more thing," Captain Blood said. "Don't think you can go questioning my agents. It won't do you any good. They're loyal to me and the Five Oh First."

That proposition remained to be tested.

Ernie and I stepped out of his office. Blood followed us down the hallway. Earlier he'd been reluctant to talk, but now he didn't seem to want the conversation to end. "And one more thing," he said again, "what was your name? Sween-o? We know about what you've done—and your contacts up north. You keep pushing this and we'll find out more."

In the middle of the hallway, I stopped and turned back to face him. "What are you talking about?" There was a low menace in my voice, one I hadn't intended, but that was there nevertheless.

Captain Blood smirked at my discomfort and lowered

his voice, too. "We'll find out what we need to find *out*, Sween-o," he said. "About you and your girlfriend."

Ernie grabbed my elbow, as if to say *don't react*.

"I don't know what you mean," I said.

"Sure you don't."

I turned and continued toward the exit. Outside, Ernie and I hopped down the wooden steps. Blood was standing on the porch. As we crossed the gravel parking lot, he said what I'd been fearing he'd say. "*And* your son. We'll find out more about him, too. You can *count* on it!"

Ernie hustled me into the jeep, started the engine, and we backed up and sped away. On the way down the incline, the three-quarter-ton truck passed us in the opposite direction. The same three soldiers were in it, heading back to their lord and master.

-18-

We drove straight to the barracks. Ernie was quiet. He knew Blood's words had rattled me.

"Don't sweat the small stuff, Sueño. We're going to take this puke down and take him down soon, before he can do any damage. You'll see."

"He knows about Doc Yong," I said, "and about Il-yong." My son.

Ernie snorted. "So what's he gonna do about it? If he goes down there to South Cholla and starts sniffing around, he's liable to end up in a dark alley with a knife in his back."

"So he won't go at all."

"He doesn't have the nerve."

I hoped Ernie was right.

Back at the barracks, I didn't feel like going to my room right away. Instead, I stopped at the CQ's desk and said, "You need a break?"

"Yeah, I wanted to walk down to the PX and buy some smokes."

"Go ahead. I'll cover for you."

The CQ took off, and I sat at the rickety field table in the main entranceway that served as his desk. When the hallway emptied, I picked up the phone and dialed. This time, she didn't answer. It was a voice I was unfamiliar with. "Female BOQ. Lieutenant Norris speaking, sir or ma'am."

In my most officious tone, I said, "Captain Prevault, please."

"Can I say who's calling?"

I remembered the name of the doctor who'd treated me at the 121 after I'd been beaned out in Itaewon. I used it.

"Hold on, sir."

I listened to the footsteps down the hallway, the knock on the distant door and then a long wait. Maybe I imagined it, but I thought I heard a door creak open, then whispered words, urgent, purposely hushed. The door closed and the footsteps returned.

"She's not in, sir. Do you want me to leave a message?"

"No, thank you. I'll contact her later."

I set the phone down and stared out the front door of the barracks. GIs pulled up in jeeps or trucks and hopped out and ran inside laughing. A couple of them dropped thirty-five cents into the beer machine and out popped a can of cold brew. When they left, I bought one for myself. Falstaff. I didn't know anything could taste so good. And it eased the pounding in my head that still throbbed right behind where the welt was most tender. After polishing off my first, I had another.

"Are you okay?" Ernie asked.

"Okay," I confirmed.

It was early morning. We were walking downhill, past the long brick 8th Army headquarters building, heading for the CID Admin Office.

"You look like you tied one on last night."

"I did. When Riley came back to the barracks, we shared his last bottle of Old Overwart."

"You're down to socializing with that loser?"

"The rye whiskey worked fine."

He studied me. "What the hell are you so worried about, Sueño? Captain Blood?"

"Nah," I said. "We'll get that puke."

"That's the spirit." Ernie slapped me on the back. "So what is it?"

"Nothing," I said, in an irritated tone of voice. That was enough to back Ernie off. I didn't want to tell him or anybody else what I was really worried about.

We walked up the stone steps that led to the CID office.

I was worried about losing everything. By holding on to Il-yong and the possibility of being part of his future, I couldn't let go of his mother, Dr. Yong In-ja, not completely. If by some miracle she returned to me and proposed that we establish a family, how could I say no? If I did, I'd be turning my back on my own child, something I'd promised myself I'd never do. On the other hand, I was being unfair to Leah Prevault, which she'd made abundantly clear last night by not taking my phone call.

I had to see Captain Prevault, and I had to be honest with her, I knew that. I'd do it today, as soon as I had the chance to break away.

Riley was already sitting behind his desk shuffling paperwork, looking none the worse for wear.

"You're *late*," he shouted.

Ernie glanced at his watch. "Two minutes."

"That's what I said. You're freaking *late*."

Ernie ignored him and breezed his way to the stainless steel coffee urn.

"The Colonel wanted to talk to you."

"So we'll talk," I said.

"You're too *freaking* late. He just left for the Chief of Staff briefing."

I sat down, grabbed Riley's copy of the *Pacific Stars and Stripes*, and opened it to the editorial section. On the left side of the page, the columnists were beating up on Nixon, and on the right side they were making excuses for him. I turned to the comics section: Andy Capp, my little island of sanity.

"You two are to go nowhere," Riley said. "As soon as the Colonel returns from the briefing, he wants to chew your butts personally."

"For what?" I asked.

"For not making progress on the Schultz case and for interfering with counterintelligence operations."

"Interfering? How did we do that?"

"You questioned Captain Blood, didn't you, at the Five Oh First?"

"Yeah."

"Without the Provost Marshal's approval?"

"We didn't arrest him, for Christ sake, we just tried to ask him a few questions. None of which he answered, by the way."

I was about to add that he'd threatened me but thought better of it. The fewer people who knew about Il-yong's mother being a fugitive from ROK authorities, the better.

"*Max nix*," Riley said. "The Colonel doesn't want you questioning field grade officers without first receiving his express permission."

Ernie returned with a mug of coffee. "He's not a field grade officer. He's a captain."

"But he's in charge of the Five Oh First, which is a battalion, so he's operating at a field grade level."

We both shook our heads. Forcing us to ask permission to talk to people was a clear indication that the PMO didn't approve of where our investigation was heading. It also indicated the elevated status that Captain Blood enjoyed amongst the 8th Army Officer Corps. Why? Was it the force of his personality? Or another, more unsettling reason? I suspected it had something to do with the almost inquisitorial power Blood had managed to accumulate. He could accuse anyone of espionage. Or if not that, of somehow being a dupe for North Korean Communist agents. Such an accusation would ruin an officer's career, or worse, send him to the federal pen.

"Fine, if we can't ask him," I said, "we'll ask you. Did you find out anything else about Captain Blood?"

Last night, while we were polishing off his bottle of rye, Riley'd agreed to make inquiries with his 8th Army contacts in Personnel.

"I called Smitty," he told me.

Sergeant Smith was another workaholic, like Riley, who invariably arrived at the 8th Army Personnel Office at least an hour early each morning.

"What'd he say?"

"Blood is overdue for a promotion. It'll be up-or-out for him at the next promotion board."

Up-or-out was the shorthand term for the US Army's policy of getting rid of officers, or enlisted men, who didn't receive their next promotion in a reasonable period of time. Once an officer was promoted to captain, he was not eligible for promotion for three years. After that, he was considered for promotion to major in each annual promotion board, held in the Army Personnel Headquarters in Alexandria, Virginia. If he was passed over for promotion three times, he'd be asked to leave the service. This meant

Captain Blood had been passed over twice; this year was his last chance. Which possibly explained how uptight he'd been about me and Ernie asking questions. A bad mark on his personnel record at this point would mean he'd be toast on the next promotion board, then tossed out of the army and back onto the street as a "silly-vilian," which maybe doesn't mean much to non-military people. But when you've been in command of over forty soldiers and over-seen a budget of tens of thousands of dollars, it's not easy to go hat in hand to an employment agency, seeking work as a temp. Sure, maybe he could build himself a new life as a civilian—many GIs who've been forced out of the service had—but with his temper and his arrogance, it didn't seem likely that Captain Blood would resign himself to pounding the pavement and begging for a job.

"By the way," Riley said, "Smitty told me Blood had a legal name change. When he joined the service as a pri-vate-E-nothing, his name was Vladimir Bludovsky, from Buffalo, New York."

Ernie slurped his coffee. "Cold up in Buffalo."

"That's what they tell me," Riley said. "And not too many guys named Lance."

I rose from my chair, walked over to the coffee pot and pulled myself a cup. Black. When I returned, I glanced at Miss Kim's desk for the first time this morning. Her vase was gone, as was its flower, and the adjacent box of tissue.

"Where's Miss Kim?" I asked.

Riley shook his head and studied the paperwork in front of him. He didn't answer.

Ernie looked at her desk too. "Everything's gone," he said. "No more Black Dragon tea."

We both loomed over Riley. "What is it?" I asked.

His voice came out garbled, as if he were choking back tears. I don't believe I'd ever seen him so emotional. Maybe the one time he accidentally dropped his bottle of Old Overwart and it shattered all over the barracks floor, but that was it.

"She quit," Riley said.

"What?" Then I said, "When?"

"This morning."

"Did she say why?"

"Not to me. The Colonel took her into his office and had a long talk with her. He didn't want to lose her, she was the best admin assistant we've ever had."

For once, Riley didn't use the word "secretary."

"So what did the Colonel say?" Ernie asked. "Why'd she quit?"

Riley shook his head more vehemently this time. "He told me that she wouldn't tell him. She just said that she had to leave the job."

If anybody was responsible for us losing Miss Kim, it had to be Ernie. Both Riley and I stared at him. Finally, I said it. "You followed her onto the bus."

"Hey, don't blame me," he said, pointing at his chest. "I

didn't do nothing. I caught up with her after her stop and she didn't want to talk to me, but I finally convinced her to have one cup of coffee with me at a teahouse. We just talked. I was a perfect gentleman."

We continued to glare at him.

"Honest!" he said. For the first time since I'd known him, Ernie Bascom was on the defensive. "She told me she wouldn't go out with me. I accepted that." He glanced back and forth between me and Riley. "It's not my fault," he said. "Or at least it's not anything I did to her." He thought about it. "Not lately, anyway."

I turned to Riley. "Do you have her address of record?"

Without hesitation, he pulled out a five-by-eight card with all her pertinent data, even her Korean National Identification Number.

"Can I keep this?"

"I wrote it out for you."

I slipped the card into my jacket pocket.

"Go talk to her," Riley said. "Tell her we need her here."

"A little late for you to admit that," I told him.

Riley's face turned red. He didn't make a rude retort, which is what I'd expected. For the first time since I'd known him, I almost felt sorry for him. Not quite, but almost.

Maybe it was to take our minds off of Miss Kim. But mainly, we knew it was time, so Ernie and I drove downtown to KNP headquarters. We wanted to check in with Mr. Kill concerning their progress on the investigation into Major Schultz's death and the whereabouts of Miss Jo Kyong-ja. I also had a few other questions for him.

After we checked in at the front desk, Officer Oh appeared almost immediately. She escorted us upstairs to Kill's office. He sat stone-faced at his desk, his jacket hanging on a hook behind him. "No progress," he told us. "No hint of the location of Miss Jo Kyong-ja, even though every KNP station in the country has been notified. Mokpo tells me you paid them a visit."

"We wanted to see her mother's home," I said.

He cocked an eyebrow. "What did you think?"

"Dirt-poor," Ernie replied.

Kill sighed. "For my country, it's been a long, slow fight out of poverty. Many tragedies."

"And no one's found an unidentified female body?" I asked.

He shook his head.

"So she still might be alive?"

"She might."

Officer Oh brought in a stainless steel tray with a bronze pot of hot water, three cups, a box of Lipton tea bags and a squat jar of Folger's Instant Crystals, plus some creamer and sugar. She set it on the long coffee table in the center of Mr. Kill's office, and he came out from behind his desk and joined us, serving himself. Officer Oh asked if he needed anything else, and he told her no, that she could leave. On her way out, I thanked her. Her face impassive, she nodded back.

Once the three of us were alone, Ernie said, "You know that crime scene is phony."

Kill didn't reply. He just stirred coffee crystals into hot water and ladled in a heaping spoonful of sugar. "Phony in what way?"

Ernie explained how there really wasn't enough blood, and that the blood that *had* been there looked as if it had been purposefully splashed. And that there wasn't a big enough mess. Not enough broken bottles or smashed wooden crates.

"Major Schultz was a husky guy," Ernie said. "If he'd been fighting for his life, there would've been more damage."

Kill sipped on his coffee. Then he set the cup down,

looked at Ernie and then looked at me. "Yes, that's what I thought, too. And after our analysis, that conclusion is confirmed. There's little doubt that the body was transported from somewhere else and left behind the Dragon King Nightclub. Probably sometime during the midnight-to-four curfew."

"Meaning it couldn't have been done with a civilian vehicle," I said.

"No," Kill agreed, "to be out after curfew, it would have to be a military or police conveyance. Something on official government business, anyway."

"Or he could've been carried there," Ernie said.

"Yes. Even during the curfew, our foot patrols can only cover so much territory. A couple of thugs could've carried the corpse there, dumped it, and done their best to replicate a murder scene. However, if that's what happened, they couldn't have carried him far."

"Too heavy and too high a chance of being spotted."

"Exactly. So I had a dozen officers canvass the area, checking for evidence, asking questions of nearby residents. I even have them checking trash-collector pushcarts for traces of blood. The circle around the crime scene keeps growing, but so far they've found nothing."

"So transport of the corpse by motor vehicle seems most likely."

Kill nodded.

We sat silent for a minute. Then I said, "Who?"

"That's the question," Kill replied. "So what do we ask next?"

He was treating us like students. Personally, I didn't mind. He'd been a homicide investigator for over twenty years, the best Korea had, and I was more than willing to learn. I'm not so sure Ernie was thrilled with us receiving the subordinate treatment, but he kept quiet.

"Motive," I said. "That's what we have to look at next."

"Miss Jo had a motive," Inspector Kill said. "He had accused her of being a thief and her landlady, backed up by the Itaewon police, was making her life hell."

KNPs can literally run a business girl out of town if she makes trouble and embarrasses them, especially when it has to do with the US military.

"She could've just moved to another GI village," Ernie said.

"Without her clothes? Without money? You saw what she already had to do, start work in a brothel. Maybe it doesn't seem like much to us, but to her it must've been a hideous shame. And she must've blamed Major Schultz for losing what little she had."

"Not to mention," Ernie added, "she claims he beat her up."

"Or his accomplice did."

"So she had a motive," I said, "but physically, I don't see how she could've done it. Yes, maybe if she'd surprised him with a knife or a hatchet, she might've been able to kill him, but how would she then have transported the body to the Dragon King Nightclub?"

Kill shrugged. "Someone could've helped her. Like the men who attacked you and made possible her escape."

My head pulsed painfully at the thought.

"Seems too elaborate," Ernie said. "Who wants to risk their life for a business girl?"

"Yes," Kill agreed. "But this involves international politics. An American field grade officer has been killed, and the Korean government is extremely embarrassed. If there's some way to wrap the case up quickly and make it seem like nothing more than a straightforward criminal matter, they'll do it. They're already pressuring me to find her and close the case."

"If you find her," I asked, "will you charge her with the murder?"

"I will have no choice," he told us. "The decision will be made, how do you say, above my pay grade."

"She'll be convicted and thrown in jail, and the embarrassment will be over."

Kill poured more hot water into his cup. "Exactly," he said. "Unless you two figure out who else might've had a motive to kill Major Schultz."

"We're working on that," Ernie said.

"You'd better work fast. Once we find Miss Jo Kyong-ja, she'll be on trial within days."

"How long do you figure the trial will last?" I asked.

Mr. Kill grimaced. "Maybe past noon," he said. "Probably not."

Ernie dropped me off at the 121st Evac Hospital on Yongsan South Post. He drove away to top off the jeep, and we would rendezvous at the barracks in an hour. We had a plan, but in order to implement it, we had to stay away from the Provost Marshal for as long as possible.

I made my way to the officers' lunchroom.

Inside the double doors, a steam table stretched along a serving line, and to the left were rows of about two-dozen Formica-topped tables. I wore the civilian coat and tie required of a CID agent on duty so no one questioned my presence. She was there, sitting alone at a table in the far corner. I zigzagged my way through the boisterous crowd of nurses in their starched white uniforms and absent-minded doctors with stethoscopes still hanging around their necks. When I approached, she looked up. Her eyes were large and moist, and when she saw me she dropped her spoon and looked away. Before she could object, I sat down opposite her.

"I have to talk to you."

"No need," she said.

"Of course there's a need." There was no one in earshot, but nevertheless I lowered my voice. I didn't wait for her permission, and just started talking fast, so she couldn't interrupt; something I don't normally do. I told her about my childhood, about my mother dying when I was small and being abandoned by my father, and what it was like growing up in one foster home after another.

"It wasn't all bad," I told her. "Many of my foster parents were good people, but at a certain age I would be shuffled to another home, ripped away from the other foster kids, who'd become like brothers and sisters to me. It was confusing. And as soon as I became a teenager, I grew as tall as a man, and stronger, and suddenly my presence made people nervous. As soon as I could, I joined the Army."

Captain Leah Prevault listened patiently, staring at her unfinished bowl of navy bean soup.

"My greatest fear," I told her, "was to have a child I couldn't take care of. And now, because of this oppressive South Korean regime, that's the situation I'm in. If I could've rectified that, if it had ever become possible for Yong In-ja and me to get back together and raise our son, that's always what I would've done. Regardless of how my feelings for her might've evolved, I'd have done it for *him*."

She finally looked up at me. "And you'd do it now."

"You've changed everything," I said.

She studied me, gauging my sincerity. "But you can't be sure."

I broke from her gaze. "Right now it's impossible for me to see Il-yong's mother. She's a fugitive. If the Korean CIA catches her, they'll interrogate her, torture her, and probably execute her without a trial. So planning our future is moot. But politics are funny. There could be a revolution tomorrow, Pak Chung-hee could be overthrown and suddenly she'd be able to come out in the open. That's why I'm hesitant."

"As unlikely as that is," she said, "you don't want to bet against the chance that it might happen."

"I never want to mislead you."

She sat quietly for a moment, then said, "So what do you want to do?"

I really, honestly searched for an answer. I detest people who default to saying they don't know the answer to a question because it involves something as difficult as thought. Or something more complex, like reflecting on your own emotions. But finally, I had to give her my honest answer. "I don't know."

"And me?" she asked. "What am I supposed to do?"

When I didn't reply, she pushed her soup away. "I have to think about this," she told me.

Helplessly, I watched her make her way through the crowded lunchroom, ignoring the few people who greeted her. One of the nurses a few tables away had been watching us. She glared at me as if I'd done something wrong. I probably had.

-20-

"Where the hell is this address, anyway?" Ernie asked.

We were in the Taehyon-dong district of Seoul, which was packed with bean curd eateries, bicycle repair shops and small stationery stores on the main road, and homes stacked one atop another like tile shingles leading up the sides of the steep hills.

"Slow down," I said, "I can't read the signs."

Behind us, impatient kimchi cabs and three-wheeled trucks honked as they swerved around us. Pedestrian crossings were packed with men pushing carts and old women balancing impossibly huge bundles atop their heads.

"How do people live in this mess?" Ernie asked.

"Pretty well, sometimes," I said. "Behind those brick walls, some of those hooches are pretty luxurious."

"Some," Ernie said. "Most not."

We turned up a narrow lane. The first few yards were paved until, about halfway up the hill, blacktop gave way to mud. The jeep's four-wheel drive churned upward. Now most of the homes were held up by walls not of brick, but of splintered wood.

"Miss Kim always looks so nice when she comes to work," Ernie said.

"Yeah," I replied.

We marveled at how she'd managed it, emerging like a goddess from a soiled cocoon. Finally, we neared the address we were looking for—117 *bonji*, 227 *ho*. Walkways too narrow for the jeep split off the main path.

"Stop here," I said. "Let me hop out and look around."

I walked down one pathway, reading the numbers painted on wood, but they were wrong, so I doubled back and tried the pathway on the opposite side of the road. About three hooches down, I found it. I ran back and waved to Ernie. He inched the jeep as close to the wall as he could, turned off the engine, padlocked the steering wheel, and joined me at the mouth of the alley.

"How we going to work this?" he asked.

I studied him. "My God, Ernie, you're nervous."

"I'm not nervous," he said. But his shoulders had risen, his stomach was pulled in and his eyes darted from side to side like a schoolboy at his first dance.

"Okay," I said, slapping him on the shoulder. "You're not nervous. I'll do the talking."

We marched through the muddy lane until we reached the gateway marked *117 bonji, 227 ho*. The family name printed next to the number was Kim. Miss Kim's family name, obviously, but that didn't mean much. In Korea, roughly a third of the country is named Kim, from three or four ancient clans. Another third of the country is named Pak or Lee, and the final third shares about a hundred different names. Was this the right Kim? According to the five-by-eight card Staff Sergeant Riley had given me it was, but there was only one way to be sure. I pushed the buzzer. A few seconds later a woman spoke through the intercom. "*Nugu seiyo?*" Who is it?

I could tell from her voice that she wasn't Miss Kim.

I leaned forward and spoke directly into the metal grate. "We're from Eighth Army," I said in Korean. "We're looking for Miss Kim who works on the compound. My name is Geogie."

I pronounced George the Korean way, dropping the hard "r" sound and abrupt consonant ending.

There was a long silence, as if the person on the other end of the intercom was stunned. "*Wei-yo?*" she finally said. Why?

At least we had the right place. I searched for the appropriate Korean words. "Because we need her at work. It is very important."

Professional responsibility was ingrained in Korean culture. I knew Miss Kim possessed that national trait.

In the background, there was muffled speaking, as if a hand was being held over the intercom. Finally, the woman's voice came back on. "*Jomkkanman-yo.*" Just a moment.

Then the buzzer sounded. We pushed through the small metal door in the larger wooden gate.

She kept her head down, as if she were ashamed or had done something wrong. We sat in a well-appointed *sarang-bang*, front room, with tea placed before us on a low folding-leg mother-of-pearl table. The oil-papered floor was immaculate, and the flowered wallpaper made a fine background for three watercolors of sparkling seascapes. The paintings leaned forward from the wall at about a 45-degree angle, as was customary in Korea so those sitting on the floor could look up and have a better view. Miss Kim wore a long, green housedress made of felt over a white cotton blouse. Her hair was tied back in a bun and clasped with a jade pin. She looked gorgeous, which I'm sure wasn't lost on Ernie. He kept reaching for his tea, nervously sipping tiny amounts and setting the porcelain cup back on the table.

"We want you back," I told Miss Kim in English.

She didn't answer.

"It came as a big shock when we found out you were gone," I continued. I motioned toward myself and Ernie. "Maybe we did something wrong?"

I thought of Ernie following her on the bus, and the fact that we'd rousted Specialist Four Fenton for bothering her after she'd expressly asked us not to.

She shook her head. "You didn't do anything wrong."

"Then why have you left us?" I asked.

Ernie raised his eyes, also waiting for her answer.

She finally spoke. "He came here."

"Came here? To your home?"

"Yes."

"Who?"

"The man who was bothering me," she said. "The man who used to wait for me after work and then walk beside me to the Main Gate."

I described him. "Thin, reddish hair, sort of curly, cheap patterned suit?"

She nodded. "That's him."

"When did he come here?"

"The night you and Ernie talked to him."

"How'd you know we talked to him?"

"He told me. He told me that you punched him. He told me that you think you're *tough*."

I was surprised for a lot of reasons. Usually, twerps who bother women back off immediately when they know someone is watching. And most GIs are afraid to venture out in Seoul any farther than the red-light district of Itaewon. They can't read the signs, they can't speak the language, and with everybody staring at them, they feel hopelessly out of place. Specialist Four Fenton had more resourcefulness than I'd initially given him credit for.

"Did you let him in?" Ernie asked.

She shook her head again. "No. We talked through the . . . What do you call it?"

"The intercom," I said.

"Yes. We talked through the intercom."

"What'd he say?"

"The same thing he said on compound when he walked next to me."

We waited for her to elaborate, but when she didn't, I figured she didn't want to repeat the probable obscenities he'd used.

"What'd he say?" I asked. "Bad words?"

She shook her head vehemently. "He never said bad words."

I was surprised. "Never? Did he ask you to do bad things?"

"Yes. Very bad things."

"Sexual things," I said.

"No." Her face flushed red, but to her credit, she swallowed and kept talking. "He asked me to do worse things than that. In fact, I didn't know the English word. I had to look it up."

I gulped down some of my tea. Ernie didn't want to ask, so I had to.

"What did he ask you to do?"

Miss Kim leaned forward, as if afraid to say the word out loud. "He asked me to *spy*." She sat back up, straightening her lower back. We both watched as she paused, breathing out and breathing in. "He said that if I didn't spy on you two, and tell him every day what you were doing, that he knew where I lived and he knew where my mother lived, and he'd be back."

Then she started to cry. Ernie and I both fumbled around for a handkerchief, but neither of us had one. Finally, Miss Kim's mother crouched into the room and slid a box of tissue across the floor. Miss Kim daintily snatched two or three sheets and dried her eyes.

"Why didn't you tell us?" I asked.

"I was afraid."

"But you kept coming to work."

"Yes. My mother and I, we need the job."

"But something changed."

I waited. She blew her nose. Not a Korean custom to do such a thing in front of other people, but she was amongst Americans now.

"Yes," she said, "something changed."

"What?"

"He came back."

"When?"

"Last night. Late. Just before curfew. He buzzed on the intercom. When I answered, he didn't say anything."

"How'd you know it was him?"

"His breathing. How do you say? Heavy."

"Maybe it was someone else," I ventured.

"No. It was him."

"How do you know?"

"Only an American would do such a thing."

She was probably right. I looked at Ernie. "It wasn't *me*," he said.

I turned back to Miss Kim. "Maybe it was the same guy who bothered you before. But please, come back to work. We need you."

Ernie reached for her hand. "We'll protect you," he said.

She studied him above the wad of tissue, doubt in her eyes. She glanced at me and I nodded in affirmation. Then she bowed her head and continued to cry.

-21-

As Ernie sped north through the heavy traffic of downtown Seoul, I studied our copy of Major Schultz's inspection report alongside my map of Kyongki Province.

According to what Miss Kim just told us, Specialist Fenton had first started bothering her about a month ago. That would've been shortly after Major Schultz launched his inspection of the 501st. It made sense. Captain Blood must have believed that a thorough inspection of his operation might lead to criminal charges and, if so, such a high-level classified inquiry wouldn't be handled by the MPs. It would be handled at a higher level, by the 8th Army Criminal Investigation Division.

"So he decided to cover himself," Ernie said, "just in case. Get himself a spy inside our organization."

"So he had Fenton go after the most vulnerable person," I replied. "A woman who was terrified of losing her job."

"Maybe that's what he thought. But he didn't bargain for someone as brave as Miss Kim."

"No."

We drove in silence. Finally, when we passed Songbuk-dong and the last remnants of the ancient northern wall, Ernie said, "How many branch offices does the Five Oh First have?"

"Five, north of Seoul." Which figured, because most US Army base camps sat between the capital city of Seoul and the Demilitarized Zone, which sliced across the Korean Peninsula about thirty miles to the north. On the far side of the DMZ, 700,000 North Korean Communist soldiers waited impatiently for the orders to flood south. So far, since the Korean War twenty years ago, they hadn't, other than small-scale incursions and the occasional commando raid or stray artillery round. The South Korean Army averaged one fatality a month at the hands of the North Koreans; the US Army, about one per year. Of course, our commitment was much smaller than the ROK's: 50,000 soldiers to their 450,000.

"So which one are we going to hit?" Ernie asked.

"Uijongbu," I said. "They've busted three GIs in the last year and a half."

Ernie whistled. "Busy little beavers."

It was unlikely that the compounds as small as those surrounding Uijongbu had one American GI selling secrets to the North Korean Communists, let alone three in eighteen months. But according to Major Schultz's inspection report, that was how many arrests had been made there. The GIs had been ferreted out by the excellent counterintelligence work of a certain Sergeant Leon Jerrod of the 501st Military Intelligence Battalion. One of the accused had faced military court-martial, *in camera*, been convicted, and was now serving a twenty-year sentence at the Federal Penitentiary in Fort Leavenworth. The other two had taken bad-conduct discharges and left the military with no pay or benefits. Better, at least, than rotting in federal prison. An appendix to the report had the dates of the proceedings and the names of the witnesses who had testified against the GIs. It was a long shot, but I was hoping to locate one of those witnesses and, after interviewing them, use the information they gave us to pressure Sergeant Jerrod into spilling his guts.

Until we knew what was really going on at the 501st, we couldn't determine the likelihood that Captain Blood or anyone else there had a motive to murder Major Schultz. They certainly had the means: These were trained soldiers who'd already demonstrated a willingness to use force. And they had a three-quarter-ton truck that could easily transport a body to Itaewon, even after curfew, and dump it behind the Dragon King Nightclub. But had there been more at risk than receiving a bad inspection report?

And that's why we were avoiding the Provost Marshal. Unless we came to him with concrete evidence, he'd never let us go forward with an investigation against a military unit and a fellow officer who could be promoted to field-grade rank within a year.

And whether or not the Provost Marshal would believe Miss Kim's story about being threatened and ordered to spy by Specialist Fenton was impossible to tell, even though she was our trusted office assistant. Ernie and I believed her absolutely. But the honchos at 8th Army had a different standard of belief based not on a person's integrity, but whether the report would reflect poorly on themselves or the Command. And having a rogue counterintelligence unit threatening innocent women and railroading GIs into prison just to acquire power and funding wasn't likely to be well received by the honchos of 8th Army. We'd need proof. The same type of proof that Major Schultz had apparently been after. At least, according to the inspection report Strange had pilfered for me. The inspection was thorough and backed up by facts, figures, and dates. If I were doing something illegal, I wouldn't want Major Schultz after me.

"Our mistake was," Ernie said, "we didn't kill that guy Fenton when we had the chance."

"We don't need to kill him, Ernie. We'll just send him to jail. That's good enough."

"We'll see," Ernie replied.

His knuckles were white on the steering wheel, and he cursed when a kimchi cab swerved in front of him, something he seldom did.

"Easy," I said. "Nobody's going to hurt Miss Kim now. We'll make sure of that."

"You're damn right we will."

The city of Uijongbu sits about fifteen miles north of Seoul, on the route known as the Eastern Corridor. Since Uijongbu is an important intersection with several major roads leading north and another slashing across mountains toward the Western Corridor, a half-dozen military compounds are located nearby.

The 501st kept their Uijongbu office manned by Sergeant Leon Jerrod at the local Veterans of Foreign Wars branch, or VFW, in a district known as Kanung-dong. The VFW was only a couple of hundred yards from the front gate of Camp Red Cloud, a compound that housed the headquarters that had been known as I Corps during the Korean War.

Ernie and I had been in this area before on other cases, and as we rolled up the MSR into the city of Uijongbu proper, I told him where to veer off. The side road led to a traffic circle that old-timers told me had been notorious during the Korean War. Truck drivers running supplies to and from the front lines stopped here and traded C-rations, heating fuel, medical supplies, and other military items for whatever their hearts desired: booze, drugs, women, you name it. Those days were over, but there was still a river of neon leading from the traffic circle through the Kanung-dong area and right up to the front gate of Camp Red Cloud. The VFW sat smack-dab in the middle of all the action.

"Nice place to be stationed," Ernie said. "Away from the

flagpole, plenty of creature comforts. What's the name of the agent again?"

I checked the appendix to the report. "Sergeant Jerrod."

Ernie didn't ask the first name. We seldom used them in the military. As an old drill sergeant once told me, "Your first name is your rank, and your last name is printed on your name tag, in case you forget it. But don't *ever* forget your rank."

Ernie parked the jeep on a side street. We climbed out and walked toward the VFW.

When we pushed through the front door, a sleepy-eyed Korean woman behind the bar looked up. She had long black hair, sagging cheeks and the unperturbed air of someone who'd been bored for the better part of her life.

"What you want?" she asked.

"Jerrod," I said.

She went back to the Korean film star magazine in front of her. "He not here."

"When is he coming in?"

"How I know?"

"Where does he live?" Ernie asked.

She looked up, her eyes widening. "You buy drink, no buy drink? That's my job."

"That and charm," Ernie replied.

"Huh?"

"Never mind."

She glared at us and turned back to her magazine.

"Do any customers ever come in here?" I asked.

"Most tick they come," she replied.

"When?"

She looked at me, greatly annoyed. "When they come, they come."

I grinned at her. The time was about fifteen-thirty, three-thirty in the afternoon. She was right—it was still early for the bar crowd.

"Do you have happy hour?" Ernie asked.

"No happy hour," she said without looking up.

"I didn't think so," he told her.

A hallway led toward the latrines out back. While Ernie waited with Miss Congeniality, I checked out both the men's bathroom and women's, just to be thorough. Both empty. I pushed through another door that led to a store-room, then an alley out back. No sign of life. Although this place was designated as a Veterans of Foreign Wars official chapter, there wasn't much to it. Just a bar. No meeting hall, no games of chance.

When I returned, I shook my head in the negative to Ernie. To the left of the bar, a stairway led up toward the second floor.

"What's up there?" Ernie asked the barmaid.

"Not your business," she said.

We both walked toward the stairs. Finally, she looked up from her magazine and said, "What you do?"

"We're gonna leave a note in Jerrod's office."

"No can do. No can go up there."

Our assumption was right. If the VFW was in this building, Jerrod's office would be, too. We ignored her and climbed the stairs. On the second floor, a short hallway led to a window. I peered outside. Nothing below but an empty alleyway. The doorway on the right was stenciled in black letters: PRESIDENT, UIJONGBU BRANCH, VETERANS OF FOREIGN WARS. The doorway on the left had another sign: PRIVATE.

I tried the handle of the office on the left. Locked.

"Did you bring your lock pick?" I asked Ernie.

"Yeah," he said. "Got it right here."

He backed up against the wall opposite the door marked PRIVATE, raised his right foot, and leapt forward, throwing all his weight into it. The door crashed open.

Downstairs, I heard the front door open and the barmaid's voice call "*Koma-ya!*" Boy! A few seconds later, there was a hushed conversation I couldn't make out until a boy's voice said, "*Nei, nei.*" Yes, yes. And then the door closed again.

Ernie and I walked into the office. It was Spartan. A grey Army-issue desk with a full in-basket and wooden filing cabinets behind and a black phone resting on a blue cloth at the edge of the desk. The filing cabinets each had a metal bar running vertically through the front handles, which were padlocked securely into place.

I started riffling through the in-box. Ernie checked the

desk drawers. Sergeant Jerrod's name was everywhere, along with the unit designation of Headquarters Company, 501st Military Intelligence Battalion.

"I think she sent someone to get him," I told Ernie.

"Get who?"

"Jerrod."

"You think he has a hooch nearby?"

"Wouldn't you?"

"With a cushy setup like this? Yeah, I probably would."

The paperwork in the in-box and in the desk drawer was routine. Personnel matters, policy directives concerning unit training and physical fitness. The good stuff pertaining to the three counterintelligence cases Jerrod had brought recently were almost certainly in the locked file cabinets. Ernie and I stared at them in frustration.

"How are we going to get in?" he asked.

"You can't kick that metal bar off?"

"Not without breaking my leg. Maybe the grumpy old broad downstairs has a crowbar."

"Maybe. But I have a better idea."

"What?"

"I think the guy with the keys is on his way. Maybe he'll open the cabinets for us."

"Maybe he will," Ernie said, "if we ask him nice."

Ten minutes later, footsteps tromped up the stairs.

Ernie and I had turned off the lights and re-closed the

door. Of course, the lock was still busted, but there was nothing we could do about that. The footsteps slowed to a halt on the other side. "Anybody in there?" called a deep but unsteady voice.

Ernie and I sat on straight-backed chairs on either side of the room's only entrance. We didn't answer. Slowly, someone pushed the door open. Then a hand reached in and flicked on the light switch. The man waited a second, then burst into the room, quickly reaching the opposite wall and swiveling around. He held a .45 automatic in his hand. His eyes were wide, his face sweaty.

Sergeant Leon Jerrod was a stout man. Not fat, but pretty wide for his height, which was about five-foot-six. Still, he looked strong and had a low center of gravity, so fighting him wouldn't be easy, and knocking him off his feet might be impossible. His hair was dark, trimmed short in a butch haircut that accentuated his round head. His eyes were round, too, bovine and wet. Of course, what Ernie and I noticed first was the barrel of his gun pointing at Ernie, then at me.

"Sorry about your door," I said.

"Yeah," Ernie added. "We were in sort of a hurry. And your charming hostess downstairs wasn't much help."

"In a hurry for what?"

"To talk to you," I said, "about a couple of cases you closed in the last few months." Both Ernie and I kept our hands motionless at our sides. Rule number one: never make an armed man nervous. "Can I reach in my pocket," I asked, "and pull out my ID?"

"Who are you?"

"I'm Agent Sueño, Eighth Army CID. He's my partner, Agent Bascom."

"Sorry for the intrusion," Ernie said, smiling.

"Yeah," Jerrod said, swiveling the gun between us and motioning with his free hand. "Let me see some ID."

We both started to reach into our jackets but he screeched, "One at a time! You first."

I pulled out my CID badge. "Slide it to me on the floor," he said.

I did.

Crouching but still keeping the gun on us, he flipped open the leather holder and held the ID up to the light. Then he turned to Ernie. Ernie reached slowly into his coat and repeated the process.

"Okay," he said, tossing the badges onto his desk. "What the hell is all this about?"

"You are Sergeant Leon Jerrod," I asked, "aren't you?"

He wasn't wearing his uniform. Like us, he was wearing blue jeans and a long-sleeved shirt.

"I'll ask the questions," he said. "What the hell are you doing here?"

"Just paying a friendly visit," Ernie said. "And looking for some backup information on that guy you put away." He turned toward me. "What's the name?"

"Do you mind?" I asked, motioning toward my jacket pocket again.

He nodded. I pulled out Major Schultz's inspection report, thumbed toward the back pages and said, "Arenas, Hector A., Staff Sergeant. Convicted by general court-martial of espionage. Twenty years at Leavenworth."

"Good job," Ernie said, smiling even more broadly.

"Just what I get paid for," Jerrod said, but I knew he felt proud.

"Do you want to frisk us or something," I asked, "before you put the gun away?"

He stared at the .45 as if just realizing it was clutched in his hand. "Oh, this. Yeah, sorry." He switched on the safety and shoved the weapon beneath his belt. "You guys gave me a start."

"Sorry about that," I said.

He grinned at us like a guy hungry for companionship. Which he probably was. I'd seen the crowd at the VFWs and AmVets around the country, and they were mostly geriatric. Korean War and World War II veterans, few within a decade of Jerrod's age. And as a counterintelligence agent, he wouldn't be encouraged to socialize with the young guys on Camp Red Cloud. He had, after all, been sent here to spy on them.

"How about we have a beer downstairs?" he said.

"Sounds good to me," Ernie said, slapping his knees.

"Me too," I said.

Ernie and I stood, towering over Jerrod. He grimaced briefly, but then laughed and backed out of the door. We followed him downstairs and ordered a liter of cold OB and three glasses from the ravishing creature behind the bar. How she felt about serving us, no one could tell. Her face remained grim at all times; I thought she'd missed her calling as an undertaker. The first beer was followed by the second, and then Jerrod suggested a round of bourbon. Ernie and I heartily agreed. We sipped on the imported whisky, but since Ernie was buying, Jerrod kept putting single shots away, and then doubles, as fast as Miss Congeniality could pour.

The way I understood it, these barrooms operated under the charter of the American veterans associations while someone else, invariably a Korean, paid for the concession. So the barmaid must've been happy to see two big spenders from Seoul, although you'd never guess it from her facial expression.

By the time the regular drinking crowd showed up, Jerrod was looped. Ernie engaged him in animated conversation—something about how the counterculture wastrels were leaching our resolve to fight Godless Communism—and while they raved, I leaned against Jerrod and unhooked the keys that hung by a metal ring clasped to his belt loop. I excused myself to use the latrine, but when I returned, I passed the two guys arguing now about whether or not *Rowan and Martin's Laugh-In* had weakened our national fiber and, while the barmaid was busy serving some old vets, I slipped upstairs.

A single key opened all three cabinets. One of them was empty, and another held Jerrod's military-issue field gear: fur-lined cap, parka, mittens, rain poncho, wet-weather overshoes. The central file had what I was looking for. The Arenas file was right up front. Behind it, farther back in the alphabet, I found the other two. I slipped the files into a large mailing envelope, then slipped the envelope beneath my belt in front. I zipped up my nylon jacket and slapped my stomach to make sure the entire package was secure. Then I relocked the cabinets, turned off the light and trotted downstairs. Ernie glanced over at me. I gave him the high sign and continued out the front door, walking quickly over to the jeep. By the time he approached, I'd already pulled the Arenas file and slid the other two files under the metal floor panel beneath the passenger seat where the jack, crowbar, flares and the other pieces of roadside equipment were stored, including a short-handled axe for chopping off ice during the brutal Korean winters.

"Got it?" Ernie asked.

"Got it," I replied.

"And his keys?" Ernie asked.

"I left them in his top desk drawer."

Ernie climbed behind the steering wheel. "He'll be so hung over tomorrow, he won't remember if he left them there himself or not." Then he turned to me. "Where to?"

I retrieved the Arenas file and, using my flashlight, quickly thumbed through it. After a couple of minutes, I found what I was looking for. "There's a bar in Songsan-dong called the Star Mountain Club."

"Yeah, what about it?"

"That's where Staff Sergeant Arenas's *yobo* used to work."

"They didn't throw her in jail too?"

"No. Since she cooperated with the prosecution, the KNPs gave her a pass. Probably because they knew she had no real connection to Communist spies."

"You're assuming a lot."

"Maybe. But if they thought she had a real connection, they would've never let her go."

Ernie started the engine. "So where's Songsan-dong?"

"On the other side of Uijongbu. We've been there before."

"That village outside Camp Stanley?"

"That's the one."

"I like that place," he said. "Nice and decadent."

We rolled out onto the main road, turned left, and passed the VFW. No commotion. Apparently, our departure was going as we'd hoped. Unnoticed.

-22-

Songsan means Star Mountain. Looming above Camp Stanley, it's a pointed peak that would provide a layer of protection from incoming artillery in case of war. The peak slants down to a narrow plateau, upon which two artillery battalions and the 2nd Infantry Division Artillery headquarters are stationed, and from there the mountain continues to slope downhill. The narrow pathway leading out of Camp Stanley's back gate was steep and lined with neon-signed bars and nightclubs jammed together like dominoes. Heaven, in other words, to an American GI. We parked the jeep at the base of the hill, about a hundred yards from the compound itself, and walked up slippery steps, passing soul music and rock and roll blaring out of open doorways. About thirty yards from the base's back gate stood the Star Mountain Club.

I entered first. Ernie followed shortly after.

The joint was for older soldiers, with slightly more sedate music, soft lighting and upholstery a few millimeters thick on all of the seats. The women working the bar were older, too—some in their thirties, a few probably in their forties. A couple of NCOs sat at the bar, and one guy lounged in a booth with his *yobo*—or at least, his *yobo* for the evening. The far end of the bar was wide open, so Ernie and I sat down. We ordered ourselves OB.

Time was of the essence, so I got straight to the point. "Where's Miss Lee?" I asked the waitress who brought us the drinks.

"Who?"

"Miss Lee Suk-myong. She works here, doesn't she?"

The woman looked startled. "Miss Lee? She long time go."

"She doesn't work here anymore?"

"No. Long time *tonasso-yo*." She left a long time go.

"Long time," I repeated, "like one month ago, two months ago?"

The woman thought about it. "Not last payday, maybe payday before that one."

Two months ago, maybe less.

"Where'd she go?" I asked.

Her forehead crinkled. "I don't know," she said. Then she looked at me more closely. "Why you wanna know?"

"When I was in the States," I told her, "my *chingu* told me he steadied her before. He told me she is a good woman."

Chingu means friend. It's not uncommon for a GI to have a steady *yobo*, to return to the States after his tour is up, and then recommend her to a friend who's on his way to Korea. If she's proven to be reliable and not a thief, some guys will look her up and, if she's available, move right in.

"You too young for her," the woman told me.

I shrugged. "Young woman, old woman, what's it matter?"

This seemed to please her. She grinned and said, "You wait."

At the end of the bar, she conferred with two of the other hostesses who were chatting and smoking. Life can be boring, even in a sex bar, and after listening to the barmaid, the three women engaged in animated conversation.

Finally, the barmaid returned. "Maybe not sure, but somebody say she move to TDC." Tongduchon, the city outside of the 2nd Infantry Division headquarters at Camp Casey.

"There's a lot of clubs up there," I said.

"Yes," she agreed. "*Taaksan.*" Many. "Maybe she get job at Cherry Girl Club."

"Is she a cherry girl?" Ernie asked.

The woman laughed with just a hint of bitterness and waved her cigarette. "Long time ago she cherry girl. Same time Yi Sing-man president." The Syngman Rhee regime had been deposed by a military coup in 1962, more than eleven years ago.

We thanked her and rose to leave. Ernie left a generous tip: five hundred *won*. Almost a buck.

"Now who's spoiling them?" I asked.

Ernie patted the envelope with the expense money Inspector Kill had given us. "My days of being a Cheap Charley are over."

"For the time being," I said.

The city of Tongduchon was about a twenty-minute ride up the road. That is, it would have been twenty minutes if it weren't for the 2nd Infantry Division military check-point. That took over fifteen minutes to clear; there was a long line of vehicles waiting to get through. When we reached the front of the line, we showed our emergency dispatch, but just our regular military ID instead of our CID badges.

The MP eyed us suspiciously, keeping his M-16 rifle pointed skyward. Then he gazed at the bumper of the jeep, which was stenciled in white with the 21 T Car unit desig-nation. He brought the dispatch back.

"You can't drive a military vehicle while wearing civilian clothes," he said.

"Why not?" Ernie asked.

He seemed flummoxed by the question. Finally, he said, "This is Division. I don't know what you all do down in Eighth Army."

"There's nothing that says we can't drive a jeep in civilian clothes," Ernie said, "as long as we can identify ourselves and the vehicle is properly dispatched."

We'd been through this before.

The MP motioned to the ROK Army MP not to move the barricade. He returned to his field radio and made a call. The radio buzzed and clicked and the MP kept his voice low so we couldn't make out what he was saying. Finally, he switched off the radio, returned to us and said, "Destination?"

Before Ernie could argue with him, I said, "Camp Casey."

He nodded and said, "They'll be expecting you at the front gate. Check in there. The Duty Officer wants to talk to you."

"Why?" Ernie asked.

"To make sure your heads are screwed on right."

"What the hell's that supposed to mean?"

The MP ignored him, turned away, and motioned for the ROK MP to pull back the crossed metal stanchions.

"It means they want to show us who's boss," I told Ernie.

He gunned the engine and we sped off.

"Butthole," Ernie said.

We didn't check in at the Camp Casey front gate.

We were still a hundred yards from it when we parked in a side alley. Just off the main road ahead, neon was punctured by silhouetted GIs parading from nightclub to nightclub in packs of three or four, as if buttressing one another in their quest for debauchery.

"What's the name of the club again?" Ernie asked.

"According to the gal at Star Mountain, it's called the Cherry Girl Club."

"How could I forget?" asked Ernie rhetorically. "Do you know where it is?"

"No idea."

"So we search."

And search we did, navigating past the drunken GIs who barreled down crowded lanes like pinballs in a brightly lit machine. Korean business girls in shorts and miniskirts pressed against beaded curtains, beckoning to passersby to enter their dens of sweet iniquity. Old women fished onion rings and sliced yams out of bubbling vats, slapping the oily concoctions onto folded wads of newspaper and collecting a few coins from half-drunk GIs. MP patrols shoved their way through the milling crowd, checking one bar after another for miscreants, overwhelmed by the boisterous humanity that threatened to envelop them.

I asked a couple of the business girls where the Cherry Girl Club was. They shook their heads, confused.

"It must be new," Ernie said.

I nodded. And if it was new, it wouldn't be here in the heart of the GI village. It would probably be somewhere on the outskirts. "Maybe across East Bean River," I said. There were a few bars over there, mostly frequented by the older non-commissioned officers. The more I thought about it, the more it made sense.

"She's no spring chicken," I told Ernie, "if the other gals who work at the Star Mountain Club are any indication."

"So she'll be across the bridge, where the lifers hang out."

"Lifer" is the derogatory term young GIs use for the older NCOs who've made the army their career.

"Worth a shot," I said.

We left the neon behind and made our way through muddy lanes to the footbridge across the East Bean River. Lights spread up and down the water, flickering from the backs of hovels and dilapidated two-story buildings that housed the working-class families who made their livings off the meager economy that Camp Casey provided. During the day, acres of laundry fluttered on lines like the flags of a Mongol army. But now, at night, back windows were lit up in a checkerboard pattern and the steady buzz of radios and television sets was interspersed with the occasional shouts of children, the clang of pots and pans and the wailing cries of infants.

On the far side, we turned north toward the branch of the Military Supply Route that ran west from Camp Casey. Eventually the road would cross the small mountain range dividing the Eastern and Western Corridors.

Finally we hit neon. Not as much as on the main drag of TDC, but enough to make us feel at home.

"There it is," Ernie said, pointing to a sign about fifty yards ahead: THE CHERRY GIRL CLUB.

We walked quickly, our hands buried deep in our coat pockets. The night was becoming colder.

■ ■ ■

We decided not to take the direct approach. Better to play it low-key and check out the lay of the land. A few NCOs in civvies sat at the bar. We steered away from them, settled into a booth, and ordered a pitcher of OB. Ernie splurged for a plate of *daegu-po*, strips of dried cuttlefish with a dip of red pepper paste.

"You're hungry," I said after the waitress brought our beer and snacks.

"So are you," he said.

Our server was a husky woman who wore short yellow pants and a pullover sleeveless blouse. She could get away with such skimpy attire because the Cherry Girl Club had an Army-issue diesel space heater on either side of the twenty-yard long barroom. Her nameplate read MISS NOH.

"We're hungry," Ernie told Miss Noh as he paid her for the beer and *daegu-po*. "Where's a good place to eat?"

"Sell hamburger here," she said.

"What kind of meat?"

She crinkled her round nose. "Maybe not good like compound."

"You've been on the compound?" Ernie asked.

"Sure. My *yobo* take me."

"You have a steady *yobo*?"

"Of course. Supposed to."

"Is that a rule here?"

She grew exasperated. "What you mean?"

"I mean a friend of mine back Stateside, he used to steady a woman here. A woman who works at the Cherry Club."

Miss Noh sat down, mildly interested. "What her name?"

Ernie told her. "Miss Lee," he said.

Miss Noh held up three fingers. "We have three Miss Lee work here."

"Three? Damn. Where are they?"

"Most tick they come. Early now. Most GI, they get off work, eat in mess hall, take shower, change clothes. Maybe they get here seven o'clock. Maybe eight."

"And that's when the other waitresses come in?" I asked.

She pondered what I'd said, processing the English. "Yeah. Most girl come in eight o'clock." She turned back to Ernie. "What's your *chingu* name?"

Ernie didn't want to say Arenas. It might ring alarm bells. "Schultz," he replied.

"Schultz?" Miss Noh pronounced carefully. Ernie nodded.

"When they come, I ask," she said.

Most of the hostesses and waitresses and business girls knew each other by either their family name or a nickname they used at the club. Seldom would their first name be offered, because that was considered to be private, almost sacred, and not something to be spread around. So it wasn't unusual that Miss Noh knew three Miss Lees but didn't bother asking for a first name, since she wouldn't recognize it anyway.

We ordered the hamburgers Miss Noh had mentioned. They were as bad as implied. But the fries were okay, as was the sliced cucumber.

As we sat in the booth, I studied the Arenas file. The case against him had been based primarily on the testimony of his *yobo*, Miss Lee Suk-myong, and that of a black marketeer named "Nam," who'd allegedly introduced Arenas to an unnamed North Korean agent. Nam, when used as a family name, is usually represented by the Chinese character for "south"—pretty ironic, for someone doing business with a North Korean agent. Quite a few things were strange about the Arenas case. First and foremost was that the 501st had busted Arenas early on, when normal procedure would've been to observe and follow him, waiting patiently for the opportunity to take down his handler and this mysterious North Korean agent. As it turned out, the agent never appeared, and they couldn't even find Nam and take him into custody. Only Miss Lee and Staff Sergeant Arenas had been arrested. The paperwork indicated that Miss Lee had made a deal with the Korean prosecutor and gotten off with time served in exchange for her testimony against her former *yobo*.

"Bullshit case," Ernie said. "If we brought something like that to the Provost Marshal, he'd kick us out of his office."

"Especially since they didn't arrest the most important

person in this whole drama. The still-anonymous North Korean spy."

Ernie poured himself more beer.

I wasn't worried about him getting wasted—I didn't figure we'd be doing any more driving tonight. When the time came, we'd just find a cheap room in a *yoguan*, a Korean inn, or even more economically, a couple of sleeping mats in a community room of a traditional establishment known as a *yoin-suk*. I'd spotted a few on the way over.

"What did Arenas give up?" Ernie asked.

"You mean, what classified information was compromised?"

"What'd I just say?"

Ernie was getting irritable. I flipped through the pages in the file. "Staff Sergeant Arenas worked at the Camp Red Cloud Communications Center. As such, he had access to classified information all the way up to Secret. He occasionally hand-carried Top Secret documents to and from the I Corps Headquarters, since he was cleared for that."

"But he wasn't supposed to read them," Ernie said.

"No. Just determine where the document should be routed, then deliver it."

"But he could've read them because he had his hands on them."

"Sure. If he was careful, he could've even made a copy. Not authorized, but there's one of those big Xerox machines in the Commo Center." I pointed at the paragraph I was scanning. "Says so right here."

"Okay, so he had access to Top Secret information. How do they know he stole any of it?"

"Testimony of his girl."

"The woman we're waiting for."

"Right."

"That's it? They didn't have anything else?"

"She says this guy Nam showed up, all good looks and nice clothes and personality, and started taking Arenas out to those *kisaeng* houses down south on the outskirts of Seoul." *Kisaeng* are female entertainers, typically skilled in the art of catering to wealthy clientele. "According to her, Arenas went along with it and even spent nights away from home."

"She was jealous that he was out with Nam all the time."

"Maybe. Or jealous of the money Arenas was spending on some *kisaeng* instead of her."

"But what about the actual leak of classified info? What does the file say about that?"

I thumbed through it, twisting the pages as I read in order to catch more of the words in the dim light. I went through the file once, then back through it again.

"It doesn't say anything about that. It only has testimony from one of the GIs who worked for Arenas, who talked about how he would sometimes sneak off to the copy room by himself, then bring back pages and not show them to anyone."

"Sounds pretty flimsy to me." Ernie glugged back more beer. "Did Arenas build up a lot of cash in his bank account, or buy money orders and mail them home?"

"If he did, it doesn't appear here."

"So the main thing is that at least one of his subordinates didn't like him, which isn't unusual, and his girlfriend was jealous that he had a rich buddy who took him to party with a bunch of *kisaeng*."

"That's what it looks like."

Ernie shook his head. "No wonder they keep these proceedings *in camera*. Who'd want that out in the world? Did Arenas hire a Stateside lawyer?"

I flipped back to the appendix. "No. He was represented by military counsel."

"Mistake," Ernie said.

"The biggest thing that the prosecution harped on was that there were Top Secret documents not properly logged in and out. This happened right in the middle of Sergeant Arenas's shift—he was the NCO in charge."

"Did other GIs have access to the login and logout register?"

I studied the statements. "Yes."

"But Arenas was the man in charge."

"For that shift, yes. He was the ranking man in the Commo Center during the hours the documents in question were supposed to have been logged in and logged out."

Ernie polished off his beer and ordered another. "So

somebody was taking shortcuts and not following procedure. Christ, we could put away half the US Army if *that's*
the standard. Does the file say why the counter-intel pukes
didn't go after this guy Nam?"

"Not a word," I said.

"Figures. They didn't want to embarrass themselves.
Maybe because he doesn't exist."

After about twenty minutes, a half-dozen hostesses entered
the Cherry Girl Club. Three were named Miss Lee. Miss
Noh wasted no time. She cornered them all as they were
taking off their coats, speaking rapidly, and once she had
their attention, she pointed toward us. After a quick trip
to the ladies' room, two of the women came over and sat
down next to us. We didn't want to waste time buying them
drinks if we didn't have to, so I immediately asked if either
of them was Lee Suk-myong. My abruptness was rude, but
I could tell by their baffled reaction that neither was the
woman we were looking for.

I watched the far side of the bar, and from the ladies'
room emerged the third Miss Lee. Her head was down and
her coat was back on. She shuffled quickly back toward the
door she'd first entered through.

"Come on," I said to Ernie, and started to get up.

The Miss Lee next to me pouted and grabbed my wrist.
I ripped my hand away and almost dumped her out of
the booth, though at the last minute she managed to keep

on her feet. Then I hurried across the barroom and hit the far door, and outside I saw our prospective Miss Lee Suk-myong hail a cab. She climbed in, and before I could position myself in front of the cab to block it, it sped off, drenching my blue jeans with water. I ran after it, glimpsing part of the license plate.

"*Damn!*" Ernie said, sprinting up to my side.

But I was already waving my arms frantically, and another taxi emerged out of the night. We hopped in and I yelled the Korean equivalent of "Follow that cab!"

He did. And then I told him to step on it, which in Korean is *bali, bali*. Quickly, quickly.

When Miss Lee Suk-myong climbed out of her cab, she was not in front of a *yoguan*, a *yoin-suk* or even a hooch, but rather the one place in town that was reminiscent of a Western-style hotel: the Tower Hotel. Six stories high and easily the tallest building in Tongduchon, it held preeminence of place. It sat across the street, and only a quarter mile south from the main gate of Camp Casey. Many of the guests at the Tower Hotel were military officers on temporary duty from elsewhere in Korea or from the United States. As such, the Tower Hotel billed the US government directly for rooms. The hotel lobby had a Western-style coffee shop, which provided food and coffee of poor quality and was therefore usually empty. The Americans who stayed at the Tower seldom ate or drank there, since they could just take a short walk across the street and enter the pedestrian gate to Camp Casey, where they could find much better, more reasonably priced food and drink at the 2nd Infantry Division Officers Club.

But the hotel also had an elegant bar called the Tower Lounge. It was carpeted and softly lit, with comfortably upholstered chairs and waitresses in short skirts, all providing an air of American-style elegance. As such, it was extremely popular not with Americans, but with upwardly mobile young Koreans.

Miss Lee paid the cabbie and entered the front door of the Tower Hotel.

We ordered our driver to cruise past slowly.

"She can't afford to live here," Ernie said.

"No."

"So what's she up to?"

"We'll find out."

I told the driver to pull over about ten yards past the hotel entrance. Ernie paid him and we emerged from the cramped kimchi cab into the cold night.

"Maybe only one of us should go in," I said. "She knows two guys are looking for her. If she only sees one, that might throw her off."

I slipped out of my jacket and handed it to Ernie. Beneath, I wore a long-sleeved blue sports shirt with a buttoned-down collar. "If I'm not wearing a jacket," I said, "she might think I'm staying at the hotel."

"Unless she took a real good look at us at the Cherry Girl Club."

"I don't think she did," I said. "At least, I hope not."

Ernie pointed to a *yakbang*, a pharmacy, on the other

side of the street. "I'll go get the jeep," he said, "it's not far from here. I'll be waiting in front of that pharmacy."

"Good."

Ernie trotted off and quickly faded into darkness. After he was gone, I turned, walked up the street, and pushed through the large glass front doors of the Tower Hotel.

Our goal was to prove what Major Schultz's inspection report implied: that the 501st Military Intelligence agents were jerry-rigging investigations to make themselves look effective, and to expand both the unit's budget and the reputation of its Commander, Captain Blood. Given the paranoia of the military officers who sat on court-martial juries—men who saw Commies behind every bedpost—it wasn't too far-fetched to think that they would set aside their better judgment and go along, at least sometimes, with the counterintelligence "experts" of the 501st. No officer wanted to be seen as soft on Communism, not if he had any ambition in this man's army.

The case against Staff Sergeant Hector Arenas seemed, thus far, to meet all the criteria of a sham trial. A guy who worked with classified documents, whose *yobo* was angry with him, and who had somehow become friends with a mysterious Korean named Nam. Money, sex, glory, and anti-Communism can all become a jumble in the fevered military mind. Under those conditions, a miscarriage of justice can occur. And I could see Captain Blood and the agents who worked for him panicking when Major Schultz threatened to expose them. But did it amount to murder?

It seemed like something was missing. There had to be more in order to push someone to hacking a field grade officer to death. But what was that something? If I could establish a motive in the Provost Marshal's mind, we might receive clearance to investigate further. But to establish that motive, I needed one last thing: the testimony of Arenas's girlfriend, Miss Lee Suk-myong. Not the official testimony she'd given to the court-martial, but her real testimony, right here in the center of Tongduchon, with no counterintelligence agents to protect her and no lawyers to promise her immunity.

I wanted to hear it straight. In Korean, English, or any other language she wanted, as long as she didn't lie.

The Tower Hotel Lounge was dimly, tastefully lit and true to form; about a half-dozen tables were occupied, mostly by Korean men in suits, and in some cases, well-attired ladies accompanying them. But mostly it was men—discussing business, I imagined, although I couldn't make out much amidst the jumble of conversation.

At a two-person table against the far wall, the woman I believed to be Lee Suk-myong sat across from a Korean man in a dark suit who blended in perfectly with the crowd. I took a closer look at her. She projected elegance, with a smooth complexion and a narrow face that tapered to a round chin. She also dressed better than I would've expected for a night's work at a joint like the Cherry Girl Club. She wore a silk dress, beige with a light blue and pink flower pattern. She appeared to be in her late twenties, maybe her thirties, but she was a woman whose delicate features held aging at bay, at least for a half-decade or so longer than her contemporaries.

The man across from her was youngish, clearly in his thirties, and sported a well-tailored suit. He leaned his elbow on the white linen tablecloth, his palm up and a cigarette balanced between his fingertips. As Miss Lee spoke, he puffed on the cigarette, narrowing his eyes to avoid the fumes.

I sat at the far end of the bar with my back to the couple, as close as I could get without attracting attention. I ordered a Heineken, and a young Korean man wearing a black vest and matching bowtie opened it and poured frothing hops into a frosted pilsner. Suddenly, I realized that I didn't have any Korean money, but when I pulled out a single US dollar, he looked at it, frowned, and told me I'd need another. I pulled out the second bill, trying to hide my outrage. In my entire life, I'd never paid two dollars for a beer, not in the US or in Korea. I reminded myself I was on an expense account and tried to calm down. The kid brought me two hundred *won* in change, which meant that I'd paid about a dollar sixty-five for the beer. A record for me.

Up-and-coming Koreans, especially those who fancied

themselves to be in business, loved nothing more than to be spotted at an expensive place, paying too much for something—anything—especially if it was imported. The Tower Hotel Lounge—and the overpriced Heineken—fit the bill.

Articles in the local press claimed Korea would be rich someday. Industries were expanding, and millions of dollars' worth of goods were being exported every year to Japan, Europe and the United States. But personally, I'd never believed it. I'd seen the poverty firsthand: farmers wrestling oxen-pulled plows through mud; old women squatting in open-air markets peddling malnourished produce; legions of young men wandering in search of jobs after completing their military service; girls barely out of middle school selling their bodies in order to provide food and rent and tuition for their younger siblings. I knew that Korea had been a great and prosperous society in the ancient past—that's why the Mongols and the Manchurians and the Japanese had coveted it so avidly, and why they'd tried to take it by force—but I didn't see how it could climb out of the devastation it had experienced during the twentieth century. Not any time soon, and certainly not in my lifetime. I fully expected that when I completed my twenty years in the army, I'd collect my five-hundred-dollars-per-month retirement and free medical and live here in Korea without an economic care in the world. But I had to admit that the Tower Hotel Lounge was as luxurious as anything I'd seen in Seoul, or in the States for that matter. And the background music was soft, the carpet plush, and the bar fully stocked with top-shelf liquor.

As I sipped my Heineken, I tried to focus on the couple's conversation about five yards behind me. I was gradually able to isolate their voices from the rest of the ones buzzing around the bar. His was smooth and calm, while hers seemed shrill by comparison. Frazzled was perhaps a better way to put it. Apparently, Miss Lee Suk-myong was shaken by the sight of two strange Americans asking for her at the Cherry Girl Club. The man in the suit seemed less concerned.

Understanding Korean conversation—especially when it isn't specifically slowed down for me—is difficult. Amongst themselves, Koreans speak so quickly words slur together, and use idiomatic phrases and terms that are often unfamiliar to me. Still, I listened as hard as I could, staring into the lowering foam in my glass.

I picked out the phrase *sinkyong-jil*. I'm nervous. Then Miss Lee said, *yogi ei ilhagi sillo!* I hate working here. And finally, *tangsin gwakatchi domang kago shipo*. I want to run away with you.

Apparently, she was into the guy sitting across from her. Maybe he'd been her real boyfriend all along, not Arenas. I strained to hear a name, but no such luck. Koreans don't usually use one another's names in one-on-one conversation. They refer to one another indirectly, most often by who they're related to: older brother, younger sister, wife, etc. So far, I hadn't discovered how these two were connected.

The man paused, probably puffing on his cigarette. Finally he spoke. "*Kokchong hajima*." Don't worry. He went on to say that it was probably nothing, but he would look into it.

Again, she asked him to take her with him. He was a cool customer. He didn't answer her right away, but although I couldn't understand the full extent of the conversation, it seemed to me that he was making her beg.

"*Jamkkanman*," he said abruptly—wait a moment—and rose from his chair and walked across the lounge, checking his wristwatch. He turned the corner, moving out of sight. I waited a few seconds and told the bartender that I'd be right back. He nodded and set my cocktail napkin on top of my glass, protecting the foam.

The mystery man wasn't in the lobby. What I did see was a sign guiding me to the men's room, so I went in. Just before I entered, I saw him. Huddled over a large red pay phone hidden in a recessed alcove in the hallway. Without stopping, I breezed past him and took care of my business in the men's room. As I washed my hands, the same guy stepped into the bathroom and headed toward the nearest urinal. I dried my hands and hurried back to the lounge. Miss Lee was still in her chair, head bowed and hands crossed over her purse, nervously twisting a pink handkerchief.

I took my seat and the man returned. This time, he didn't sit down.

"*Kaja*," he told Miss Lee. Let's go.

In the mirror, I could see her eyes light up. "*Jinja?*" she asked. Really?

"*Jinja*," he replied.

As they walked out of the lounge, I picked up my almost full-pilsner and chug-a-lugged it down. The bartender stared at me in disgust. I didn't care. For almost two bucks, I wasn't going to let a perfectly good beer go to waste. After a quick burp, I hurried into the lobby.

Out front, the valet trotted off while the guy in the sharp suit waited with Miss Lee. Within a couple of minutes, the valet returned in a black Hyundai sedan. He jumped out and held the door for the mystery man who climbed in behind the steering wheel. Fending for herself, Miss Lee sat in the passenger seat. As far as I could tell, no tip changed hands. That's Korea for you. Americans were generally expected to tip, but not necessarily even wealthy Koreans. Ernie and I preferred to follow the Korean custom, as a sign of our deep respect for the culture.

-24-

We were in the jeep now, following Miss Lee and Mr. Fancy Suit west out of Tongduchon into the rugged hills dividing the Eastern and Western Corridors. These roads were two-lane affairs with plenty of mud and gravel interspersed at inconvenient spots, just waiting to toss unwary motorists into a ditch. Every couple of miles or so, another small farm village with straw-thatched homes pressed right up against the edge of the road. Only occasionally did we see a streetlamp. Ernie wanted to turn his high-beams on, but didn't dare because he didn't want to be spotted by the couple in the Hyundai sedan ahead of us. So far, he was doing an excellent job, keeping their brake lights visible as they swerved around bends.

Ernie was the best driver I'd ever seen. He could wend his way through the manic Seoul traffic like a shark slicing through tuna, all the while seeming completely unconcerned; leaning back in his seat, fingers touching lightly on the bottom of the steering wheel, appearing for all the world to be a Zen monk in a trance. But when he put on speed he was fearless, absorbing road conditions and traffic like a UNIVAC computer processing data.

The brake lights ahead of us flashed red and then stopped. A turn indicator blinked. The guy veered left.

"Where the hell is he *going*?" Ernie asked.

"Off the beaten track," I replied.

The road between the Eastern and Western Corridors was heavily traveled, but as far as I knew, there wasn't much on either side except rice paddies and hills. I'd never noticed a cross street until now.

We turned left and followed for about a half-mile and the road narrowed, barely wide enough for two cars and no white dividing line down the middle. Ernie downshifted. "Slope," he said. The engine growled as we rolled steeply downhill.

The forest around us was pitch black. Drooping branches of evergreen trees reached out to grab us. After a few minutes, Ernie said, "How long since we passed a village?"

"At least three miles," I replied.

"We're out in the boonies now."

I couldn't argue with that. Since leaving Camp Casey we'd climbed mostly uphill, winding through country roads. I figured we'd been traveling almost a half-hour and were about halfway to the Western Corridor. But now we were descending into some sort of valley. The road twisted and turned, leaving us blind to anything more than a few yards ahead. Ernie switched on his high beams. "I don't give a shit," he said.

He was right not to; it didn't matter if they realized we were behind them now. Out here, there was no way to blend in with the traffic because there wasn't any. Suddenly, just within visibility, a yellow sign loomed indicating a sharp turn in the road with a red arrow pointing to our right. Ernie slammed on the brakes, downshifted once again and, expertly maintaining traction, took the corner.

As we pulled out of the turn, he listened for a moment and said, "What's that?"

To our left was the sound of water rushing over rocks.

"Whitewater," I said. "It's a river."

"So if I hadn't made that last turn, we would've crashed over an embankment."

"Like they told us in driver's ed classes, this ain't the States."

"Who needs the States?" Ernie said. "Boring."

Now the road ran evenly along the edge of the river. Up ahead, through trees, I spotted lights. "We're almost there," I said.

Ernie slowed. A few yards on, we passed a sign. It was composed of a huge slice of tree trunk, varnished and carved with giant Chinese characters and smaller *hangul* lettering.

"What's it say?" Ernie asked.

Only a dim bulb illuminated it.

"I can only make out the Chinese characters," I said. "One says 'chamber,' and the other says 'heaven.'"

"What the hell does that mean?"

Ernie rolled slowly into a half-acre gravel parking lot strewn with Korean-made sedans, almost all of them black. Beyond that, lit up like a Macy's Christmas display, was a traditional Korean building with a large wooden entrance gate, stone stairway and tiled roof with shingles upturned at the edges.

"Freaking Disneyland," Ernie said.

"Better than that," I replied. "It's a *kisaeng* house." A place where businessmen could relax with beautiful, elegant hostesses to attend to their every need.

"Nice," Ernie said. He switched off the jeep's headlights and found a place to park away from the other vehicles. "Far enough from Seoul that the wife can't find you, but close enough that you can drive up here in less than an hour."

We climbed out of the jeep and stood in awe of the glimmering edifice.

"Must be expensive," Ernie said. He patted the envelope with what was left of our expense account.

"Don't even think about it," I said. "We'd run through that before we sat down. Besides, a class joint like this doesn't allow *Miguk*s." Americans.

"Good," Ernie replied. "I'm glad they maintain high standards."

We walked through the parking lot, hoping we could spot the sedan that belonged to Mr. Fancy Suit. But we hadn't been able to make out his license number, and all the vehicles looked alike. Ernie placed his palm on the hoods of a few of the cars. Most of them were cold. Finally he found one that was still warm.

"This must be it," he said.

I pulled out my notebook and jotted down the license plate number.

Then we looked at the entranceway. Inside, gorgeous women in traditional Korean gowns, *chima-jeogori*, flitted back and forth on seemingly urgent errands.

"You think they'll like us?" Ernie asked.

"I'm sure they'll be charmed," I replied.

We trotted up the stone steps.

When we entered, a woman in a beautifully embroidered white silk dress almost dropped the silver tray she was carrying, which would've been a shame, because balanced atop it was a bottle of Johnny Walker Black scotch, a bowl of ice with tongs, and four crystalline shot glasses.

"*Andei,*" she said, her mouth falling open. Not permissible.

I smiled at her and waved, and we were just about to search the private rooms that stretched down the hallway when Mr. Fancy suit, accompanied by three other Korean men in suits, stepped out of what looked like an administrative office. They walked right past us, as if we weren't there, and Ernie and I watched them go. The four of them trotted down the steps and Mr. Fancy Suit turned to the other three, bowed, and said some words of farewell. Then he hurried across the gravel lot and climbed into the still-warm sedan that we'd surmised was his. He started the engine, backed out a few yards, and sped off into the night. The other men walked back into the *kisaeng* house.

"Excuse me," I said to them in English.

They were grim-faced and businesslike. A couple had huge calluses on their knuckles, as if they'd spent years practicing martial arts.

I continued to speak in English. "The woman who came with that man. Miss Lee. I'd like to speak with her."

No hint of understanding on their blank faces. I started to repeat myself in Korean, but one of them put out his hand, the palm flat toward me, to indicate that I shouldn't speak. Then he moved away, but as he did so, he crooked his finger for me to follow. In Korean custom, it's an insult to do that to an adult. An adult should be beckoned by waving your hand palm downward. Still, I overlooked it and followed the three men down the hallway. Ernie followed a few yards behind, and I motioned for him to wait here.

We passed the office the men had emerged from and turned right down another hallway, this one much shorter than the first. We passed a busy kitchen on the left, then pushed through a swinging door into what appeared to be a community dressing room. On raised platforms, oil-papered floors were festooned with flat cushions. On a few of them sat young women in front of huge mirrors. None seemed surprised by our entrance. Apparently, there was plenty of traffic in and out of this dressing room. One of the women I recognized: Miss Lee Suk-myong.

The man who had crooked his finger at me said, "Miss Lee!"

Then he held out his open palm face-up, as if leaving me to her. The three men turned and stalked out of the dressing room. The woman put down a thin brush and turned to look at me, eyes wide.

"Miss Lee Suk-myong?" I asked.

She nodded silently.

"May I talk to you?"

She nodded again. Then she rose from the cushion, walked to the edge of the raised floor and sat down, spreading her silk skirt in front of her like a huge flower. It was an elegant move, practiced. She gazed at me expectantly.

"Hector Arenas," I said.

She winced.

"You knew him?"

She nodded. So far, I'd spoken nothing but English.

"You were his *yobo*."

She sighed and then said, "For a little while."

"How long?" I asked.

She thought about it and then said, "Maybe four months."

"You speak English well," I said.

"Before, I worked in bar in TDC. Montana Club."

"Difficult work," I said.

She nodded. "Very noisy."

I pictured the Montana Club, country western music cranked up to the highest volume humanly possible.

"Do you work here now?"

"Yes. Now I start. No more Cherry Girl Club."

"Why not?"

She scrunched her shoulders together. "I don't like."

"You don't like Americans?" I asked.

"They okay. But too much trouble."

"Trouble like me and my partner showing up today?"

"Yes." She waved her hand. "I want forget."

"Forget what happened to Arenas?"

"Yes."

And forget the time she spent in a Korean jail. But I didn't mention that.

"So the man who drove you here, the man in the nice suit, is he your boyfriend?"

She shrugged. "No." But she said it tentatively, as if she wasn't sure.

"But he got you this job here?"

"Yes."

"So he has a lot of money?"

She didn't answer.

"Is his name Nam?"

Again she didn't answer.

"He's the man who used to take Arenas out to places like this, to *kisaeng* houses. He's the one who they say introduced him to somebody from North Korea."

Her eyes were tightly shut now.

"Am I right?" I asked.

After a long pause, her eyes popped open and she stared up at me.

"You dummy," she said. "Everything dummy." She raised her hand to indicate the vast world around us. "You go now. You know nothing."

I leaned toward her. "Miss Lee, when Arenas was on trial, did they tell you to say that he had sold things to a North Korean?"

"You know nothing," she repeated. "Everything *they* say, not me."

"They?"

"American soldier, he say."

"What was his name?"

"I don't remember."

"What did he look like?"

"Big man, like you. But how you say . . ." She curled her arms in front of her chest like a bodybuilder flexing.

"Stronger," I said.

"Yes. Big."

"He told you what to say?"

"Yes. If I no say, no get out of jail."

"And Arenas, he never sold anything to a North Korean?"

"No." She searched for a word, her English reaching the limits of her vocabulary.

"Say it in Korean," I prompted.

"*Bandei*," she said.

"Opposite."

"Yes, opposite. Arenas see that somebody else talk to North Koreans."

"Who?"

She looked at me as if I were stupid. "Who you think?"

"Nam?"

"No, not Nam. He just businessman. Make money."

"Then who?"

She twisted her lips, staring at me in exasperation. And then I knew who she was talking about. "The big American?" I asked. "The man with the muscles?"

She nodded, as if relieved.

I stopped and absorbed that for a while. She'd just accused Captain Lance Blood, a commissioned officer in the United States Army, of accepting money from a North Korean agent in exchange for information. This was an entirely new level of shit hitting the fan. If Miss Lee was telling the truth, Lance Blood and his boys from the 501st were not only railroading GIs into Leavenworth, but they were doing so to cover their own espionage. Their own betrayal of their oath of enlistment and their own acts of treason.

For a moment I wavered, feeling the knot in my head; less painful now, but still throbbing.

I considered arresting Miss Lee, or at least taking her in for questioning. But then I remembered I had no jurisdiction. She was a Korean civilian, not a GI. Taking her into custody would be illegal, and might taint any future prosecutions. I decided to contact Mr. Kill. He'd know what to do. Still, for all the effort Ernie and I had put in, I wanted something tangible.

"Will you write that down for me?" I asked. "What you just said."

She shook her head negatively and hugged herself as if she were suddenly cold.

"We'll protect you," I told her.

Once again she looked at me as if I were an idiot.

"If you're worried about someone hurting you," I said, "then why are you telling us this?"

"No matter," she said.

"It doesn't matter?"

"No more," she said. "It doesn't matter."

I was confused. "What exactly doesn't matter?"

She spent a few seconds planning her English sentence and then she said, "It doesn't matter if you know. Doesn't matter. No more."

I wasn't sure what she meant. Maybe she meant she'd just broken up with Nam and nothing mattered to her anymore, so she'd sold him and the entire operation out. Or maybe she meant that the people involved were beyond prosecution.

I was about to press her further, but apparently the thugs who'd allowed me back here had decided I'd had enough time with Miss Lee. They came up behind me and said it was time to leave. She scurried off. I could've resisted and had Ernie back me up, but what was the point? For whatever reason, they'd allowed me to talk to Miss Lee, and she'd dropped a bombshell. Were these guys involved? Maybe not, but they weren't about to let me spend more time with a girl who made money for them by the hour. Fisticuffs weren't likely to change that, and they might even make things worse.

The smart move was to notify Mr. Kill. He had jurisdictional authority—and plenty of it.

I tipped an imaginary hat to the three dour-faced gentlemen and found Ernie waiting in the hallway. We trotted down stone steps to the parking lot.

"You find her?" Ernie asked.

"Yeah."

"What'd she say?"

"First," I said, "let's get the hell out of here."

Ernie could tell that whatever she'd told me had freaked me out. He didn't ask more questions. We jumped in the jeep; he started it up and drove us away, gravel spitting out from behind our wheels.

At the yellow sign in front of the river embankment, Ernie turned left. By then I'd briefed him.

"She says it didn't matter," he said. "What the hell does that mean?"

"I'm not sure."

Ernie veered left, taking the sharp turn with more authority now that he knew what to expect.

"It doesn't sound good," he said.

"No. Did you bring a gun?" I asked.

"I should've. You're always the one talking me out of it."

"They're more trouble than they're worth."

"I bet you wouldn't mind one now."

I shrugged.

"The whole case against Arenas is phony," Ernie said. "He ought to be released from Leavenworth."

"This information won't do much good though, if she doesn't recant her previous testimony."

Ernie shifted into low gear and churned up the slippery road. His high beams flashed on dark branches.

"All we need is her statement," I continued. "As soon as we find a pay phone, I'll call Mr. Kill. He'll be able to take her into custody and convince her to write one."

Ernie thought about it for a while. "Why was it so easy?"

"What do you mean?"

"I mean, this gal Miss Lee must've been threatened and been placed under tremendous pressure when she testified against Arenas. Why would she suddenly tell us the truth?"

"I don't know."

"And why'd that rich guy, whatever his name is, drive her all the way out here to have her switch jobs? Why tonight? Just because we showed up?"

"What other reason would they have? She was about to start a shift at the Cherry Girl Club, but when she saw us she ran to Nam, and then he made a phone call and drove her out here."

"And she said that it didn't matter if she told us the truth."

"That's what she said," I replied.

Ernie thought about this for a while. He swerved around a dark corner, too fast, I thought, but I knew what he was relying on. If another vehicle was on the road, he'd see the flash of their headlights long before he saw the vehicle itself.

I thought about it, too. Miss Lee had claimed that it wasn't Arenas who'd contacted the North Koreans, but Captain Blood. What sort of double-agent game was being played?

Were Ernie and I stumbling into something that could foil a long-planned sting operation? I didn't know—we didn't have clearance for anything pertaining to counterintelligence. What I did know was that the more I learned about the agents of the 501st MI, the more I thought it plausible that they were covering up something much bigger than an inflated budget. They had fabricated evidence that had resulted in more than one innocent man's court-martial and conviction, and if Miss Lee could be believed, Captain Blood was on the take from North Korea. This was one hell of a motive to murder the man who was about to expose them, Major Frederick Manfield Schultz.

Ernie screamed.

Out of the narrow road in front of us, a boulder emerged from the darkness, but it didn't keep to its lane. Instead it veered to our right, rolling directly into our path. Ernie slammed on the brakes, but the boulder kept coming. What most drivers would've done was plow over into the safety of the ditch on the right, but Ernie Bascom wasn't most drivers. Instead he veered to the left, across the boulder's path. It was then that I realized that it wasn't a boulder, but a truck. A truck with its headlights off. Whoever was driving adjusted to Ernie's surprise maneuver. Before we could veer into the safety of the far left lane, the truck turned back toward us. We were on a collision course. We'd be clipped by the front bumper of the truck right where I sat, in the passenger seat.

Unexpectedly, Ernie stepped on the gas. His little jeep

was kept finely tuned by the mechanics at the 21 T Car motor pool, all of whom received a cut of the money realized from the quart bottle of Johnny Walker Black that Ernie paid to the Head Dispatcher each month. The jeep leapt forward. The bumper of the truck headed straight for me, but because of our sudden increase in speed, it missed the front and slammed into the rear.

The impact jolted me out of my seat, and I was overcome by the sensation of flying through darkness. A sensation that was abruptly replaced by a jarring slam, maybe into a tree trunk. Briefly, I experienced pain—plenty of it—and then, mercifully, oblivion.

The first thing I realized was what Miss Lee Suk-myong had meant when she'd said it didn't matter. It didn't matter what she told me because she and her boyfriend didn't expect me to live through the night. All they wanted me to do was leave the *kisaeng* house and get back on the road, where my hash would certainly be settled.

But because of Ernie's expert driving, I was still alive, or at least I hoped I was.

I wasn't sure how long I'd been unconscious but I tried to raise myself, conducting inventory as I did so of my arms, legs, and the other appendages that are so important to a young man. All still apparently intact. What else did I need? Maybe a head that didn't feel like it was being crushed by King Kong's foot.

I rose to my feet. Somewhere I heard groans. I pushed myself away from the adjacent tree and turned. It had suffered a large gash from the impact of the front fender of Ernie's jeep. The roadway loomed a few feet above me, and on the far side a small fire glowed.

The jeep? I looked around before spotting it upright in a shallow ditch just yards away. Unsteadily, I pushed myself from tree to tree until I reached it. Ernie was still in the driver's seat, his head slumped forward. The dim glow from the distant fire shone on his face, and it appeared that his nose was bleeding. The back of the jeep on the passenger side had been caved in by the truck. But after being hit, the jeep slid sideways down the incline and landed against another tree. The trunk stood indented into the chassis right behind Ernie's head. I hobbled around to his side, reached in, and pulled Ernie upright. His eyes popped open.

"What the . . ." he said.

"Don't talk now."

I felt his arms. They didn't appear broken, and his legs seemed all right, too. But because of the odd angle at which he sat, his feet were twisted to the side. I pinched his nose and tilted his head back. Blood ran down over his lips and into his mouth. Oddly, his round-lensed glasses were still in place.

I slapped him.

"Huh?"

If I'd had smelling salts, I'm sure I could've brought him fully awake. I didn't, so I made do and slapped him again.

"Knock it *off*!" he said.

"Are you hurt?" I asked.

"I am now." He rubbed his cheek where I'd slapped him.

"Can you climb out?"

"Yeah, I think so." He flexed his arms and fingers, then moved his legs. "Everything seems to be working."

"I'll carry you."

I kept one hand under his left armpit, and with the other I held onto the edge of the jeep. He lifted himself gingerly and climbed out. Once on solid ground, we continued to cling to tree trunks and branches and, like two old men using walking staffs, we made our way uphill to the road.

On the far side, a military vehicle had plunged into the ditch. We walked unsteadily across pavement and peered down.

"A three-quarter-ton," Ernie said.

I squatted down and read the white stenciling on the rear bumper. "Headquarters Company," I said. "Five Oh First MI."

"For Christ sake," Ernie said. "These boys play rough."

The engine still rumbled, low and threatening. Quickly, we dropped down the incline to salvage what life we could.

At the first farmhouse we reached, I banged on the wood plank door, but the farmer who peered out told me there was no telephone in the village. He pointed down the road. When I asked him how far, he said three kilometers.

I trudged back to the pavement, where Ernie sat hunched over.

"Oh, great," he said when I told him the news. He glanced around at the surrounding darkness. The only things that moved were the clouds drifting in front of the half-moon above. "Must be past curfew," Ernie said. Then he thought to check his wristwatch. Broken. He slipped it off and tossed it away.

During daylight hours, dozens of ROK Army and US military vehicles traveled back and forth between the Eastern and the Western Corridors. It would've been easy to catch a ride, or even use one of their field radios to contact the local MPs.

"The driver was alive," I said.

"He won't be much longer," Ernie replied, "if we don't get an ambulance out there."

We'd stopped the bleeding, cleared his air passage and did everything the Army First Aid Field Manual told us to do. We'd even treated him for shock by elevating his feet, loosening his belt and wrapping him in a tent-half of canvas—one half of a full pup tent—we found in the bed of the truck. But that had been all we could do, so we left to find help. He probably had internal injuries. Although we couldn't see much in the dark, he seemed to be turning sheet-white.

As if Ernie had conjured up a guardian angel, headlights appeared in the distance. We both stood in the middle of the road, waving our arms. We were blinded by the high beams but held our ground. When the vehicle stopped, two armed soldiers hopped out. As they approached, I could see that they were ROK Army—their helmets were stenciled with the word HONBYONG, Military Police.

I told them what had happened. They radioed for an ambulance and told us to climb in. We didn't fit very well. At the turnoff from the main road we had them stop, and they left one of their MPs at the roadway to guide the ambulance in. The rest of us bounced down the narrow road. When we reached the wreck, the driver was still breathing. For the first time since the accident, I finally had the presence of mind to take a closer look at his face. His nametag confirmed it—Fenton, Specialist Four. The same guy who'd threatened Miss Kim.

-26-

The ROK MPs helped us back Ernie's jeep out of the ditch, and after hoisting Fenton into the military ambulance, we drove back to Camp Casey. The steering was off, but Ernie managed to get us there in one piece. We were patched up at the Aide Station. No serious injuries, just bruises and superficial cuts. After a lecture by the on-duty doc about how lucky we were and a scolding on defensive driving, we were sent on our way.

The next morning, as I sat at my desk at the 8th Army CID office, I spoke to Mr. Kill by phone.

"Apparently," he said, "the customers at the *kisaeng* house were directed by the staff to leave via another road out."

"Meaning they were in on it," I said. "They knew what was going to happen."

"Yes, although they're denying it, saying it was just the shortest route for customers returning to Seoul."

"What about Miss Lee?"

"Nobody seems to have heard of her. She was gone by the time we arrived, as were most of the *kisaeng*. Management claims they've never heard of a Miss Lee Suk-myong."

"What about Nam?"

"Unfortunately, they hadn't heard of him either. However, thanks to your description of the sedan and, more importantly, the license plate number, we should locate this fellow, whatever his name is, soon."

Highest priority had been placed on the all-points-bulletin for that sedan. Mr. Kill was later able to confirm that the owner's name was indeed Nam, so we knew our mystery man wasn't using a pseudonym. Still, after two days of waiting, there was no sign of the vehicle. Miss Lee Suk-myong seemed also to have vanished from the face of the Korean Peninsula.

Specialist Fenton's injuries were serious enough that he was put on an air-evac chopper out of Division and was now recovering at the 121st Evacuation Hospital in Seoul. When we tried to interview him, Captain Blood interceded with the Provost Marshal, and after conferring in private session, Colonel Brace denied us permission to speak with Fenton.

"A sting operation," Staff Sergeant Riley explained. "The Five Oh Worst has been working on it for months, hoping to round up a North Korean agent, and you two stepped right in the middle and screwed everything up. Congratulations."

So all our work had come to nothing. Miss Jo was still at large, the clock ticking down to her unjust conviction.

Vindication for Hector Arenas was dead in the water. No one at 8th Army wanted to hear about it, not without evidence more concrete than the alleged testimony of Arenas's former *yobo*. Captain Blood rode high at 8th Army, and all our requests to examine other aspects of the case, including his inflated budget, were turned down by the Provost Marshal.

"No probable cause," Riley told us.

The fact that the 501st had tried to kill us was written off as a figment of our overheated imaginations. I believed that Nam had called somebody from the Tower Hotel, who had in turn notified Captain Blood. Nam had led us on a merry goose chase to the isolated *kisaeng* house while Blood ordered Fenton up north in the three-quarter-ton truck with the express purpose of running us down and making it look like an accident. The only problem was, I couldn't prove it. Not without interrogating Fenton. And even then, only if he slipped up or admitted what he'd done, which seemed unlikely.

The only good thing we'd accomplished was bringing Miss Kim back to work. Her hand lotion, box of tissue, and Black Dragon tea were all on her desk where they were supposed to be. She quietly went about her business, typing up reports, translating memos into Korean, patiently filing the massive amounts of paperwork that spewed from Sergeant Riley's desk.

And no one was harassing her. At least, they didn't appear to be.

-27-

Using a red cloth, the Korean mechanic wiped grease from his fingers. "*Andei*," he said. No good.

We were at the motor pool of the 21st Transportation Company (Car), or 21 T Car. The Head Dispatcher had assigned his ace mechanic to check out Ernie's jeep, but it was a total loss. The frame had not only been twisted, but cracked. It was beyond repair. According to him, we were lucky that we made it back to Seoul.

I slapped Ernie on the back. "There're more jeeps in the Yellow Sea," I told him.

"Yeah, but we've been through a lot with this one."

He was right. It had been almost two years now, and we'd used that jeep on more cases than I could remember.

"All good things come to an end," I told him.

"For Christ's sake, Sueño. Stop with the platitudes already. You're making me feel worse." He surveyed the vast expanse of the motor pool, inhaled and pulled his belt up. "Let's get a drink."

So we did. In the Dispatcher's Office. The Korean honcho kept a bottle of soju there; the imported scotch was reserved for resale only. But soju was good enough for us. We wiped out a couple of shot glasses with our thumbs and toasted the death of Ernie's jeep, on its way to the great junkyard in the sky.

When we returned to the CID office, there was more good news.

"They're slapping you with a Report of Survey," Staff Sergeant Riley told us.

"For what?" Ernie asked.

"For reckless driving that resulted in the totaling of two military vehicles. Not to mention almost killing Specialist Fenton."

"Reckless driving?" Ernie said.

Riley shrugged. "You were on the wrong side of the road."

"So was the other guy."

"Tell it to the judge," Riley said.

I poured a cup of coffee from the stainless steel urn and returned to Riley's desk. "Was this Captain Blood's idea?"

"Don't know," Riley replied, "but I wouldn't be surprised. He's not happy that you almost killed his right-hand man."

"His right-hand man almost killed *us*," Ernie corrected him.

"What a loss that would've been," Riley said.

Miss Kim grabbed a tissue and walked quickly out of the office.

■   ■   ■

Leah Prevault and I sat on a wooden bench in the small garden behind the 121st Recovery Ward.

"Nobody believes you," she said.

"Nothing we haven't been through before," I told her.

She placed her soft hand on mine. "I've been thinking about what you said. About your commitment to your son, and how important it is to provide a stable family for him."

She pulled her hand away and continued.

"I admire that. It's a wonderful thing. Nobody knows how it will be resolved at this point. We need to give it some time."

"You mean you want to stop seeing me?"

She took a deep breath. "Yes. For now."

"How much time?" I asked, too abruptly, regretting my harsh tone.

She sat still for a moment. "I'm not sure," she said finally.

I stood, angry. So angry, because what she was saying made sense. My relationship with Yong In-ja had to be resolved; go or no-go, for better or for worse, one way or the other. But even trying to find her risked exposing her to the Pak Chung-hee regime, which would stand her up against a wall and fire away the moment they located her.

"Okay," I said. "Let me take care of this."

"Don't do anything rash."

"You mean like turn her over to the Korean government,

so they can torture and murder her without anyone knowing about it?"

Tears came to Captain Prevault's eyes.

I stared at her a while, clenching and unclenching my
fists. I sighed and said, "I'm sorry," then walked away.

"There must be a way," I told Ernie.

"To do what?"

We sat in the 8th Army Snack Bar, for once without
Strange. In the serving line, I'd ordered a BLT with coffee,
which still sat untouched in front of me as Ernie wolfed
down his scrambled eggs and home fries.

"To climb out of this rut we're in. To find out who murdered Schultz."

"Most of the world thinks they know it's Miss Jo."

"Okay, but we know better."

"Do we?" Ernie asked. "We're still missing a little thing
called evidence."

"And we have to get off the dime with this Five Oh First
case," I continued, undaunted. "Arenas is an innocent man,
rotting in prison. And it's possible that Captain Blood is on the
take from—" I lowered my voice. "—North Korean agents."

"You don't think they'd let us investigate *that*, do you?
Even if it were true, the Eighth Army honchos wouldn't
want to hear about it. Not until their tour is over and they're
safely back in the States. They don't want to be anywhere in
the area when that blows up."

"Fine, you're right." I took the first bite of my sandwich and chomped on it for a while, thinking. With my mouth full, I said, "We can't just stay in limbo like this."

"You think the Five Oh Worst will take another shot at us?"

"Not yet. Blood has convinced Eighth Army not to investigate, so we're neutralized for the moment."

"But when things die down, he'll come after us."

"Probably. We're a threat to him."

"And if we swing back into action right away?"

"He'll come after us right away. He can't afford for any-one to find evidence that will force Eighth Army's hand."

Ernie thought about that. "They killed my jeep."

"Almost killed us."

"And tried to force Miss Kim into spying for them."

"And sent Arenas to Leavenworth, plus who knows how many other innocent men."

"Okay," Ernie said, shoveling the last morsel of potato into his mouth. "You've convinced me. By the way, how's it going with you and Captain Prevault?"

"Don't ask," I said.

"That good, huh?"

We finished our grub and went to visit our favorite armorer.

"You gotta keep it well oiled," Palinki told us. "Not too much oil. Just enough so it's smooth, like a baby's skin. But not slippery."

Staff Sergeant Palinki was a huge man. Over six feet tall and maybe three hundred pounds, most of it muscle. He was Samoan from Hawaii and loved the Army almost as much as he loved armaments. He handed the .45 to me with both hands, the weapon looking toy-like in his calloused palms.

"Thanks for cleaning it, Palinki," I said.

We were underground in a reinforced cement bunker, behind the bars of the 8th Army Military Police Weapons Room.

"No problem, bro. Keeps me busy. After I finish reading all the comic books, nothing else to do."

"You oughta volunteer for regular MP duty," I told him.

"No." He shook his head negatively. "Doc says no."

"Bad back?" I asked.

"No. Not that kinda problem." He pointed his forefinger and his huge square skull. "This kinda problem."

"Mental?"

"Yeah. I get mad, then nobody know what I'm gonna do. Not even me."

Over a year ago, Palinki had almost murdered three GIs he'd caught attacking a Korean schoolgirl in Itaewon. I, however, saw that as a good thing, not a mental problem.

"You wanna get back on the street?" Ernie asked.

"Sure. Better than this place." He waved his open palms at the dungeon surrounding him.

"My friend Sueño here knows a shrink."

I groaned inwardly.

Palinki's eyes lit up. "Yeah. Maybe you talk to him. Get Palinki a good eval."

"Not *him*," I said. "*Her*."

"Even better. Pretty lady all love Palinki."

He broke into a gold-capped smile.

I slipped the .45 into my shoulder holster. "I'll see what I can do," I told him.

On the way out, he shouted after us, "You don't forget Palinki now, you hear?"

"What'd you do *that* for?" I asked Ernie once we got outside.

"He's a good man. You have a connection."

"I *used* to have a connection."

"That bad, huh?"

I didn't answer. We climbed in the new jeep Ernie'd been issued at 21 T Car. He started it up, cursing all the while. "Hear that?" he asked. "Carburetor problems. Why'd they give me this piece of shit?"

The engine sounded fine to me. But the upholstery was standard Army-issue canvas, not the black leather tuck-and-roll that Ernie had paid to have installed in his old jeep.

"I guess we'll just have to make do," I told him.

"I guess we will. But if they don't give me something better than this, I'm taking my Johnny Walker back."

■ ■ ■

Technically, Ernie and I were still assigned to the Schultz murder case. But where it stood officially was that the perpetrator was Miss Jo Kyong-ja, whose whereabouts were still unknown. The Provost Marshal didn't want us running all over Korea searching for her—that was the KNPs' job—so he'd put us back on black market detail, our default assignment. This kept us from conducting unwanted interviews, and any arrests we made would look good at the Chief of Staff daily briefing. All of this was to give the impression that we were really going after what the honchos saw as the primary crime problem in the Command: the illegal resale of duty-free goods by NCO wives. Violent capital crime was of little consequence when compared to the goal of keeping the PX and Commissary swept clean of *yobo*s, even though they had official dependent ID cards and were authorized to shop there. Go figure. That's the military mindset. But Ernie and I had different goals.

Blood had taken one shot at us and if we did nothing, he'd bide his time and try again, possibly with success. It was undeclared war: Ernie and me versus the 501st MI Battalion. The Provost Marshal and his right-hand man, Staff Sergeant Riley, were trying to pretend that nothing was wrong. But to us, the danger was real. I usually chose not to carry a weapon. But after our visit with Palinki, I felt better with the heft of the .45 hanging in a shoulder holster beneath my jacket.

-28-

We drove to the Korean National Police Headquarters in downtown Seoul. Within minutes, Officer Oh ushered us into Inspector Kill's presence. He noticed the bulge of the .45.

"You're ready," he said.

I nodded.

"We found Nam," he said.

Ernie and I were led downstairs to the below-ground interrogation rooms. Through a two-way mirror, I saw that Mr. Nam wasn't looking so spiffy now. His collar was open, his tie askew, and his hair a mess. The worst part was the way that his expensive suit was wrinkled and twisted around his body, as if he'd recently spent a lot of time in odd positions. His eyes had lost their luster. Instead of the easygoing confidence I'd previously seen, they now had the wary jitteriness of a hunted rabbit.

"What'd you *do*?" Ernie asked.

Inspector Kill gave Ernie a slightly offended look. "We questioned him."

"What was the charge?"

Kill shrugged. "Possible involvement in a crime."

Ernie already knew all this. Under the rules of procedure set up by the Pak Chung-hee government, the Korean National Police didn't need probable cause to bring someone in. They only had to feel the need to question him. I think Ernie was just smarting from the loss of his jeep.

"How long have you had him in custody?" I asked.

"This is the second day. I was waiting for you two to show up so we could search Nam's office together. If what he's telling me is accurate, Eighth Army personnel are deeply involved."

"Involved in what?" Ernie asked.

"North Korean espionage."

Mr. Kill slipped on his jacket and led us upstairs. In front of KNP headquarters, Officer Oh was already standing next to the blue government-issue sedan. She held the door open as Mr. Kill climbed in front. Ernie and I squeezed into the back. As we pulled away, two cops saluted and Officer Oh switched on her flashing red light. We made excellent time through Seoul traffic, entire phalanxes of kimchi cabs pulling out of our way. Even up north, at the 2nd Infantry Division checkpoints, we swerved around the waiting line and were waved through with no delay.

"Finally getting the respect we're due," Ernie told me.

"I'm pretty sure it's not us," I replied.

"Maybe not," Ernie said, chomping on his ginseng gum.

■ ■ ■

It was a nondescript *bokdok-bang* in a back street of Tong-duchon. *Bokdok-bang* means real estate office, of which there are tons in any Korean city. They're used not only for purchasing real estate, but often for something as simple as renting a hooch. Their activities are typically highly local-ized; an agent can easily walk a client to see the properties he has listed because they're all within a few blocks.

Using the keys she'd confiscated from Nam, Officer Oh popped open the padlock that secured the folding metal awning and rolled it upward until her arms were stretched high above her head. Ernie's eyes never wavered from her figure. I stepped in front of him, hoping he wouldn't embar-rass us. Or, more accurately, wouldn't embarrass *me*. I don't think Ernie Bascom was capable of being embarrassed.

The front of the *bokdok-bang* was a sliding wooden door with small glass panels. Mr. Kill slid it open and stepped into the office without taking his shoes off. The floor was cement and therefore considered a public space, not a home where immaculate cleanliness always had to be maintained.

The filing cabinets were made of wood, a type I'd seen so often before that they were presumably mass-produced in Korea. Mr. Kill and Officer Oh took the lead in open-ing the drawers and riffling through the paper files. We let them handle it because everything was written in *hangul*. Ernie and I sat on the short couch opposite the small desk.

A coffee table held two huge glass ashtrays with the OB logo on them and an octagonal cardboard box containing tightly packed wooden matches. The ashtrays were full, and after a few seconds of smelling the stale odor of burnt tobacco, I couldn't stand it any longer. I took them outside and emptied them in the gutter.

When I returned, Mr. Kill pulled up a straight-backed chair and placed a thick folder on the coffee table. Officer Oh continued to search the files.

"It's in code," he said, thumbing through sheets of loose pulp. "Or more exactly, in abbreviated form."

"Shorthand," I said.

"Yes." He pointed. "Initials. Some of them in English."

"Those are the Americans involved," Ernie said.

Kill nodded. "Maybe. And the locations, all of them the names of the nearby Korean villages. Not the names of the American military compounds." Kill read them off. "Unchon-ni, Tuam-dong, Yonpung."

"Unchon-ni is Camp Kaiser," Ernie said, "and Tuam-dong is way the hell up north."

"Camp Arrow," Mr. Kill said.

"I've never heard of that one," I told him.

"It was small, very remote. Probably closed before you even arrived in the country."

"So what does this mean?" Ernie asked.

Kill explained. It was, at its heart, a real estate deal.

When the Vietnam War had really begun to ramp up in

the mid-Sixties, the US Army was steadily drawing down in Korea. The First Cav had been pulled out and sent to Southeast Asia, next was the 7th Infantry Division, and now the only remaining US division was the 2nd Infantry. They'd inherited the mission of protecting the two corridors leading to Seoul, and the ROK Army had taken the rest, defending the DMZ from the Yellow Sea in the west to the Eastern Sea on the far side of the peninsula. (What Koreans patriotically call the Eastern Sea is known to the rest of the world as the Sea of Japan.)

Because of their drastically reduced mission and forces, many US Army compounds dotting the countryside were abandoned. Probably the largest was Camp Kaiser in Unchon-ni, which had been closed less than two years ago. But there were others. These camps featured some unbelievable luxuries for rural Korea, like a modern electrical grid, hot and cold running water, fuel storage facilities, central heating, and a communications network that ran all the way back to Seoul. Most of these bases were handed over to the ROK Army. But because of the disposition of forces vis-a-vis the North Korean Army on the opposite side of the DMZ, some of the base camps—or parts of them— were no longer needed. That's where Nam came in. He was fundamentally a real estate hustler. Once the Korean government had possession of the former American bases, it was theoretically auctioning them off to the highest bidder. But in reality, the fix was in. Money changed hands with government officials. That was Nam's area of expertise. He had contacts everywhere: in government, the ROK Army, private business, and even the US Army. Somewhere along the line, Nam had run into one of the 501st operatives and was reported up the line. Captain Blood immediately saw Nam's usefulness to his counterintelligence operations; Blood and Nam became buddies.

Blood provided Nam with introductions to the senior officers who decided what to salvage and what to leave behind at the defunct camps, thus determining their overall value. Nam contacted buyers—Korean businessmen and government officials—and made money as the go-between. Did money change hands under the table? Yes, in some cases hard currency was handed to American officers, most of whom had returned to the States by now. In other cases, favors were traded, like a night with an attractive hostess—maybe even Mr. Nam's girlfriend, Miss Lee Suk-myong. According to Nam, Blood wasn't interested in the women, but he did want a share of the money—for 501st operations, he claimed. Building a slush fund to hunt down more North Korean spies.

All of this was interesting, but corruption wasn't unheard of in either army. And could the fear of exposure really have led to Major Schultz's death? As for the crimes themselves, these allegations would be difficult to prove, especially if the money had been transferred in small, untraceable bills. And the offerings of sexual favors, of course, left no record at all. So Captain Blood might have been nervous about Major Schultz's inspection report, but he'd have plausible deniability. Blood was ambitious, and such a report could negatively impact his promotion potential, but it still seemed that murder—for such a clearly intelligent man—would be an extreme miscalculation. Smarter, if he did get busted, just to hire a good attorney.

"*Jo join pei kopunei-yo*," Mr. Kill said, slapping his knees. I'm hungry. "Let's go to a noodle shop."

That sounded good to Ernie and me. We all stood. Officer Oh begged off. She bowed to Inspector Kill and apologized, but said she wanted to continue searching the files. He told her to come find us if she got hungry, and she said she would.

Outside, it didn't take long to find a chophouse. It was late afternoon and the dinner hour hadn't started, so we were the only customers. Kill ordered tea. He hadn't really been hungry; he'd just wanted to talk to us away from Officer Oh.

"I don't want her involved in this if it's not necessary," he told us.

Ernie and I ordered tea as well, and once it was served, Mr. Kill told us the rest of the story. The real estate scam had been going on for some months, a prime operation with clandestine contacts between the upper echelons of the US military and top levels of the South Korean government. It didn't take long for someone to realize that this could be used for something more than just abandoned bases.

"That's where a highly skilled spy known as Commander Ku came in," Kill told us.

"Who's he?" I asked.

"A North Korean agent, we presume. He or one of his operatives approached Nam and offered a significant sum of money for the use of his best offices to gather information. No one told Nam the nature of this information, but somehow they had caught wind that the Five Oh First was one of his real estate co-conspirators. Commander Ku wanted a one-on-one meeting with Captain Blood."

"About what?"

"We're not sure. Nam suspects it has to do with Camp Arrow."

"The compound closest to North Korea?"

"Yes. Tomorrow night, we're setting up a sting operation in Mukyo-dong." The pricy nightclub district in downtown Seoul, too expensive for the average GI but hugely popular with the monied Korean elite. "Nam is contacting both Captain Blood and this Commander Ku. We expect to learn much more. We want you there."

We both nodded. This could be huge. Anything involving North Korean espionage could be dangerous, even fatal. Who was a spy, who was a counter-spy, who was a double agent . . . All of this was often left unclear, and keeping Officer Oh as far from it as possible was probably a good idea; she was young and had a bright future ahead of her. We finished our tea and returned to the *bokdok-bang*. Just a few blocks away, we heard a woman's scream.

Without hesitation, Kill took off running.

I turned to Ernie. "Officer Oh."

"Yeah," he replied. He pulled his .45.

"Put that thing away," I told him, but we were sprinting now, watching Mr. Kill round a corner ahead of us.

Smoke billowed from the *bokdok-bang*. The double-door was slid open and inside Officer Oh flailed away with her blue coat, trying to bat out the fire. Two men were trying to stop her until they spotted Mr. Kill barreling toward them. They were young, barely out of their teenage years, but both were husky and towered over Mr. Kill. They took martial arts stances. Kill plowed into the biggest one head-first. The thug let out a woof of air. Somehow, Kill maintained his balance, swiveled, and kicked the other punk in the groin. Then, with his right fist, he popped a jab into the first one's nose. Blood spattered through the smoke. Within half a minute, both of them rolled to the ground, holding their faces and trying to protect their stomachs.

Ernie and I ran up to help, but it was too late. Both thugs had been reduced to pulsating puddles of goo. All we could do now was cuff them, just in case.

"Remind me not to mess with Mr. Kill," Ernie told me out of the side of his mouth.

Now that the attackers were down, two neighbors appeared: one with a fire extinguisher, the other with a pail of water. Soon we were dousing the flames that had originated in the filing cabinets. Mr. Kill pulled Officer Oh outside and was speaking to her calmingly.

Apparently, while she was concentrating on reading the files, she'd been surprised by the two men. One of them punched her and she was dazed for a moment. When she regained control of her senses, the flames were already consuming the file cabinets. She then did her best to put them out.

By now, the local KNPs had arrived. Mr. Kill showed them his identification, and the uniformed men bowed. He asked them if they knew the two young men, and they did; they were a pair of local strong-arm thieves. One was in good enough condition to be slapped alert, and in a groggy voice, whining like a child, he explained to his KNP interrogator that Nam had paid him and his cousin to keep an eye on his office. And if anyone besides Nam tried to gain access to his files, they were instructed to burn them.

One of the cops asked him why they'd hit a female police officer and he replied, "She's smaller than us."

The KNP laughed, and then frowned, and leaned over and slapped him on the side of the head. The young thug whined again, the only mode of self-protection he'd have available to him for quite some time.

■   ■   ■

Officer Oh was checked out at a local clinic with a clean bill of health. Though she protested, Chief Inspector Gil Kwon-up insisted on driving and she sat in the front passenger seat, which is the seat of honor in Korean custom. We didn't talk much on the way back to Seoul, except to tell her how well she'd done. Thanks to her efforts, most of the records had been salvaged. Still, she was embarrassed by the fact that she'd been overcome by such obvious idiots.

Back at the KNP headquarters in Seoul, Ernie and I promised Mr. Kill that we'd meet him in Mukyo-dong tomorrow night. We marched off in search of the jeep. The old lady of the *pindeidok* stand was still watching it, but she complained that the thousand *won* Ernie had paid her wasn't enough after parking all day. He handed her another bill and she smiled and bowed.

What we'd learned today was significant, terrifying. If we could just make the Provost Marshal believe that Nam was telling the truth, we'd get the go-ahead to audit the 501st financial records. But I didn't believe that the word of a slippery Korean street hustler would be enough to make Colonel Brace doubt the integrity of a fellow officer. He wouldn't stick his neck out on such flimsy evidence; we needed corroboration.

Mr. Kill's sting operation in Mukyo-dong was one way to provide one channel to that corroboration, but that would have to wait until tomorrow night. I told Ernie about another way. He listened and nodded. "Worth a try," he said.

He started the jeep's engine and we wound through the heavy Seoul traffic back to Yongsan Compound.

-30-

The long hallways of the 121 Evacuation Hospital were dim, lit only by an occasional yellow bulb. We entered not through the big front door of the 121st, but the emergency room entrance around the back. The medics there had seen us often enough and knew we were in law enforcement, so they hardly noticed as we pushed through double swinging doors into the main precincts of the huge military hospital.

"Which room is he in?" Ernie asked. I told him.

"It's down here," he said pointing. We followed the signs. Eventually we reached Ward 17, Room B. The door was open and we entered, pushing past gauzy beige curtains in search of bed number three.

Specialist Four Wilfred R. Fenton, known to Ernie as "the twerp," was snoring.

"Hate to wake him," Ernie said.

But he reached out and pinched his big toe. Hard. Fenton's eyes popped open. "What the . . . ?"

Ernie tipped an imaginary hat. "Top of the mornin' to ya."

Fenton stared up at him, apparently trying to decide if he was really awake.

According to the doctors at the 121st, Fenton's prognosis was good. Some parts of his internal plumbing, the Latin names of which I couldn't pronounce, had been bruised, but bleeding had been minimal, and since he'd received medical attention quickly, all he needed now was rest and monitoring to make sure no infection developed. Two or three more days of bedrest was the word we were given. At that time, the Provost Marshal would decide whether or not to charge him, but it wasn't looking like the decision would go our way. Road conditions in Korea are atrocious, and GIs are seldom charged with reckless driving or other roadway violations—even when a Korean civilian is hurt or killed. Prosecution for doing their jobs—driving through ice and snow and mud—is seen by the 8th Army honchos as a sure way to kill morale.

And besides, the Provost Marshal believed the 501st's cover story. Fenton claimed to have been on his way up north to participate in a counterintelligence operation involving an espionage suspect, the details of which were classified. It was Ernie and me who'd blundered into the middle of things and messed up their plans. If the accident was anyone's fault, it was ours.

Of course, Ernie and I knew it was a blatant assassination attempt that had happened to end with Fenton in a hospital bed and us standing over him. This was perhaps why Ernie pinched Fenton's toe so viciously, though I also suspected it was for Miss Kim.

Full consciousness lit up his eyes. He pushed himself upright, frightened. "What do you guys want?"

"Don't scream," I told him. "We're not gonna hurt you."

"Not like you tried to hurt us," Ernie added, smiling.

Fenton repeated himself. "What do you want?"

"We want information," I said.

Reflexively, Fenton said, "I don't know nothing."

I ignored the statement, pulled up a chair, and started to talk in a low monotone. When Fenton tried to edge away, Ernie slapped him on the side of the head and pushed him back. Intimidated, Fenton sat like a schoolboy, giving me his full attention.

I explained what Nam had told us about working with Blood on the disposition of closed military bases. When I finished, I paused and allowed Fenton time to respond. He was still terrified. Ernie loomed over him, glaring, mumbling incoherently, as if the hatred he felt couldn't be formulated into words. Fenton was probably afraid that Ernie would rip out one of the needles in his arm or, worse yet, punch him in the stomach and reopen his internal wounds.

Fenton glanced at Ernie nervously, then back at me. "So what? That don't mean nothing."

Some agent. He'd just confirmed what Nam had told us. Blood and Nam were indeed associates.

"I guess beating up a business girl in Itaewon doesn't mean anything, either," I said.

Fenton glared at me distrustfully, wondering what I was getting at.

"Major Schultz had a problem," I continued. "A business girl in Itaewon ripped him off and was lying to everyone about his sexual prowess."

"Or lack thereof," Ernie added.

"So Captain Blood offered to help," I said. "They went out to Itaewon together and slapped the girl around a little, to persuade her to shut the hell up. Blood was hoping that by becoming close buddies with Schultz, he might influence him to go a little easy in his inspection report." Fenton frowned but didn't contradict me. "But despite Blood's best efforts," I said, "Schultz wasn't playing ball. He wasn't going to ease up on his negative inspection report. Blood felt betrayed."

Fenton looked away.

With his forefinger, Ernie poked him in the side of the head. "Are you listening to the man?"

Reluctantly, Fenton turned his gaze back toward me.

"So Blood killed him," I said. "Or maybe it was you. One thing's for damn sure, you're the one who drove the body to Itaewon."

Fenton reached toward the night table and in one swift movement threw something at me. I dodged and it missed me but liquid splashed everywhere, some of it spraying on my pant leg. It crashed against the far wall but didn't break, and more liquid gushed out. Then I realized what it was: an Army-issue blue plastic water carafe. I bent over and picked it up while slapping moisture off my knee.

With both hands, Ernie grabbed Fenton's head and dug in his fingers. Fenton pulled his arms free of the needles on hanging tubes and struggled to break Ernie's grip.

A nurse ran into the ward. Captain's bars were pinned to her neat white smock, and her nameplate said Schulman. Ernie quickly released his grip and stood away.

"What are you doing here?" she asked. When we didn't answer, she said, "I don't know what you two are up to, but visiting hours were over at eight. This man needs his sleep." She glanced at Fenton. "And he shouldn't be bothered while he's recovering."

"Yes, ma'am," Ernie said, stepping even farther from the bed.

"Well, vamoose!" she said, planting her hands on generous hips.

"We're on our way," I said. Then I turned and whispered in Fenton's ear. "Think about it. If you spill what you know, you can cut a better deal for yourself." When he ignored me, I decided to raise the stakes. I leaned in closer and said, "Nam told us about Commander Ku."

We drove away from the 121st Evac through a sleepy South Post, and then we crossed the MSR and entered the Yongsan Compound Main Post.

"You think Fenton will rat on Blood?" Ernie asked.

"He'd be crazy not to," I replied. "Taking a little money on the side is one thing. You just hire a Stateside lawyer and keep your mouth shut, and you might be all right. But working with a North Korean agent, that's serious biz. And if Fenton had anything to do with it, he's going down too."

Ernie whistled. "I'll say. Why'd they do it, anyway?"

"Blood's a glory hound," I said. "Now that he's grown the battalion so much, he thinks he can get away with anything. I'm sure Fenton and some of the other guys went along because they believed—like most GIs would—that they'd be all right as long as they could claim they were just following orders. Plus, they probably liked the extra cash and being treated like royalty on the occasional trip to the *kisaeng* house."

"Still," Ernie said, "didn't they realize how serious this was? It's a betrayal of the whole country, not just Eighth Army. I'm not all that fond of our rah-rah I-love-the-flag bullshit, and I can understand selling booze and cigarettes down in the ville, but working with North Korean spies? That's a level of hurt I'd never want to get involved with."

"Nam said it was gradual. First the real estate deals for some side money, then Commander Ku and the much bigger rewards for military intel. Maybe they were even blackmailed, or the Five Oh Five guys Blood didn't trust were kept in the dark. However it happened, Captain Blood and the Five Oh First did it, and we're gonna bring them down. For Major Schultz and Miss Kim and Miss Jo, and a lot of other reasons."

"Think they'll give us a medal?"

"Hell no. Eighth Army gives medals for hiding dirty laundry, not airing it."

-31-

The next night we were in downtown Seoul, where the air was chilly but clear. We stood loitering in the heart of Mukyo-dong, the city's most expensive entertainment district. Neon flashed down the long, winding roadways and well-dressed matrons carrying embossed shopping bags, their high heels clicking on pavement. Above us, the Dancing Lady Scotch Corner sported a spangled neon effigy of a beautiful, long-haired woman whose hips glowed as they swiveled from side to side.

"We should've asked for more expense money from Mr. Kill," Ernie said.

"Why? We're not going inside."

"But I feel poor out here," Ernie replied. "I'm a shot-and-a-beer kind of guy."

"So get yourself some soju." I pointed at a heavily laden vending cart, a *pochang macha*, being pushed by an old man along the edge of the narrow road.

"Maybe I will," Ernie said.

And he did. He ran off and stopped the old man, communicating mostly with hand gestures, miming opening a bottle and pouring it down his throat. I also heard him say the word soju, rice liquor, which was probably the main reason the man understood him. He stopped his cart, reached beneath the canvas overhang, and pulled out a small crystalline bottle of Jinro. Ernie handed him a couple of small bills, thanked him, and trotted back to my side.

I checked out the metal cap. "You forgot to have him open it," I told Ernie.

Startled, he stared at the soju and ran back to the old man, holding the bottle out and pointing at the cap. The old man grinned, stopped his cart again and reached deep into loose pants pockets to pull out a bottle opener. He popped the cap and handed it to Ernie. Ernie thanked him again and hurried back to where I was standing at a dark wall beneath a cement power pole.

"That's what I like about you, Sueño," he said. "Always thinking."

He glugged a swig of the powerful rice liquor, then offered the bottle to me. I took it out of his hand, wiped the rim, knocked back a sip or two, grimaced, and handed it back.

"Rotgut," I said.

"Gets the job done," Ernie replied.

I wasn't worried about Ernie getting wasted. We'd spent most of the day at KNP headquarters going over the plan with Mr. Kill and Officer Oh. They had three or four rookie cops lined up to act as customers in the Dancing Lady Scotch Corner when the meeting went down and plenty of backup in the surrounding alleyways.

Officer Oh showed us the latest technology in recording equipment. I expected something from Japan, but she pointed proudly to the label. "*Dokil*," she said. Germany. Korea was inundated with electronics from Japan, which was a little surprising because the Japanese colonization from 1910 to 1945 still conjured up resentment, sometimes even hatred. Still, the price and quality of Japanese products was hard to beat. There was talk of new Korean electronics companies that would one day equal or surpass Japanese technology, but I thought that a very ambitious goal. Officer Oh must've gone out of her way to find something made in Germany, which possibly said something about her family history. Some families had done better under Japanese colonization than others—and those who'd refused to knuckle under had suffered for it.

Inspector Kill told me earlier that Nam had only reluctantly agreed to set up the sting. What he'd been threatened with to force his compliance, we didn't know, but it couldn't have been good.

There was a secret communication system in place. First, Nam reached out to Blood. They had previously arranged a signaling mechanism: Nam visited one of the branch offices of the 501st outside of Seoul during certain times and used a code word to indicate that he wanted to parley with Blood. The 501st agent on duty contacted the captain through normal channels and used another password, and then Blood would leave the compound. At a randomly selected phone booth, he would call Nam directly at his *bokdok-bang*—real estate office—in Tongduchon to set up a time for the meeting. Inspector Kill had somehow managed to reroute this number to KNP headquarters in Seoul.

Nam had told Captain Blood that Commander Ku was nervous about a few things—namely me and Ernie poking our noses into their business—and wanted to discuss them with Blood. Blood had rejected Nam's earlier suggestions for a meeting place and only relented when Mukyo-dong was thrown into the mix—it appeared he liked his bars exclusive and discreet. The rendezvous was set up for 10 P.M. at the Dancing Lady Scotch Corner.

Then Nam contacted Commander Ku. This method was more complicated, utilizing blind drops and several other steps standard to international spy craft. One of Ku's representatives called Nam, also at the number that was supposedly his *bokdok-bang*, and referred to everyone involved in cloaked terms as if they were part of a typical real estate deal. Nam claimed that Blood had requested the meeting. He hadn't, of course, but Nam was Commander Ku's only connection to Blood, so there was no way to verify the claim. Ku had agreed to tonight's meeting at the Dancing Lady Scotch Corner.

Ernie sipped his soju.

"We need to move farther away," I told him.

"Is it ten already?"

"Twenty minutes till."

"Okay."

Although foreigners—mainly businessmen, English teachers, and a smattering of tourists—did frequent Mukyo-dong, Mr. Kill had warned us to stay away from the action. Nearly the entire nightclub had been wired with Officer Oh's recording devices. The four rookie cops would be scattered around the premises, and as soon as Captain Blood and Commander Ku started talking business—and Inspector Kill decided there was enough evidence to make the arrest—a KNP squad a few blocks away would be notified and proceed to sweep in. Ernie and I were there not just to observe, but to have the honor of formally arresting Captain Blood when the time came.

The Provost Marshal would probably pop a gut when he found out about this operation, mainly because we hadn't informed him. But once Captain Blood was under arrest for espionage and the evidence was presented, Brace would have no choice but to go along with us. The next step would be for him and the Chief of Staff to jockey over how to split blame for the case—and credit for the arrest.

At first, Nam had been reluctant to even mention Commander Ku's name. But Inspector Kill had persuaded him with the assistance of a ham-fisted interrogator named Bang, who seemed to enjoy roughing people up. I couldn't ascertain whether Bang was his real name or not, but he was apparently a legend in the interrogation circles of the Korean National Police. Nobody could resist his persuasion for long. Eventually, even though there were no visible bruises on Nam, he'd revealed everything he knew about Commander Ku.

Ku was a North Korean agent, as we'd figured. But he'd somehow managed to operate successfully in South Korea for over a decade without being caught. He'd entered the country in 1962 during the chaos of the riots that would evolve into the eventual overthrow of the Syngman Rhee regime, and had remained for the dozen years since. You'd think that in all that time, a North Korean Communist might have been persuaded to change sides, but these guys were brainwashed. As far as they were concerned, the people running South Korea had betrayed the country by collaborating with the brutal colonization of the Japanese military. Even the current President, Pak Chung-hee, had been trained at the Manchukuo Imperial Japanese military academy. According to Nam, Commander Ku was dedicated to his Great Leader, Kim Il-sung, and would be happy to murder anyone who stood in his way.

When Nam was asked what Commander Ku looked like, he claimed he'd never actually seen him face-to-face. On the phone, he'd always conversed with subordinates who were supposedly in near proximity to their commander. But he had neither seen nor spoken to Commander Ku, so we weren't sure who exactly we were looking for.

Ernie and I climbed the steps of an office building to a door marked CHILSUNG IMPORT COMPANY. We knocked and it opened. We were quickly ushered into a dark room. On the far wall, the window was open, but everyone stood about six feet back from it. Officer Oh sat on a stool at a small table with a telescope sitting on it. She motioned for us to look. I went first, and then Ernie. With all the ambient light from street lamps and blinking neon, the telescope provided a clear view of the front door of the Dancing Lady Scotch Corner. From a speaker on a desk, the clink of glassware and the murmur of conversation sifted through knitted cloth.

"Nice equipment," Ernie whispered.

"Way better than what we've got," I replied. Which was next to nothing in the MP Supply Room. When we needed a tape recorder we went down to 8th Army Audio-Visual and checked the equipment out, which involved a hassle of updating signature cards and the like. If the equipment was even available.

Officer Oh resumed her seat. The other KNPs shuffled around the room nervously. Twenty minutes later, Officer Oh waved her hand, leaned back, and motioned for me to take a look.

Captain Blood, wearing a navy suit and red tie, entered the front door of the Dancing Lady Scotch Corner. A few minutes later, I thought I heard someone say a few words in English through the speakers, but they were drowned out by the general hubbub of conversation. Officer Oh stepped over to the glowing radio-control-like device next to the speaker and fiddled with a knob before the conversation came across more clearly.

"Here you are, sir," said a male waiter in English with a Korean accent.

Presumably after money changed hands, Captain Lance Blood said, "Keep the change."

We waited an hour. Several groups of businessmen had entered the Dancing Lady Scotch Corner, but as far as we could tell, no one had sat down at the table with Captain Blood.

"He's not gonna show," Ernie said.

"What went wrong?" I asked.

"Ku smelled a rat. Maybe Nam had a special code word to let him know he'd been compromised." Ernie turned to me. "Or maybe Fenton told them."

"Fenton?"

"Yeah. We dropped Commander Ku's name last night to spook him into confessing, but maybe it just made him more set on keeping the whole thing quiet."

A sinking feeling rushed through my gut like a tide of suds and bleach. I grabbed the soju bottle out of Ernie's hand and downed the last glug.

Officer Oh waved to us again. She adjusted her headset and spoke to me in Korean. "Target on the move. One of our operatives thinks contact may have been made inside the men's room. He's checking it out now."

I squinted in front of the telescope. A double door opened, Captain Blood shoving through. "He's running," I said.

"Follow him," she ordered into a handheld microphone.

After he'd turned a corner, three plainclothes Korean cops, converging from different directions, followed Captain Blood. Ernie and I thanked Officer Oh and hurried downstairs. On the sidewalk, we pushed through the growing late-night crowd. Blood was out of sight now, but I thought I spotted one of the KNPs tailing him. We jogged to catch up. And then we were running because the cop in front of us was running.

When we found the KNP officers, they were screaming at one another in Korean, gesticulating and calling for a vehicle. From what I could understand, a US military truck—one matching the description of a three-quarter-ton—had rolled through the narrow road and Captain Blood had made a mad dash for it. He'd jumped up onto the running board before the driver had gunned the truck's engine and sped away.

I grabbed one of the cops and asked, "Did anyone see Commander Ku?"

He didn't understand me at first, so I repeated my question in Korean. "No," he replied in English. "Only Captain Blood. He go alone."

"And the guy driving the truck? Did you see him?"

The man shook his head and jerked himself away.

The next morning in the 8th Army CID office, Ernie and I did our best to avoid the Provost Marshal. We didn't want to answer his questions. Not yet. The accusations against Captain Blood and the 501st were so fantastic that we didn't expect anyone to believe them. Taking money from a North Korean agent was too much to even be mentioned until we had proof.

Riley was talking to someone on the phone and then he said, "Okay. I'll check," and slammed down the receiver.

"What'd you guys do with Fenton?"

"What?"

"That was one of the nurses from the One Two One Evac, mad as hell, wanted to know if you guys helped him leave the recovery ward."

"He's not there?"

"That's why she called. Said two CID pukes were snooping around the One Two One the night before last. Couldn't have been you two, could it?"

"We were there," I said.

"Then what'd you do with him?"

Ernie stirred sugar into a mug of hot coffee. "I know what I would've liked to do with him."

"When did they notice he was missing?" I asked.

"At roll call last night. The nurse on night duty remembered you two being there."

"Smart cookie," I said. "But we didn't help him get away. When we left he was still in bed number three."

"So you're saying he took off by himself?"

I didn't answer. "By the way," I asked, "where's Miss Kim?"

Her desk was empty.

"You guys oughtta get to work on time, maybe then you'd know what the hell is going on."

Ernie set down his coffee cup. "What is it?"

"Who the hell do you think is in there with the Provost Marshal?"

"Miss Kim?"

Riley shook his head at us like we were hopelessly deficient in every positive attribute, especially brains. Before he could answer, Colonel Brace, the Provost Marshal of the 8th United States Army, stormed out of his office.

"Sueño," he said. "Bascom. Both of you get in here. *Now!*"

We hurried in. When I saw her, sitting in one of the comfortable leather armchairs, I nearly stumbled and fell flat on my face. Instead, I steadied myself with the doorknob, and as I hesitated, Ernie bumped into me. We must've looked like two stooges.

I stepped forward, knelt, and took both her frail hands in mine. I didn't even have to ask the question. She looked into my eyes and started crying.

Colonel Brace followed us in. "You've already met, I see. This is Miss Kim's mother." She looked smaller, much paler now than when she'd served us tea at her house.

The Colonel stood upright, as if concentrating on maintaining his posture, and then barked, "You will, immediately if not sooner, commence a search for that young lady. And I don't need to tell you that you *will* find her. Is that understood?"

Ernie and I answered in synchrony. "Understood, sir."

The Head Dispatcher at 21 T Car checked his records. "Yeah," he said. "Replacement vehicle. Before they have three-quarter-ton, all totaled. Last night he check out 'nother three-quarter-ton."

"Let me see the register."

He turned it toward me. Fenton, Spec Four.

"Thanks," I said.

Ernie was about to start complaining about his new jeep when I grabbed his arm. "No time," I said.

"Why? They're *gone*. What's your rush?"

I'd never seen Ernie like this. It was as if he were

suffering from shock, unable to process that Miss Kim had been taken.

Her mother had told us that Fenton showed up at their home late last night and ordered Miss Kim to come with him. When she said no, Blood climbed over the front gate, pushed their hooch door in and proceeded to tie her up, gag her and carry her out to the truck. Her mother watched all of this helplessly as Fenton held a gun to her head.

Ernie was yelling now. "What's the *freaking* rush? We don't have any idea where they took her."

"So we start searching," I said, "that's the rush."

I was about to punch him, hoping that would calm him down. Instead, he shook his head, took a deep breath, and said, "Yeah. Let's do it."

We topped off the jeep and drove to Headquarters Company of the 501st Military Intelligence Battalion. The building was locked down, the heavy metal doors padlocked from the outside. But Riley had called in some favors, and a detail from the Post Engineers arrived just as we did. With crowbars and bolt cutters, they started in on the door. Within minutes it creaked angrily, then swung open as Ernie and I entered, guns drawn.

The place was empty. We switched on the lights and did a quick sweep of every room, including the Orderly Room, Commander's Office and even the small phone booth with its classified satellite connection to D.C. No one there. I searched Captain Blood's desk, but found nothing that could help us locate Miss Kim. I pulled back the curtain covering the giant map on the wall. It was a mosaic of smaller Army-issue maps that, when pasted together, covered the entire southern half of the Korean Peninsula. I studied it carefully.

In yesterday's interrogation, Nam had mentioned the biggest deal of his career, which involved the former US Army Anti-Aircraft Artillery base of Camp Arrow. I found it on the map. It sat atop a line of hills just south of the Imjin River, near Liberty Bridge. Its mission had been to defend the bridge from air attack and, just as importantly, stop enemy aircraft as they flew past on their way to the capital city of Seoul. Advances in anti-aircraft-artillery technology and the overwhelming American superiority in air power had made the placement of Camp Arrow obsolete. As a result, it was one of the first base camps abandoned by the US military during drawdown. Still, because of its lack of strategic importance, the ROK Army didn't want it, and because it was in such a remote location, no civilian buyer could be found. According to Nam, Blood had made a point of inspecting the facility and even moved some equipment in, which was how Nam had originally met him.

What Camp Arrow did provide was a clear view of the traffic, mostly military, crossing Liberty Bridge. That's when Mr. Nam found a real buyer. An agent for an anonymous Korean man he later came to know as Commander Ku contacted him about renting space on the compound. It would be an excellent produce transshipment point, he claimed. Nam didn't see how it could be, pushed right up against a tributary of the Imjin River like it was, and in that area, the northern side of the river was used strictly for military training, so no agriculture was allowed. But as they say in Korea, "*Sonnim-un wang ida.*" The customer is king. So he didn't argue. When Commander Ku became aware that the seller was the 501st MI, he insisted on meeting Captain Blood. After Blood took a few interviews with Commander Ku's men, according to Mr. Nam, the two went into business together.

Each Army-issue map composing the mosaic was about three feet by three feet. I reached up and grabbed the one held in place with a red pin representing Camp Arrow. Carefully, I pried loose rows of staples until I was able to pull that section of the map off the wall.

"That's where they went," I said.

"How do you know?"

I pointed to the contours of the ridgeline. "You could hold off an army from there."

"That's why they put Camp Arrow there in the first place," Ernie said.

"He's waiting for us."

"Why?"

"To deal."

"Deal for what?"

"Miss Kim's life."

The phone rang. Ernie and I looked at one another. It rang again. I reached for it.

"Sueño," I answered.

"If you want to see her alive, you're going to call off the KNPs. And I want Nam brought up here to me. Now."

"Why?" I asked.

"You're not stupid, Sueño."

So my hunch was correct. Even if Nam had signed a statement that implicated Captain Blood in espionage, it was just a piece of paper. Eliminate the live witness, and a good attorney could go to work to destroy the credibility of a statement that they'd claim was signed under duress. So Mr. Nam was the key to this whole mess. What Captain Blood wanted to do now was put a bullet into Nam's skull and throw him into the Imjin River.

"If we bring Nam, you'll turn Miss Kim over to us?"

"That's the deal. But only you and Nam. No KNPs." He confirmed that he was at Camp Arrow.

"I need my driver."

Ernie winced.

"No dice," Blood replied. "You and Nam. That's it."

"How am I supposed to pry him loose from the KNPs?"

"You're a clever guy, Sueño. You'll think of something. Eighth Army has clout with the Korean government."

"Okay," I said. "But it'll take time to convince them to turn him over to us and drive up there. At least a couple of days."

"You have until twenty hundred hours." Eight P.M. "Tonight. If you're not here by then, we'll toss what's left of her in the river."

"I want to talk to her," I said.

Instead, there was a scream so loud even Ernie could hear it. Blood hung up.

"Who screamed?" Ernie asked. When I didn't answer, he said again, "Who *screamed*?"

"Easy, Ernie," I warned.

But the answer sat uneasily, weighing on both of our chests. The voice unmistakably belonged to Miss Kim, and we had just a few hours to save her.

-33-

Ernie downshifted the jeep over a patch of black ice. The temperature had dropped by ten degrees Fahrenheit. According to the Armed Forces Korea Network, a cold front was moving out of Manchuria down the Korean Peninsula, and the full force of the storm traveling with it was expected to hit at midnight.

Nam wasn't with us. After Captain Blood hung up, I called Inspector Kill and explained the situation. He refused to turn Nam over to us for a rogue mission without KNP involvement. What he did promise to do was meet us in Tuam-dong, the old village that once served Camp Arrow. He, Nam, and a troop of armed KNPs would be waiting there.

"We'll stay out of sight," he told me. "We'll turn Nam over to you up in Tuam-dong, and then two of our officers will conceal themselves in your vehicle as you bring Nam into the camp."

Miss Kim's scream replayed in my head. Her life was at

stake. I had no choice but to agree to Inspector Kill's plan. Once we made our way to Camp Arrow, I'd play it by ear.

Ernie wound around another curve and said, "Where in the hell *is* this place?"

I aimed the beam of my flashlight onto my map. It wasn't late, only mid-afternoon, but the sky was so overcast that visibility was poor. "Not too far now. Before we hit Liberty Bridge, we'll head on up into the hills."

Freedom Bridge was the largest and most famous bridge across the Imjin River. Once you crossed the Imjin there, the next stop, a few miles farther on, was the heavily fortified Demilitarized Zone, the only buffer between us and the 700,000-man-strong Communist army of the Democratic People's Republic of Korea, also known as North Korea. Normally, the farthest north civilians could get was along the southern banks of the Imjin River. A park and national shrine had been set up by the Korean government just south of Freedom Bridge to commemorate the heroic multi-national effort that had kept South Korea a free country during the Korean War. Tour buses drove up there, people took photos by the fast-flowing Imjin, and happy couples even stood for formal wedding pictures, the military bridge lined with explosives serving as the backdrop. The waters of the Imjin sometimes held floating mines launched south by the citizens of the Communist North.

Liberty Bridge, by contrast, didn't have tourists.

It was in an area that was restricted to civilians unless

you lived in one of the farm villages dotting the nearby hills. And Liberty Bridge wasn't nearly as scenic as Freedom Bridge. Instead of being suspended elegantly twenty yards or so above the flowing water, Liberty Bridge was a cement platform on concrete stanchions that was elevated just a few feet above the normal flow level of one of the tributaries of the Imjin. Why this was so, I wasn't sure, but it was probably because this originally made it a more difficult target for North Korean air and artillery assault.

The men who guarded the bridge wore rubber overshoes because on any windy day, of which there were many in the narrow valley, the choppy surf from the river washed across the roadway and soaked their combat boots.

Ernie must have made good time, because when we reached the village of Tuam-dong, Inspector Kill and his officers hadn't arrived yet. We parked near a large wooden building just a few yards from Liberty Bridge. The side wall had been whitewashed with just a single coat. Beneath the thin layer of paint, the old sign could still be made out: PINK DRAGON CLUB. And on the other side of the street, THE SMILE BAR and NUMBER ONE CHOP HOUSE. All closed and shuttered since the American base had been mothballed.

The bridge itself was guarded by ROK Army soldiers. In the distance, we watched them pace the length of the low-slung cement. On the embankment closest to us, two of their vehicles were parked—one a two-and-a-half-ton truck, probably for transporting the guards, and the other a jeep with a long radio antenna for the officer in charge. We stepped away from the jeep and studied the hills that ran parallel to the river. Though a heavy mist rolled slowly in, there was still enough sunlight to see most of the terrain features.

"There," I said, pointing.

Ernie shielded his eyes with his hand like a Sioux warrior searching for the 7th Cavalry. "A Quonset hut," he said, "a few more buildings, and a guard tower."

"If it's an anti-aircraft camp," I said, "a lot of the construction will be below ground as protection from incoming rounds."

Ernie pointed to the right. "There's the access road."

A crumbling two-lane dirt path wound up the hill like a snake climbing toward his lair.

"They'll see us coming," I said.

"If we drive."

"You've got a better idea?"

"I don't know if it's *better*, but it's different."

"Hike up there?" I asked.

"Exactly."

"Hard enough for us," I said. "I doubt Nam could make it." Mr. Nam was a thin, elegant-looking guy, but he didn't appear too strong physically.

Ernie turned to me. "Who said anything about Nam?"

"They want to make an exchange. Kim for Nam."

"I don't particularly give a shit what they want."

"So what are you saying?" I asked.

"I say we drive around to the other side of these hills, hike up to the compound, and take her."

That wouldn't be easy, but I liked the sound of it. I was tired of the arrogance of Captain Blood and the 501st. Who the hell did they think they were, taking money from freaking North Korean spies, then harassing and kidnapping an innocent woman?

"We should've brought a rifle," I said.

Ernie glanced toward the bridge. "Maybe those guys will loan us one."

The drive around to the other side of the ridge was the hard part. There were no roads. Where there were flatlands, they were mostly filled with rice paddies, and even though they'd already been harvested and were fallow now, the winter had yet to hit in full force, so they weren't frozen and it was impossible to drive across them. The wheels would wallow in axle-deep mud. So we had to keep searching until we found a turnip patch. The farmer, mad as hell because his plants hadn't yet matured, cursed us and waved his hoe in our direction as Ernie sped across what amounted to a couple of acres of budding vegetables. Finally we reached a solid path, and another farmer riding a wooden cart pulled by an ox nearly had a heart attack when he saw us. His first thought was probably that the Korean War had

started again. When Ernie honked, the guy was so pan-
icked that he pulled his cart off the entire path to let us pass.
By way of amends, we smiled and waved as we passed, but
I figured it would take him and his ox a lot of effort to pull
that cart out of the ditch. Using dead reckoning, we finally
figured we were on the opposite side of the compound. We
parked the jeep beneath a pear tree and climbed out.

"It's up there," I said.

"I can't see anything."

"It's there, though."

"I hope you're right."

"Come on, we only have about an hour of daylight left."

Ernie grabbed the M-16 rifle and the two clips of ammunition that the ROK Army Lieutenant at Liberty Bridge had
so graciously loaned us. Well, not *so* graciously. He'd said
no, absolutely. After all, the first thing an infantry soldier
learns is that his weapon is like his life: never to be given
away under any circumstances. But this circumstance was
that Ernie had pulled his .45 on him. When the Lieutenant still hesitated, Ernie fired a round that zinged past the
Lieutenant's head and landed in the cold waters of the rushing river. Using my best Korean, I apologized as I quickly
grabbed the rifle and ammo.

If we'd been anybody else, the guards on the bridge
probably would've opened fire and killed Ernie and me.
But we were Americans, and everyone in the ROK military
knew that you left Americans alone, unless you wanted to

bring the wrath of the Pak Chung-hee government upon yourself. It was a hell of a chance we'd taken, but it worked.

And it was guaranteed that as soon as we left, the Lieutenant fired up the radio and reported it.

"So the KNPs are on the way, and the ROK Army is pissed," Ernie said.

"Yeah," I replied. "All we have to do is make sure Miss Kim is safe before anybody arrives."

"With guns blazing," he said.

We started climbing.

-34-

In the dark, the compound appeared deserted. No lights shone, which confirmed to me that they were underground. We low-crawled up to the chain-link fence that bordered the compound, which was rusted and deformed in places. We made our way along it until Ernie found a loose section that he propped up about six inches with a forked tree branch. On my back, as they'd taught us in Basic Training, I wriggled beneath the fence until I was inside. Then I knelt and pulled the fence higher for Ernie to slide through.

We crouched and studied the compound. Ernie pointed, and we silently approached the big Quonset hut.

We knew there'd be an underground storage area for the anti-aircraft ammunition, as well as an underground command bunker. It made sense that Captain Blood would use the bunker for our "deal." It was safe, quiet, and secure, and no one from the outside could see those lights.

The sky was spangled brightly with stars. It's like that near the Korean Demilitarized Zone. There are few internal combustion engines operating in the area, no factories, so the air is pure. Wildlife thrives up here. Certain species of crane and mountain hare are extinct in South Korea as far as scientists can ascertain, except along the DMZ. There are even rumors that a few Siberian tigers roam the mountains in these parts, but that's probably just GI myth.

We found the ammo storage facility. A huge, flat zig-gurat-like structure. We gazed down the stone steps. At the bottom of a filthy pit, the iron doors were closed, but I could hear rats squeaking in the shadows around it. This was no place for humans, especially not highbrow ones like Blood. We continued our search.

About twenty yards away, we discovered the entrance to the underground command and control center. It could have been my imagination, but I thought I saw a sliver of light seep from beneath the thick, metal-reinforced door. A shuffling noise from within confirmed my suspicions.

"How do we get in?" Ernie whispered.

I thought about it. "We could wait until somebody comes out," I said.

"That'll be too late."

He was right. We had to find a way in, preferably one that would take them by surprise. How to break in unno-ticed to a heavily fortified military command center, I had no idea.

Then it dawned on me that routine operations would be conducted above ground. Only if the base were under attack would everyone in the headquarters make a mad dash for the underground bunker.

I pointed and said, "Let's search over there."

There was a square, tin-roofed building not twenty yards from the cement steps that led down to the command center. Ernie crawled to the door, reached up to twist the knob, and pushed it open. Nothing. Dark inside. We crouched through but didn't turn on the lights. Instead, we opened the tin shutters and let moonlight filter in. There was a coffee maker on a table against the wall. I felt it.

"Warm," I told Ernie.

We searched the entire building. Empty except for evidence, like crumpled C-ration wrappers in the trash bin, that someone had been here recently.

"They were here," Ernie said, "and moved to the command center."

"Afraid we're going to dump a mortar round on them?"

"I guess so."

"But they must have a lookout," I said. "Someone to warn them when we're approaching with Nam."

Still crouched down, Ernie peered out the window. "On that side of the compound," he said.

There was the camp's guard tower, a wooden structure about fifty feet tall with a wall of sandbags around the top. It faced north and had an unobstructed view of both the Imjin River and Liberty Bridge.

"There," Ernie said, pointing.

"Do you see anything?"

"No," Ernie replied. "But he's probably there. Sitting low so his head's not peeking above the wall."

"If we wait long enough, he'll stand up," I said. "Or someone will come out of the command center to relieve him."

"That could take hours," Ernie said.

"I'm sure he has a field radio up there or some other way to communicate."

Just as I'd uttered the words, a tiny red light glimmered through wooden planks.

"He's there," Ernie said. "We can't wait. We have to take him down now and use him to gain access to the command center."

"Good idea," I said, "but how?"

"I'll climb up."

"He'll shoot you before you get halfway up the ladder."

"No he won't."

"Why not?"

"He'll think what all GIs think when they're pulling guard duty."

"Which is?"

"That I'm there to relieve him."

"Earlier than scheduled?"

"Sure. We all grew up watching Walt Disney."

"What's that got to do with it?"

He looked at me like I was dense. "We keep wishing upon stars, praying for miracles."

■ ■ ■

Ernie was halfway up the wooden ladder of the guard tower when a raspy voice whispered down at him. Ernie said something short and guttural in response. I was hidden in the nearest building, within earshot, so if I couldn't understand what he was saying, the guy at the top probably couldn't, either. I heard him ask, "What?"

Ernie let out another unintelligible grunt and kept climbing. I expected a shot to ring out, wounding Ernie and sending him on a fatal fall several stories to the ground like in the movies. But much to my surprise, nothing happened. Ernie was right. The guy didn't believe that an enemy would be so bold as to just climb up to the tower, and though he couldn't understand anything Ernie was saying, the mind has a tendency to fill in the blanks with what it wants to see and hear. This guy had decided that he was being relieved early, that he'd be able to climb down from that freezing, lonely, uncomfortable tower, return to the warmth of the underground command center, and have a cup of hot coffee with some C-rations out of a can.

Our target at the top of the tower was standing now. His silhouette was clearly outlined by the night sky. I propped the M-16 rifle on the window sill and centered his head in the front sights. If he saw through the act of the good fairy who'd come to relieve him and tried to fire on Ernie, I was fully prepared to blast his cranium into tiny shards of bone. Fortunately for him, and for Ernie, the guy was oblivious. Ernie reached the floor of the tower and, a few seconds later, his silhouette appeared opposite the guard's. In their close quarters, Ernie used his .45 to good advantage, threatening the guard with it, and a few seconds later waved the captured rifle over his head to signal that he'd taken control of the tower. I ran to the base and waited as the two of them—guard first—climbed down the ladder. When he stood before me, I leveled the M-16 at him. As he turned, I pulled off his helmet and tossed it into the dirt.

Scarcely looking better than he had in the hospital, here was Specialist Four Wilfred R. Fenton, Counter Intelligence Agent, 501st MI Battalion.

"Assume the position," I told him.

He did, leaning up against the guard tower. Ernie brought out a length of rope he'd found in the command shack and reached for Fenton's wrists. Faster than I figured he could move, Fenton turned and swung his right fist around in a huge arc. Ernie tried to duck, but the punch caught him at the top of the head, and much to my surprise, Ernie dropped to the ground. Fenton charged me. I could've shot him, but if whoever was in the bunker heard it, that might be the end of Miss Kim. Instead, I backed away, and his roundhouse punch landed on my shoulder. This should've been ineffective, but pain rang through my left shoulder like a ten-thousand-volt shock of lightning. Then I saw them: brass knuckles in his right palm. Ernie was trying to raise himself to his feet, but before he could, Fenton swung at me again.

I was backing up quickly now, trying to regain my wits from the disorienting anguish emanating from my left shoulder. I lowered the rifle at Fenton. He grinned and kept swiping at me, knowing that I wouldn't pull the trigger. I backed away again, this time to my right, tracing an arc around the base of the guard tower. I was trying to turn him around and stall. As he continued in pursuit, he dared me, "Shoot! Go ahead, shoot!"

Ernie was up now. But he was still too groggy to raise himself completely. Instead, he knelt in the dirt holding his .45 with both hands. I feinted toward Fenton, and the move startled him just enough for him to stand still for a moment. Ernie fired. Fenton's chest pushed out as if he'd been stabbed in the back with a lance and continued to explode forward. Above the gore, he gave me the strangest look, grinning as if pleasantly surprised, and then pirouetted in a large, graceful circle, balancing on the toes of his dirty combat boots, and collapsed to the ground.

A bloody mass of flesh had erupted in the center of what should've been Fenton's chest. His carotid artery had stopped beating and his wide, surprised eyes were glassy in death. A wicked-looking pair of homemade brass knuckles lay loose in his fingertips; probably something he'd made in high school metal shop. I ran to Ernie.

"I'm okay," he said, pushing my hand away, but he clearly

wasn't. I helped him stand, leaning him against the guard tower and making sure he switched on the safety of his .45. Then he threw up. When he finished spitting, he wiped his mouth with the back of his hand and said, "They must've heard that."

I nodded. "Yeah."

What to do now? Miss Kim was in the command bunker with Captain Blood and perhaps more soldiers, and had been alerted to our presence. Our only option was to talk.

I loosened the sling of the rifle and slipped it over my head. With the M-16 secure against my back, I climbed the ladder of the guard tower. At the top, I knelt before the blinking field radio. I picked up the mic and started punching buttons. Something buzzed. Then a voice yelled, "What the hell just happened?" I paused for a moment, and he screeched again, "What the hell's going on, Fenton?"

I swallowed to moisten my dry throat and said, "It's all over, Blood."

"Who's this?"

"Who do you think?"

"Sueño. What'd you do with Fenton?"

"We've subdued him. Do you have Miss Kim?"

"Of course I do. And if I let her go, I get free passage out of here. No KNPs, understood? You two are going to escort me out."

"Where are you planning on going? This is South Korea. You're boxed in."

"Not completely," he said.

And then it struck me what he was planning. Korea was a peninsula, bordered by sea on three sides. Its only embarkation points were Kimpo International Airport and the port cities, including Inchon and Mokpo and Pusan. But he knew the Korean authorities would be ready to apprehend him at all of those exits. The only other way out of the country was across the heavily reinforced Demilitarized Zone. It was delusional for Blood to think we could make it across, even if he'd enlisted Commander Ku's help.

"You get it now, Sueño? That's why I brought you up here. So you could escort me across Liberty Bridge and up north with your emergency dispatch and Criminal Investigation ID."

"We'd never make it across," I said. "We'd be shot dead or blown to pieces by a land mine."

"Better than rotting in Leavenworth."

I had to think fast, stall him.

"Look, Blood," I said, "your situation's not hopeless. Turn Miss Kim over to us. That'll show your goodwill. Then hire a Stateside lawyer, keep your mouth shut, and once the JAG people take over the case, cut a deal."

There was a long pause.

"You don't know, do you?"

"Know what?" I asked.

"Nam didn't spill."

Then there was another pause, a long one this time. In

the background I heard Miss Kim say, "I'm here, Geogie."
Then a loud slap, sounding almost like a crack.

"Shut *up*!" Blood told her. "Keep your trap shut."

"*Dalun salam do issoyo?*" I asked. Are there other people there?

"*Aniyo*," she replied. No.

A loud crash rang through the receiver, so loud I instinctively moved it away from my ear. Then another. "I told you to keep your trap *shut*!"

Miss Kim shuffled away from the radio.

"Hurting her isn't going to do any damn good, Blood."

He picked up the mic and growled, "Don't tell me what to do." He inhaled to calm himself, and then continued. "The KNPs will keep after Nam. He'll spill eventually."

"Spill what?"

"My deal with Ku."

"Which was?"

"Maybe too rich for my own good. But this was my last chance at that promotion to Major. If I didn't make it, I was out on my ass. I couldn't walk back out into civilian life with *nothing*. After all that hard work, all these years of sacrifice. It's wrong to put a person in that position. Whatever happens, it's the Army's fault. They forced me to do this."

"Do what?"

"What the hell do you *think*? What would the North Koreans pay anything for? What's the most important information they could want?"

I tried to figure it out, but I was too worried about how to save Miss Kim and stop Blood from carrying out his insane plan. "I don't know," I said. "Why don't you tell me."

"Fine," he said. "I will. Hold on a minute."

He set the mic down and lowered the receiver volume, and then I heard a vague rustling in the background. Miss Kim said a couple of words. I couldn't make out what they were, but she was clearly being compliant. She was trying not to make him angry.

What followed was silence. I started to fiddle with the knobs, wondering if the radio had gone on the blink. Just as I was about to give up, cement scraped loudly on cement.

I leapt to my feet and looked down. Someone was opening the door to the command bunker. I quickly began climbing down the ladder. Ernie, who'd had two years of combat experience in Vietnam, had done the right thing. He'd grabbed Fenton's rifle and made his way to the opposite side of the bunker. That way, once I reached the ground, we would have whoever was emerging in a crossfire.

Before I was halfway to the ground, red tracers lit the night and a line of bullets stitched the dirt below me.

From a prone position, Ernie fired.

Whoever had let loose the first burst ceased their assault. I reached the bottom and lay flat on the ground in the open, aiming my rifle at the dark opening. And then something emerged, low and dark, running to my right away from the command center. I followed it with the crosshairs of the M-16, but realized that Blood's bulk was accompanied by someone else's small frame. Ernie held his fire because he was afraid of the same thing, that the second person was Miss Kim.

The dark figures ran to a large Quonset hut near the main entranceway and disappeared around the corner. Both Ernie and I sprinted after them, but before we reached the domed building on the far side, an engine coughed to life.

"The three-quarter-ton!" Ernie shouted.

The Quonset hut was twenty yards long, and we reached the end just as a pair of headlights burst to life around the corner. We were temporarily blinded. The engine roared and the truck careened toward us. Neither of us fired, again for fear of hitting Miss Kim. The truck scraped the tin edge of the Quonset and would've hit us if we hadn't tumbled backward. Then it sped off. We stood by helplessly as the taillights swerved in a semicircle, heading for the main gate of Camp Arrow and the road that led downhill to Tuam-dong. We ran to the gate, but before we could get there, the bumper of the three-quarter-ton smashed into the wood-frame and barbed-wire construction and burst it open. The big doors were still rebounding as we ran through them. We stopped at the cliff overlooking the winding mountain road, watching red taillights swerve down the sinuous path. In the distance, a string of bright lights shone across the expanse of Liberty Bridge.

"There's movement down there," Ernie said.

He was right. Tons of it. At least a dozen vehicles. "KNPs," I replied.

"Will Kill know to stop him?"

I raised my M-16 and pointed it toward North Korea. I fired off three quick shots, then three slower shots, and three quick shots again. Then I changed the clip and repeated the process, signaling SOS.

Now all we could do was stand and watch. A line of police vehicles moved toward the intersection between the road from Camp Arrow and the Main Supply Route.

"He's not gonna stop. They'll blast him with everything they've got," Ernie said.

If the KNPs ordered Captain Blood to halt and he didn't, they would almost certainly open fire. And if he shot at them first, which I believed he would, the Korean National Police would unleash every ounce of artillery they possessed.

"We have to stop him," I said. We couldn't live with ourselves if Miss Kim got caught in the crossfire. We had promised to protect her and we had failed.

Ernie raised his rifle. "I can hit his gas tank," he said. "That'll force him to stop."

"If you manage to aim that well," I said, "it'll explode."

Ernie lowered his rifle. "Yeah," he said. "Well, maybe the KNPs will use caution."

"Yeah, maybe."

It was a bet against the odds. But all we could do was watch. And hope.

"Look!" Ernie said. I squinted but couldn't see anything. "In front. They're fighting."

And then I spotted it in the weak moonlight. The truck was slowing and occasionally veering away from the road, then back onto it. On the left side of the cab, the burly figure of Captain Blood, nothing more than a shadow from this distance, seemed to be swaying from side to side. But in the right side of the cab I couldn't see anything.

"She must be lying down on the seat," Ernie said, "kicking him."

It was the smartest thing she could do. Captain Blood's upper body strength was clearly much greater than Miss Kim's, but her legs were almost as strong as his arms. And if she braced herself against the door and kicked with all her might while Blood was trying to navigate down a steep mountain road, he'd more than have his hands full.

The three-quarter-ton truck reached level ground, but there was a deep depression before the road rose again and hooked up with the main highway. The truck slowed. Probably because of Miss Kim's assault, Blood seemed to be having trouble shifting into a lower gear. Before he could pick up speed again, a dark figure rolled out of the side of the cab.

"It's her!" Ernie shouted. "She jumped out of the damn truck."

But Blood didn't stop the three-quarter-ton. On the contrary, he seemed relieved to be rid of his troublesome hostage. He revved the engine so loudly we could hear it all the way from the edge of the cliff, and the truck picked up speed as it breached the rise, the back wheels sliding until it straightened up and sped directly toward the center of the line of KNP vehicles. Gunfire erupted. The truck rammed into a blue patrol car and plowed to its right, then more gunfire rang out and the three-quarter-ton swiveled almost completely around, its engine whining as if in anguish. Just as it was about to regain traction, more bullets whistled through the night, and the front of the three-quarter-ton burst into flame. Still trying to escape, the burning truck left the KNP vehicles behind, but as its distance from the broken line of cars increased, the flames leapt higher, fanned by the air. For a moment, it seemed as if Captain Blood might get away. Until the explosion.

The truck, now a giant ball of fire, inexplicably continued to speed in a straight path down the road. Finally it wobbled and careened sideways, struggling to regain traction. It stabilized temporarily, but then lost control again, sliding and eventually flying like a burning comet off the edge of the road down a gradual incline of at least a hundred feet. Near the bottom, it shuddered to a stop before imploding. The flames roasted and growled, charring metal and presumably flesh on the shore of the churning river.

Ernie and I ran downhill from Camp Arrow so fast that

both of us stumbled and fell a couple of times, skinning our knees and our palms. Finally, we reached the ravine where Miss Kim had jumped from the three-quarter-ton, and using a flashlight, I found her. She was moaning and bruised, but alive and breathing.

"Geogie," she said when she saw me.

"Yes," I replied, kneeling close. "Stay still. Help is on the way."

Then she spotted Ernie. For a moment her eyes held a pleading look, but then it was as if she remembered something, and she abruptly turned away. Ernie grabbed her hand anyway and held it until a small Korean ambulance rolled up the rocky dirt road.

We waved the medics over and supervised as they hoisted her onto a stretcher. Like praetorian guards, Ernie and I escorted the stretcher until it was slid safely into the back of the medical van. The door was shut. We both stood and watched as Miss Kim was driven away.

35

When Fenton's first three-quarter-ton truck had been totaled trying to run us down after we'd left Miss Lee's *kisaeng* house, the KNPs had taken it into custody. Since it was a military vehicle, they were generally supposed to turn the wreck over to the US Army right away, but in this case, they waited. I had asked Mr. Kill to have his forensic team analyze it to test my theory: that it had been used to transport Major Schultz's body to the alley behind the Dragon King Nightclub in Itaewon.

Two days after the incident at Camp Arrow, Ernie and I sat in Mr. Kill's office as he broke the news.

"No traces of blood, hair, or anything else that would indicate a human body was transported in that truck."

"So it wasn't the Five Oh First who murdered Major Schultz?"

"I'm not saying that," he replied. "I'm only saying they didn't use that truck to transport his body to Itaewon."

"But what else could they have used?" I was thinking

out loud now. As far as I knew, it was the only truck they had signed out, but I could double-check that. Kill didn't bother to answer. Then something else struck me. "How's Nam holding up?" I asked.

"Not well."

"You set Bang on him?"

"Yes."

I shifted uncomfortably in my chair, trying not to think of the torture Interrogator Bang was inflicting on Mr. Nam.

After Blood's corpse had been found in the smoldering remains of the three-quarter-ton, I told Kill that the 501st commander had been about to receive a massive payday from the North Koreans in exchange for classified, top-priority information.

We settled on nuclear-tipped missiles. There'd been a lot of speculation in the European and Japanese papers about the US bringing nuclear weapons to the Far East, both in the form of land-based tactical missiles and guided missile systems aboard the ships of the US Navy's 7th Fleet. Every time a US aircraft carrier pulled into a Japanese port, a group of anti-nuclear demonstrators was gathered there to greet them.

But the US military's policy was to neither confirm nor deny such rumors. In Korea, the Pak Chung-hee regime simply didn't allow anti-nuclear demonstrations. And they censored the subject in the press, so the Korean public was largely unaware of the controversy. Nobody in the US was particularly interested. But the North Kore-ans were, and they routinely accused the US of bringing nuclear missiles into South Korea. There was no doubt that the US had brought in regular tactical missiles.

Raytheon was the subcontractor for the Depart-ment of Defense's missile maintenance contract; I'd even played poker with a couple of their civilian technicians. But even in those private games, with plenty of beer and liquor flowing, no one was gauche enough to ask the Ray-theon techs about the weapons they were installing. Such things simply weren't discussed during a civilized game of chance.

But this theory gave me something to look for when I searched the 501st records. I soon discovered a close con-nection between Captain Blood and a half-dozen officers of the missile command near Chunchon, which gave cre-dence to the idea. Would all of these officers have willingly divulged classified information? Probably not. But if he was there under the guise of a counter-espionage investi-gation, he could probably have learned a hell of a lot—for instance, whether the missiles were in fact nuclear-tipped. And if so, where they had been deployed, how many there were, whether they were moved periodically. This informa-tion would be worth a small fortune to the North Korean Communists.

But we didn't have time to construct an airtight case against Blood. Besides, he was dead, and as far as 8th Army was concerned, any crimes he'd committed could just as well remain hidden. The honchos were already constructing the cover story of the roadway accident that took his life. If they stuck with that, he'd receive an honorable posthumous discharge and someone—it was unclear who—would inherit his Serviceman's Group Life Insurance. Most importantly, of course, 8th Army wouldn't be embarrassed.

Meanwhile, our North Korean spymaster, Commander Ku, was almost certainly spooked. We had to work with what we had and act quickly.

"Maybe we can convince Mr. Nam to cooperate," I said.

"He's more afraid of the North Koreans than he is of us," Kill replied. "If they discover he's compromised, they'll kill him on sight."

"Unless he has something to offer."

Ernie crossed his arms and studied me. "Wait a minute, Sueño. This spy stuff is not our department."

"Whose department is it?" I asked.

"The Five Oh First, but . . ."

"Captain Blood's gone, and we don't know who else in their squad was involved in this mess. It's up to us now."

Kill's eyes narrowed. "What do you have in mind?"

"Set Mr. Nam free. When the North Koreans come after him, he can offer them a deal."

"What deal?"

"He can offer them access to somebody new. Somebody who knows about the missiles."

"And who would that be?"

"I'm not sure yet," I told him. "But I'm working on it."

It took two months. During that time, Nam was released, and he immediately set about liquidating his real estate holdings and other business interests. After paying his debts, he was as poor as a church mouse, but it was worth it to him—the Korean government had agreed to let him off with less than a year of jail time if he cooperated in the capture of Commander Ku. From an outside perspective, it looked like the KNPs had let him out so he could raise enough money to pay off everyone involved; the cops, Mr. Kill, and the judge overseeing the case. Nam no longer had any way of contacting Commander Ku directly—all the old phone numbers to Ku's go-betweens had been disconnected—but we figured that Ku and his operatives would be watching. When they saw that he was rapidly selling everything for cash, they'd reason that he needed the money to pay his way out of trouble.

Mr. Kill set up a liaison between Nam and himself, an incredibly dangerous job. Officer Oh had taken it on voluntarily. She'd be temporarily relieved of her regular duties as Kill's assistant, and would masquerade as a bargirl named Pei in Yongju-kol, one of the largest and most raucous GI villages in Korea.

Miss Lee Suk-myong, Nam's girlfriend and erstwhile *kisaeng*, had been found, arrested and placed in solitary confinement, away from the action so she wouldn't inadvertently spill the beans.

Nam began to lead a progressively more dissolute life, convincing even his family that he'd fallen on hard times and was spiraling downhill fast into drink and despair. Kill had several operatives keeping an eye on him, and they said that Nam was playing his part so well that he might become the first Korean Oscar-winner.

Commander Ku eventually nibbled. Not directly, but via one of his men.

Nam was beaten to a pulp.

It was Officer Oh, or Miss Pei, who found him facedown in the mud in a back alley. The man who'd done the beating had been waiting for her. As "Miss Pei" knelt in her high heels to help Nam up, the huge thug stepped out of the shadows. She reached for the knife that she kept in her purse.

Instead of attacking her, the man simply pointed at Nam and said, "Saturday at midnight. Tell him to be at the Sejong Inn in Munsan. If he's not there, we'll come looking for him. It won't be good."

With that, the man tromped away into the darkest part of the alley, splashing mud on Miss Pei's nylons.

36

I'd been brushing up on tactical missiles.

When I asked Strange about it, he just about had a heart attack.

"Do you realize how highly classified that information is?" he asked. His empty cigarette holder bobbed on his moist lips. "It's Top Secret Crypto-freaking-*zipto*. As high as you can get, then a little higher. You can't be messing with that."

"Why not?"

We were sitting at our usual table in the crowded 8th Army Snack Bar. He leaned in closer. "The word is, we've equipped some of those missiles with nuclear warheads, just to show those North Korean Commies who's boss."

"All of them, or just some of them?"

He sat up straight. "How would I know? When a document like that comes through my distribution cage, it's hand-carried by an officer of at least captain's rank or higher."

"You don't get a chance to peek?"

"Nope. And no desire to peek," he added. "I like living here and not in a cozy cell in Fort Leavenworth."

"You got something against Kansas?" Ernie asked.

"A lot of things," Strange replied.

"Like what?" Ernie asked.

"Like it's cold and then it's hot, and the land's too flat, and there are too many agricultural misdemeanors."

"'Agricultural misdemeanors?'"

"Farm boys chasing livestock."

I sipped on cold coffee and set the mug back down. "Would Captain Blood have had access to information about the missiles?"

"At the Five Oh First?" Strange thought about it. "No way. They're counter-intel. They wouldn't have a need-to-know."

"What if they claimed someone was haunting the installations that housed the missiles?"

"Still no need-to-know," Strange replied. "Whether or not the missiles were nuclear-tipped wouldn't be their concern."

"So if Blood wanted to get that information, how would he go about it?"

"He'd have to talk to someone in the missile command. Someone with rank. Or . . ."

"Or what?"

"One of the silly-vilian technicians at Raytheon might be able to clue him in."

This confirmed my earlier suspicions. "How much do they know?"

"They're the ones who hook up the wires and check the fuse boxes and whatever in the hell else. Without them, nothing ignites, nothing flies, and nothing goes *kaboom*."

I paid for Strange's hot chocolate. We must've really shaken him, because we managed to leave before he asked if we'd had any *strange* lately.

The Raytheon technicians were mostly middle-aged men. Ernie and I were too young, and our hair too short, to be believable as veteran electronics workers. We brainstormed candidates for the role and finally found the perfect one right under our noses: Staff Sergeant Riley.

When we first proposed it to him, he said he was way too busy and besides, he had a date on Saturday night.

"A date with a bottle of Old Overwart?" Ernie asked.

"And a dolly to pour," Riley replied.

"Tell her to take a rain check."

"I don't have any way to call her. She doesn't own a phone."

"So who does? When she arrives at Gate Five and you don't show, she'll get the message."

"If I stand her up, I might never see her again."

"A great loss for romance."

Riley thought it over and finally said, "Fine. What do you want me to do?"

By the time we turned Riley over to Nam, he was drunk. They made quite a pair: Sergeant Riley in civvies, a coat and tie, stumbling half-looped through a narrow Munsan alley-way, and former real estate magnate Mr. Nam still hurting from the beating he'd taken at KNP headquarters, wobbling just as badly, but a lot less fluidly.

Mr. Kill had decided that we couldn't afford to risk exposing the operation by posting officers nearby.

"North Korean operatives are well-trained and very disciplined," Kill told us. "Commander Ku will probably have the Sejong Inn staked out for at least two days before the meeting. Anything suspicious and they'll abort."

"How will they react to Nam bringing an unknown American to the meeting?"

"If nothing else spooks them, they'll be curious. They know Nam is on the take and desperate for money. They might figure he's trying to speed up negotiations so he can get his hands on quick cash."

"Maybe."

"It's risky. But we have to force Commander Ku to commit quickly. If we give him too much time to think, he might back away."

The Sejong Inn was well chosen. First of all, Munsan was about forty kilometers northwest of Seoul, just a couple of miles from the North Korean border. The inn itself sat in the center of a labyrinth of tiny hooches in a dirt-poor section of the town, with a dozen narrow pedestrian alleyways running off in every direction like the legs of a monstrous spider. About an hour before midnight, as Riley and Mr.

Nam staggered their way through the unlit lanes, we sat with Mr. Kill in the Munsan Police Station, studying a map and outlining possible escape routes.

"In order not to frighten him away, we had to keep our forces very far back," Kill said. "Should he flee, Ku will be able to escape fairly easily."

"Unless we get lucky," Ernie said. "One of your roving police cars might spot him."

"They might. The problem is, we don't know what he looks like."

Ernie nodded. "How long do you figure this meeting will take?"

"No more than a half-hour. I told Nam that if it takes longer than that, he can expect us to come in."

"Why only a half-hour?" Ernie asked.

"Commander Ku will come straight to the point. He'll want to find out what information they're offering, and once he knows that, he'll offer a sum. They'll either agree to the deal or they won't."

"If they don't?"

Mr. Kill shook his head. "He'll kill them."

I leaned forward on the wooden bench, putting my elbows on my knees. "You've known the North Koreans to operate that way before?"

Kill nodded grimly. "But Nam knows too. He'll agree to whatever Commander Ku offers. He might try to wheedle a little more out of him for show, but he'll agree."

I suddenly felt guilty about pressuring Staff Sergeant Riley into taking this assignment. But we'd prepped him with some buzzwords that missile technicians might use: radiation casing, booster gas canister, high explosive lens, tritium and deuterium. If they asked him to explain the more technical aspects, he'd play cagey and pretend not to want to reveal too much classified data until the money was forthcoming. Drunk and greedy wasn't too much of a stretch for Riley. And he'd promise to provide not only the wiring diagrams the techs used, but also their schedule of maintenance visits, which compounds they were going to visit first and how long they'd be there. All this had been faked, of course, but we were hoping that the North Koreans would believe that they could use the information to pinpoint the location of any missiles equipped with something other than conventional warheads.

The time for the meeting came and went. Nothing happened. Apparently, the owner of the Sejong Inn had a phone. Riley called us just before midnight.

"No-show," he growled. "You're wasting my time."

"Maybe they're checking the place out," I told him. "Be patient."

"Well, I'm not waiting around. Some old broad here is bugging the crap out of me, trying to talk me into buying fresh octopus. The little fucker keeps pushing his tentacles up over the edge of the bucket. Creeps me out."

"All right. We're on our way."

I set the phone down and looked at Mr. Kill. I'd been

holding the receiver a few inches from my ear and he'd heard what had been said. His face had turned pale. Without speaking to me, he barked an order at one of the uniformed officers waiting outside his office. The man stepped into the open doorway, listened to the commands, bowed, turned and ran down the hallway.

"What is it?" I asked.

Ernie was on his feet.

"No time," Mr. Kill said, immediately up and sprinting toward the door. Ernie and I ran after him.

Inspector Oh, out of her nightclub apparel and back in uniform, slammed on the brakes as Mr. Kill hopped out, Ernie and I in hot pursuit. These catacomb-like pedestrian lanes weren't wide enough for cars. They were barely wide enough for Mr. Kill, Ernie, and me to hop single-file through the darkness, avoiding open sewage drains and slapping at low-hanging cobwebs.

Ahead I saw the blue and red neon sign that blinked in *hangul*: SEJONG INN. Footsteps, men shouting and the waving beams of flashlights converged all around us. Mr. Kill was apparently familiar with these dark passageways, and pulled ahead a few yards. I was about to speed up and close the gap when a small figure burst out of an indentation in the darkness. I skidded to a halt, Ernie bumped into me. From the glare of moonlight, I looked down on a round, wrinkled face. One eye seemed to be closed shut.

"You buy?" she asked, holding up a bucket that smelled of the sea. A small tentacle gripped the metal lip. She smiled a gap-toothed smile and tilted back the lid. Inside, murky water sloshed. Something fleshy, lined with what seemed to be at least a dozen suction cups, wriggled and groped for the sky. I touched a meaty shoulder covered in felt and moved her gently to the side.

"Not now, *ajjuma*," I said.

She offered the bucket to Ernie. He wrinkled his nose and said, "Maybe later."

We continued running toward blue and red neon. We took one wrong turn and then another, but finally reached the pathway in front of the gate that led into the small courtyard of the Sejong Inn. Over a half-dozen uniformed Korean National Police officers milled about, waving their flashlights, checking the grounds in front of the low wooden porch. Ernie and I slipped off our shoes and walked inside.

Behind an open oil-papered sliding door, Staff Sergeant Riley sat cross-legged on the vinyl floor. On a cushion opposite him sat Mr. Kill.

"She was an old *hag*," Riley told him, "trying to sell us octopus."

"Did she speak English?" Mr. Kill asked.

"A little. Broken English, like she'd been selling useless shit to GIs for centuries."

"And Nam went with her?"

"He said he wanted to buy some whatever-you-call-it."

"*Nakji*." Octopus.

"His wife likes it." Riley shuddered. "I don't know how anybody can put those creepy little suction cups in their mouth. *Gross*."

Chief Homicide Inspector Gil Kwon-up reached into his shirt pocket and pulled out a rumpled pack of Turtleboat cigarettes. He offered them around to me, Ernie, and Riley but we all refused. We weren't health freaks or anything, but somehow none of us had ever acquired the habit—too busy boozing, I suppose.

Kill pulled out a cigarette, lit it, and puffed contentedly. Then he looked at Riley and said, "You're lucky to be alive."

"What do you mean?"

"That woman," he said, "the one you called an old hag. She's a high-ranking officer in the North Korean People's Army."

"*Her*?"

Ernie and I glanced at one another.

"Yes. The woman who was trying to sell you fresh octopus. I believe she is the operative Mr. Nam has been calling Commander Ku."

"He never said Commander Ku was a woman," I replied.

"Maybe he didn't know. Or maybe he held back, hoping to make his escape. If so, it worked."

"But . . . they can't have gotten far," Ernie said. He was about to admit that we'd just seen her outside, but swallowed his words. Professional pride, I suppose.

Kill shook his head. "She must have had an escape route well planned. Yes, we might get lucky and stumble upon them, but if I were a betting man, I'd save my chips. She's gone, and even if she weren't, I don't know that we'd be able to bring her in. Not alive, anyway."

I thought about what Kill had just said and realized that, even within the past few minutes, she could have traveled far outside the perimeter the KNPs had set up. There wasn't anything more I could do, but I did have one question: "Why'd she go to all this trouble just to pull Nam's butt out of the fire?"

"They want to interrogate him, of course. See what we wanted. But also they want to send a message to those who cooperate with them that if they're caught, they won't just be left to their cruel fate."

"What will the North Koreans do with him?"

Kill shrugged. "Maybe put him on a new assignment, give him a new identity down here in the south. Or smuggle him north."

"They can do that?"

"There are plenty of fishing boats in the Yellow Sea. We can't monitor them all."

I turned to Riley. "So what'd she ask you?"

He shrugged. "Routine stuff, like where I was stationed. Told her I was a civilian. She seemed impressed and asked me how much money I made."

"What'd you say?"

Riley quoted a fantastic sum.

"Sure, in your whiskey-fed imagination you make that much," Ernie said.

"Hey!" Riley replied. "I was undercover."

"Did you tell her you repaired missiles?" I asked.

Riley nodded. "I told her about the canisters and deuterium and all that stuff."

"What'd she say?"

"She said I don't look that smart."

Ernie barked a laugh. Even Kill seemed amused. Riley's face turned red, and he looked like he wanted to punch somebody.

"You did a good job," I told him, standing up. "Let's get out of here."

Before we left, Riley accepted one of Mr. Kill's cigarettes. Officer Oh drove us back to the Munsan Police Station, where Ernie, Riley, and I switched to the new 21 T Car motor pool jeep.

"Hey," Riley said, when he climbed in the back seat. "What happened to the tuck-and-roll?"

Ernie flipped him the bird. "Sit on it and rotate, Riley."

"I risk my life for God and country, and this is the thanks I get?"

A few minutes later, we were on the Main Supply Route, rolling south. Riley made himself comfortable on the canvas seat in back, and soon he started to snore.

"Octopus," Ernie said.

"Yeah," I replied. "We should've bought some."

37

Even if we hadn't succeeded in collaring Commander Ku, we'd established a link between North Korean espionage agents and Mr. Nam—a known associate of Captain Blood, on whom the late Major Schultz had filed an official investigation report. This effectively established a motive for murder, other than the revenge narrative that had tied Miss Jo Kyong-ja to the crime. And it made much more sense that someone with a large set of connections and resources, rather than an Itaewon business girl, had pulled off the murder of a high-ranking officer.

But I still didn't think we had enough evidence to present our case to the Provost Marshal. Because of all the murmured invective and disapproving looks we'd received when we reported on the facts behind the deaths of Captain Blood and Specialist Fenton, I wanted more before I laid the Schultz murder case on Colonel Brace's desk.

"Like what?" Ernie asked.

"Proof that Captain Blood transported Major Schultz's body to Itaewon."

"The guy's dead. What difference does it make now?"

"I want to make sure that the wrong person doesn't take the fall."

"You're too much of a humanitarian, Sueño. Besides, the KNPs already checked out the Five Oh First three-quarter-ton. They found nothing."

"But Schultz was moved out there somehow. There has to be evidence."

"Where?"

"I'm working on it," I told him.

Ernie rolled his eyes.

The next morning, Riley was at work bright and early. I arrived before Ernie. Just as I was about to proceed back to the coffee urn, Riley said, "I remembered something last night, after you let me off at the barracks."

I sat down in front of his desk. He grabbed a neatly paper-clipped stack of documents and set them at the center of the blotter in front of him.

"What?" I asked.

"Colonel Jameson."

"The J-2." Schultz's boss. "What about him?"

"The octopus lady."

"Commander Ku?"

"Yeah. In all the excitement, I almost forgot."

"Forgot what?"

"She asked me if I knew him."

"Knew who?"

"Colonel Jameson."

I sat up in my chair. "A high-ranking North Korean agent asked if you knew Colonel Jameson? By name?"

Riley frowned. "That's what I just said."

"Why? In what context?"

"Said he likes octopus. Always buys from her." I noticed that my jaw had dropped open. Riley tossed the stack of documents back into his in-box. "Okay, it seemed weird to me too. But you know how these vendors are. They drop the name of a big-time colonel or a general, hoping to impress you so you'll buy whatever it is they're selling. In all the excitement, I forgot about it."

I sat there for a while in shock. The "octopus lady" had purposely relayed Jameson's name. She knew we'd notice. But why?

"Did she say anything else?"

"No. I thought about it all last night. That's all she said."

Now I knew what I had to do. When Ernie walked in the door, I stopped him before he could pilfer Riley's copy of *The Stars and Stripes*.

"Come on," I told him. "We have work to do."

"Could you have your team analyze another vehicle for me?"

"It's not normal procedure," Mr. Kill said.

We were in downtown Seoul at the KNP headquarters,

after having parked near our usual friendly *pindeidok* dealer.

"I know," I replied. "But our only forensic analysis team is in Camp Zama, Japan. The Provost Marshal would never authorize bringing them here on a hunch of mine."

Inspector Kill called in Officer Oh, who drew me a map of where to take the vehicle and told me when to bring it. We were scheduled for eight P.M. this evening.

When we picked up the green army sedan, we found another surprise. Beneath the front seat was a hatchet. Mr. Shin, Colonel Jameson's driver, told me he used it sometimes to hack ice off the car in the winter. I placed it in a plastic evidence bag and asked the KNPs to analyze that, too.

Strange wasn't happy. He didn't like me and Ernie showing up at his place of business.

"You're blowing my cover," he whispered through gritted teeth and iron bars. He worked in a heavily fortified cage in the center of 8th Army Headquarters. Not ten yards down the carpeted hallway was the mahogany entrance to the suite of offices that housed the 8th Army and US Forces Korea and United Nations Command Commanding General, a job originally held by Douglas MacArthur.

"What do you want?" he asked.

I told him.

"Not easy to get."

"I'll owe you."

"That you will." He grinned a hideous grin and waggled his cigarette holder.

Two days later, the report came back from the KNP forensic lab. I showed it to Ernie.

Miss Kim was back in the Admin Office. Nervous and undergoing therapy, both physical and psychological, but hanging in there. She had a brace around her right ankle where she'd damaged some tendons from kicking the hell out of Captain Blood. She was forced to use aluminum crutches to get around, but still wore a nice dress and a high heel on her left foot.

Ernie handed the report back to me. We knew what we had to do.

"He's on temporary duty back home," Ernie told me.

"When will he be back?"

"Tomorrow. The flight's due in at zero six hundred hours."

"We'll be there."

"I'll gas up the jeep."

The Military Airlift Command passenger terminal at Osan Air Force Base was Spartan. A small snack bar with hot coffee and a short order grill sat at one end of the building, an information counter and rows of benches filled the big central waiting room, and at the opposite end, arriving passengers came in and were inspected by both the US Air Force security personnel and a small contingent of bored-looking ROK customs officials.

He was carrying a briefcase, standing tall in his khaki uniform and smiling broadly when he emerged into the main lobby. Apparently he'd expected his driver, Mr. Shin, to be waiting for him. As full colonel and Commander of 8th United States Army J-2 Military Intelligence, Colonel Emmett S. Jameson was authorized a green army sedan and a full-time Korean civilian driver. But Mr. Shin had been ordered to stay home today; Ernie and I would be picking up Colonel Jameson. He'd been traveling on TDY, temporary duty orders to Fort Hood, Texas, for two reasons: to escort the body of Major Frederick Manfield Schultz home to his grieving wife and children, and also to attend intelligence briefings with the commander of Fort Hood and his staff. Strange told us that the briefings were mostly bullshit—authorized by the 8th Army Chief of Staff to provide an official reason for the travel, but actually intended to give Colonel Jameson enough time to make sure that Major Schultz was properly buried and that the needs of his surviving family were taken care of.

For whatever reason, the task didn't seem too onerous. Colonel Jameson was smiling and in good spirits even after a long military flight on a C-130 cargo plane. His smile disappeared when he saw us.

We wore our dress-green uniforms, and our CID badges were prominently displayed on our jacket pockets. Both of us were outfitted with web belts, holsters and Army-issue .45s.

"Colonel Jameson?" I said.

"You know who I am," he said. "Where's my driver?"

"We'll be escorting you back to Seoul," Ernie told him. "Please drop the briefcase and place your hands on this table."

"What's the matter with you two? Have you gone crazy?"

Ernie grabbed the colonel's arm and twisted him around. I yanked the briefcase away, and within seconds his hands were handcuffed behind his back. The Korean customs officials, the Air Force security officers and the few passengers loitering around the Arrival Gate went completely still.

I read him his rights.

"What's this all *about*?" he asked, moisture filling his eyes.

"You know what it's about," I said.

"I don't, *dammit*," he said, stamping his foot. And then he spit at me.

That did it. Ernie grabbed him and shoved him, face first, up against the cement-block wall. I wiped the saliva from my face.

Commander Ku, or "the octopus lady," as she was known to Riley, had purposely dropped a dime on Colonel Jameson. At first, I'd asked myself why. If he *was* on the North Koreans' payroll, as Captain Blood had been, they would've wanted to protect him and, after the 501st fiasco blew over, reestablish contact. They had to have a very good reason for throwing away such a well-placed turncoat. Then it dawned on me. In Commander Ku's eyes, Jameson had proven himself unreliable—he'd risked the entire operation by acting irrationally. The murder of Major Frederick Manfield Schultz had led to further scrutiny of the 501st, and Commander Ku believed Jameson had committed the deed for personal reasons; namely, his own relationship with Schultz's wife. Now the North Koreans wanted Jameson out of the way, prosecuted as a killer so he'd lose all credibility. But why not just cut him off, take him off their payroll quietly? Too volatile. He knew too much, and the situation could blow up if he turned against them. If, however, Colonel Jameson was proven to be a murderer, 8th Army wouldn't want to publicize it, and wouldn't want to compound the damage to their own prestige by admitting that he'd also worked for the North Koreans.

But it had also occurred to me that this could all be disinformation. Commander Ku might be trying to throw a monkey wrench into the smooth functioning of 8th Army headquarters by casting suspicion on our highest-ranking intel officer. That's why I'd asked Mr. Kill to help us prove Jameson's involvement in the murder one way or the other.

Ernie still held Colonel Jameson pressed up against the wall.

"What you did," Ernie told him, "is eliminate a rival.

You've been after Schultz's wife for years, and when you heard about the complaint he filed against Miss Jo, you figured this was your chance. You could eliminate him and make it look like she was the one who did it."

"You're *crazy*," Colonel Jameson sputtered.

"Not crazy," Ernie said. "The beauty of your plan was that you knew whoever looked into the murder would be suspicious of the Five Oh First after Schultz's inspection threw heat on them. And they'd see how volatile Captain Blood was. So you had two red herrings to throw us off."

"I'll hire a lawyer," he said, "and have you brought up on charges for defamation of a superior officer. I'll ruin your careers."

"Go ahead," Ernie told him. "There's not much to ruin. We also have a forensic report on your vehicle. And testimony from your driver, Mr. Shin, that you kept the keys that evening, and even though he drives you to all your official functions, you told him to take the night off. You picked up Major Schultz to go to the Eighth Army Officers Club together. But you never got there. Instead, you argued about his wife. He knew what was happening between you two, which is why he resorted to paying for a night with an Itaewon business girl. You had a hatchet under the driver's seat. Mr. Shin had it for protection, but also to get rid of ice in the middle of the winter. *You* used it on Major Schultz. You also used the ceremonial bayonet you keep behind your desk. Both of them were checked out by the KNPs and have traces of his blood type. And Mr. Shin says that the next day, when he realized that the sedan had been soiled and cleaned by someone, he was too afraid to mention it."

Colonel Jameson was silently bawling now. Ernie shoved him forward, but halfway out of the terminal, he dropped to his knees and started screaming, rolling his eyes and gnashing his teeth. "I didn't *want* to do it," he said. "He made me. Fred made me do it. He wouldn't leave her alone, even when he knew wc loved each other. He wouldn't leave her *alone*."

"His wife, you mean?" I asked.

Jameson stared at me with wide eyes. "Yes. She's the one who caused all this."

I didn't see it that way, but this was no place to argue. The crowd inside the terminal had backed away from the three of us as if we had the plague.

Ernie and I grabbed Colonel Jameson under the armpits and hoisted him to his feet. Outside the terminal, we threw him in the back of Ernie's new jeep. He tried to climb out, so we were forced to shackle the steering wheel chain to his handcuffs. All the way back to Seoul he leaned forward, rattling the chain, arms outstretched, like a penitent praying for forgiveness.

-38-

We still didn't know the whereabouts of Miss Jo. Nor did we know the identity of the two men who had helped her escape from us in Itaewon. This remained a mystery for just over a week after the arrest of Colonel Jameson. The prosecution was going smoothly. As promised, he'd hired a Stateside lawyer, and so far he hadn't said anything, which was smart of him. If more evidence couldn't be gathered, it was possible he'd get off with a lesser charge, like manslaughter, but that wasn't up to me and Ernie. We'd done what we could.

We'd also started the ball rolling on the possible exoneration of Staff Sergeant Hector Arenas and the other GIs who'd been railroaded by the 501st MI. All of the 501st-inspired prosecutions in the last few years were being quietly reviewed by the 8th Army JAG office. In addition, Sergeant Leon Jerrod, the 501st agent in Uijongbu, and some of the other operatives were under investigation. From what I'd heard, they were all sweating bullets.

▪ ▪ ▪

I moped around the office after duty hours, trying to work up the courage to call Leah Prevault. But what would I say to her? My situation hadn't changed. I was still in doubt as to what to do. And then the phone rang.

It was a female voice, one that I recognized: Miss Jo Kyong-ja, no longer on the KNP's most wanted list. "Ten P.M.," was all she said. "The Double Oh Seven Club. Come alone."

Then she hung up.

I felt a chill go through me. For a moment I considered not going, or at least having Ernie follow and watch my back, but in the end, I really didn't have much choice. If I ever wanted to figure out who had rescued Miss Jo and why, I had to be there. We'd exonerated her, so the danger in my going alone was somewhat limited.

When I arrived at the Double Oh Seven Club, I ordered a beer. I sat alone at a table for about twenty minutes, nursing it. GIs and business girls gyrated on the dance floor, a Korean rock band clanging behind them. Finally one of the business girls approached me.

"You want dance?"

"No, thank you," I said, trying to smile. "I don't dance."

"Then go to OB Beer hall. Drink one beer. When finish, go outside."

In a whiff of perfume, she left.

■ ■ ■

The OB Beer Hall was a stand-up bar just off a large bus stop, with counters and small round tables at elbow height. Waitresses in white bandanas brought mugs of OB draft to tired Korean businessmen who were reading newspapers and waiting for their municipal buses to pull up. I stood alone at a table and quaffed down a frosty mug of OB. I saw why they'd told me to come here. The entire front was wide open, the room well-lit, and from across the street, anyone standing in the darkness could see who was inside. When I finished my beer, I zipped up my jacket and walked out into the cool night air. A cab pulled up. In the back sat Miss Jo Kyong-ja, staring straight ahead. I opened the front passenger door and climbed in. The cabby zoomed off.

Neither one of us talked. Finally, the driver came to a stop in the Mapo area of Seoul, in front of a pool hall sitting atop a noodle shop. Miss Jo spoke.

"You pay," she said, and climbed out of the cab. After handing the fare and a small tip to the driver, I looked around. I didn't see her. I walked a few paces from the noodle shop and looked back into a narrow alley between buildings. She stood about ten yards in, huddled in her long coat. When I followed her into the darkness, she turned and started walking. Fast. We wound through alleyways and narrow pedestrian lanes for what seemed like twenty minutes. Finally, she stopped and pointed. "There," she said. "Go upstairs and wait."

"How long?" I asked.

But she didn't answer, instead just turning and hurrying off. I scanned the dark passageways. There didn't appear to be any danger yet, so I walked in the direction Miss Jo had pointed and climbed a rickety flight of wooden stairs. At the top was a door. I opened it and walked in without bothering to knock. A dim yellow light glowed into some sort of storage room beyond, reeking of mold and rust. I crossed the room and stared out of a dirty window. More buildings, more filthy apartments, more of the squalid life of Seoul.

A rat scurried behind a mattress leaning against the wall. In the towering storage cabinets sat cobwebbed items that I preferred not to touch. I waited. What was all this about? I thought I knew. I hoped I was right. But it was like when Ernie had climbed that watchtower at Camp Arrow. We hope for the best, but we might get the worst.

Finally, the door creaked open.

Behind it was the best thing I could've hoped for.

They'd heard about Miss Jo, she told me, and the murder of Major Schultz.

"We pay attention to everything going on at the Eighth United States Army."

"And also what's going on with me?" I asked.

She shrugged. "Our sources already knew that people more powerful than Miss Jo were involved. Possibly the Five Oh First and the agent known as Commander Ku."

"That's why you sent those two operatives to save Miss Jo," I said, "when we had arrested her in Itaewon?"

She nodded.

"Why was she so important to you?"

"Because we knew," she said, "if you turned Miss Jo over to the KNPs, even though Inspector Kill might have his doubts, accusing her and prosecuting her for the murder would be too convenient. The South Korean government would want the motive for the murder of an American officer to be nothing more than greed and personal revenge. They wouldn't want the American public to think his death might've been due to espionage."

"Because that might hurt the Pak Chung-hee regime's image in the West. And increase the call to bring our boys home."

"And cut off your generous American aid," she said.

Doctor Yong In-ja had once been chief of the Itaewon branch of the Yongsan District Public Health Service; she'd later been my very serious girlfriend and mother to our son, Il-yong. Moonlight filtered through the dirty window, illuminating her face. She looked beautiful. Ernie would've laughed at me for thinking so: She had a round head, wore round glasses and kept her straight black hair cut short. But she had flawless pale skin, and her broad smile lit up the world when she was happy. She was brilliant and, more importantly, dedicated to her cause. A cause that aimed to establish a third path in Korean government. Not Communism. Not authoritarian militarism, like the Pak Chung-hee dictatorship. But a way that was democratic and independent of foreign influence. Her contingent was well established and had roots all the way back to the resistance movements in South Cholla province during Japanese colonization. As such, both the North and the South Korean governments hated the group and, more often than not, killed its leaders on sight.

"Our contacts in the police department," she said, "told us that you visited Mokpo. It was discussed at our leadership counsel. Your presence in Mokpo made no sense. It didn't advance your investigation. They couldn't figure out why you'd come."

"But you knew."

"Yes," she replied. "I knew. It was dangerous, to me and to our son." She took a deep breath and continued. "We wanted Eighth Army to investigate the Schultz murder because we hoped you'd find the spies in your ranks."

"Your plan worked."

She stood and lifted the wooden crate upon which she was sitting, then placed it closer to me. She reached out and took my hand. "I am marked for death," she told me. "Only a revolution here in South Korea can change that. You and I can never marry." She paused, letting that sink in, and added, "That is our fate."

I nodded.

"Every time you search for me, it puts me in danger. You must promise." She squeezed my hand. "Don't ever try to find me again."

"It's difficult," I answered, stricken.

"Yes. But you understand why."

"I understand. That pain I can bear. What I can't bear is not seeing our son."

"I know that." Then she called out something in Korean. I was so confused by then that I didn't realize what was happening. The door opened. The two Korean men who'd dropped from the roof in Itaewon were standing outside.

Big guys. Tough. But they didn't enter. Instead, one of them waved his hand and a very small person walked through the door. He hurried to his mother's side. Through the skylight above, a moonbeam shone on his face. My son. Il-yong. The First Dragon.

-40-

I told no one except Leah Prevault, who held my hands tightly the entire time.

"So you don't expect to see him again?"

I shook my head sadly. "Not until South Korea is a free country, not just free in name only."

"And you agreed with her, that it's best that he stays with his mother?"

"I agreed." For a moment the pain of not seeing my son again—intertwined, I suppose, with the pain of my own mother dying when I was young—almost overwhelmed me. Leah realized it, gave me a moment and then hugged me.

"You're a brave man, George Sueño."

"Not brave," I said.

She smiled and said, "Then how would you describe yourself?"

"Trapped," I said.

"Why so?"

"Because my son's mother can't step out in the light of day."

She paused for a moment, working up her courage, then asked, "Would you marry her, if you could?"

"She and I are beyond that now. Too much has happened. Besides, I don't think *she* would marry *me*."

"Why not?"

"She's completely dedicated to her cause. An American husband would just get in her way."

Leah sat quietly for a moment. "But if you put in marriage paperwork with her, wouldn't the government leave her alone?"

"No chance. Marriage between a GI and a Korean woman requires a security check, conducted by the ROK's Central Intelligence Agency. If a woman is found to be a Communist, they deny her permission to marry, as well as permission to leave the country. And probably locate and arrest her."

"But she's not a Communist."

"No, not technically. But right now, if you believe in trade unions and autonomy for an entire province, the Pak Chung-hee government sees no difference between you and a North Korean."

"So there's no way out for you two?"

"No. Even if we wanted to, marriage wouldn't be allowed. The arrangement I'd want is some sort of shared custody of Il-yong. Then I could apply to get him a dependent ID card and healthcare on the base. Things like that."

"And see him occasionally."

I nodded.

"But you can't," she said.

I shook my head.

"So what will you do?"

I stared into her big green eyes. They betrayed her wisdom and kindness. "Stay here in Korea," I said, "keep extending my tour as long as I can. Try not to let my feelings bounce around so much that they kill me."

"What's he like," she asked, "your son?"

"To American eyes, he looks Korean. But the Koreans can tell in an instant that he's ethnically mixed. He's just a little too big, his hair's light brown, and his facial features—the eyes, the nose, the cheeks—are different from the pure race. Softer, maybe, on the cheekbones. More pronounced on the eyes and nose."

"Koreans view themselves as a pure race?"

"Very much so. Which is one of the reasons that half-American children have such a hard time growing up here. But more important than that is the fact that most of the half-American kids in Korea grow up abandoned by their fathers. This is much more of a stigma than any genetic difference. Koreans believe that children should live with their father. Who you are, who your ancestors are, and what you're likely to be able to accomplish in this life, is all defined by your patrilineal ancestry."

"Ancestral worship," she said.

"Ancestral reverence," I corrected her.

"But if you don't have ancestors you can point to because you don't live with your father . . ."

"Then you're nothing."

She tightened her grip on my hand. "Your son, he won't be nothing."

"How do you know?"

"Because he'll be like you."

Continue reading for a preview from the next
Sueño and Bascom mystery

THE NINE-TAILED FOX

-1-

Brigadier General Hubert N. Frankenton, Chief of Staff of the 8th United States Army, frowned as he stared at a wall-sized map of the Korean Peninsula. After pondering it for a minute, he slapped his pointer at a red dot and said, "The first soldier disappeared here, from Camp Kyle near Uijongbu." He turned toward his aide, a captain, and asked, "What was his name?"

She checked her notes. "Werkowski." She then recited his rank and unit as everyone at the conference table dutifully scribbled it down.

"Quartermaster unit," the Chief of Staff murmured, as if to himself. "The next disappearance," he continued, "happened here, at a supply-and-maintenance outfit of the Nineteenth Support Group."

He pointed to an area closer to the Yellow Sea: a compound known as ASCOM, the Army Support Command near Bupyong.

"And the most recent disappearance happened way the

hell down south in the village just outside of Hialeah Compound, near Pusan." The largest port city in South Korea, about two hundred miles from Seoul.

The Chief of Staff pulled up his khaki pants and paced the room. The only person with the bravery—or rank—to venture a comment was my boss, Colonel Walter P. Brace, Provost Marshal of the 8th United States Army.

"These disappearances," Colonel Brace said, clearing his throat and lowering the timbre of his voice, "might not be related, sir. It's possible these fellows have gone AWOL and will turn up eventually, drunk and broke and begging to be taken back."

General Frankenton nodded his head, still pacing, his hands clasped behind his back.

"It's possible, Walt," he agreed. "I hope that's what happened. But none of the facts in these cases jibe with your typical AWOL. None of the soldiers involved took anything with them. Their overnight bags were found in their lockers. Only one of them disappeared just after end-of-month payday, when most soldiers go AWOL. According to Data Processing, none of them have used their ration control plates to buy anything out of the PX since they left, which they would normally do in order to raise a little money on the black market." He waved his pointer in a circle in the air as if it were a divining rod. "And most importantly, the shrinks tell me none of the missing men appeared to be under any particular stress from personal problems or an important upcoming inspection. In fact, in all three cases, these men's commanders couldn't say enough good things about them. Ideal troops, they were called. Reliable and dedicated to their units. Top soldiers. And yet they disappeared without a trace, and apparently with no advance planning."

The general sat down heavily at the head of the table. "And I don't need to tell you," he said with a sigh, "that we're catching holy hell from their families and their congressmen back home."

After a respectful silence, one of the officers ventured an inquiry. "Do we suspect North Korean activity?"

General Frankenton winced.

In the more than twenty years since the Korean War, the warring nation had been divided along the DMZ; the Communist North Korean regime on one side and the authoritarian Pak Chung-hee military regime on the other. Just thirty miles north of Seoul, 700,000 Red soldiers waited impatiently for the order to invade, just as they did in 1950. On the southern side, 450,000 Republic of Korea soldiers stood guard, resolutely prepared to repel any foolhardy aggression. Meanwhile, North Korean commando units made the occasional clandestine foray into South Korea, spreading death to the unwary, and spy activity was a regular feature of life in this intense corner of the Cold War.

The Chief of Staff pondered the question about North Korea, lacing his fingers in front of his belly. "It's always possible," he said. "But North Korean spies usually go after well-thought-out targets. Ones with access to classified information, most often. These three fellows, while good soldiers, worked in nothing of a sensitive nature and had no hand in anything the Communists are likely to want."

The officers lining the mahogany conference table grew quiet. The Chief of Staff stood again and paced the length of the room, though his highly polished low quarters made no sound on the plush wall-to-wall carpet.

My name is George Sueño. I'm an agent for the Criminal Investigation Division of the 8th United States Army, stationed at 8th Army headquarters in Seoul. My investigative partner Ernie Bascom and I sat in two straight-backed chairs against the outer wall of the conference room. Why we'd been ordered to stand by, I wasn't quite sure. These classified briefings were usually for brass only, not lower-level enlisted scum like us. Ernie was more nervous than I was. He avoided headquarters when he could, and suspected that we were about to be railroaded into something we wouldn't like.

The Chief of Staff stopped pacing and seemed to jump out of his reverie. His eyes searched the room and eventually focused on me.

"Agent Sueño," he said, pronouncing my name correctly, with the "ñ" like the "ny" in "canyon."

"Yes, sir," I said, sitting up straighter.

"You know the ville," he stated—the GI villages, red-light

districts packed with bars and nightclubs and whore-houses, that sat outside each of the over fifty US military compounds in South Korea. "Very well, from what your boss tells me." He glanced over at Colonel Brace. "What do you think would make young troopers like these disappear without a trace?"

All heads at the conference table turned to stare at me. Ernie fidgeted in his seat.

"A woman," I replied.

The conference room broke into laughter. Smiling, the Chief of Staff turned away. After the laughter died down, he turned back to me and said, "I think you're right. I think that should be the first avenue of approach. I'm told you and your partner here, Agent Bascom, are both pretty good at blending in out in the ville."

Ernie clicked his ginseng gum but didn't answer.

"We manage, sir," I replied.

"More than manage," the Chief of Staff said. "You can speak, read, and write Korean, and your partner here seems to have a knack for communing with the underclass of whatever group you encounter. That's why I invited you two here." He hiked up his pants again. "From what I'm told, you're the two best damn investigators we have in-country."

I didn't answer.

The conference room had gone deathly silent, every head still turned toward us. Some of them with blank, wide-eyed stares, waiting greedily for me to make a fool of myself. Others with frowns, annoyance that someone so low in the hierarchy should be anointed with the Chief of Staff's attention. There are few things officers hate more than enlisted men being praised above them, and on the rare occasion when it happens, they plot their revenge carefully. I was more than just comic relief. I was a pig being fattened for a luau.

Oblivious to the pique bubbling about him, the Chief of Staff swiveled to study the map, then turned abruptly back to me. "Given what we know so far, Agent Sueño, where would you start your investigation?"

"Pusan," I said without hesitation.

"Why?"

"The disappearance from Hialeah Compound was the most recent, sir. Just two days ago. We're most likely to find people there who saw something and, more importantly, still remember what they saw."

The Chief of Staff nodded. "How much time do you need to get down there?" he asked.

"If you give us a chopper," I told him, "we can leave now."

He grinned slightly at the answer, then said, "Better change out of those monkey suits," nodding at our dress-green uniforms.

"Yes, sir."

He turned to his assistant, the female captain. "Call the One-Oh-Five Aviation Unit and schedule these two men a chopper. I want them in Pusan before noon chow."

"Yes, sir," she said, rising to her feet. A nice-looking woman with reddish-brown hair knotted tightly atop her head and a name tag that said RETZLEFF. "Come with me."

Ernie and I followed her out of the conference room. Without being told, another of the officers had stood and was handing out sheaves of paperwork. Each thin stack was topped with a light blue cover sheet stamped TOP SECRET.

All the eyes that had been studying us before now completely ignored us. Behind us, the door shut silently.

In Captain Retzleff's office, we were issued for official use only reports that had been generated by 8th Army Personnel, containing the backgrounds of the three missing GIs as well as the MP blotter reports of their disappearances. She lifted her telephone.

"How soon can you be at the helipad?" she asked.

"Thirty minutes," I told her.

She started to dial. After a brief conversation, she hung up the phone and turned to us. "General Frankenton may seem calm, but in reality, he's very upset. Soldiers don't just disappear like this. Not in his command."

"Not until now," Ernie said.

Her eyes narrowed. "Everyone says you're a wise guy, Bascom."

"Everyone's right," Ernie replied.

"The only question is," she continued, "can you find the three missing men?"

"If anybody can find them, me and my partner can."

Generous lips turned up in a half-smile. "Do you agree?"

"Guaranteed," I replied.

"You two are pretty cocksure of yourselves, aren't you?"

"We haven't failed yet," Ernie said, exaggerating perhaps a tad.

The grin faded, and Captain Retzleff paused. In the end, she decided to say nothing except: "You're dismissed." She turned her back on us and strode toward the conference room. As he watched her leave, Ernie clicked his ginseng gum more rapidly than usual.

We exited through the main doors and hurried toward the jeep.

"Why'd you mess with her?" I asked.

Ernie shrugged. "Those officers in the conference room were laughing at us. I wanted to show her that we couldn't be pushed around. Besides, I wanted to spend more time looking at her."

"You're going to get your low-ranking butt in trouble one of these days."

"She'd be worth it."

Fraternization between officers and enlisted personnel was a court-martial offense—a fact that I knew only too well, given my most recent relationship with military psychiatrist Leah Prevault. Ernie hopped into the jeep and switched on the ignition. I slid into the passenger seat.

"Colonel Brace ain't going to like it," Ernie said, "having the Chief of Staff assign two of his men to an investigation."

"Why not?"

Ernie turned and studied me. "Are you *dingy dingy*? It makes him look incompetent, like the Chief of Staff has to reach down and do his job for him."

I shrugged. "I think you're making too much of it."

"You'll see." He backed the jeep out of its parking spot. Then he asked, "Why'd you pick Pusan? That bit about finding witnesses to the last disappearance was a bunch of bull."

"Simple," I told him. "Pusan is farthest from the flagpole."

As we drove past the two-story brick 8th Army headquarters building, off to our left sat a seventy-five-millimeter howitzer used for ceremonial purposes and three flagpoles with the banners of the United States, the Republic of Korea, and the United Nations Command waving against an overcast backdrop.

"You should've asked for per diem," Ernie said.

"I can't think of *everything*. Why didn't you speak up?"

"Too many honchos."

"You afraid?" I asked.

"Very. Afraid I'll strangle one of them." Ernie's fingers tightened on the steering wheel. "We've got to find these guys."

"Why?"

"To prove we're not the bozos the brass thinks we are."

We drove to the barracks. Twenty minutes later, in our running-the-ville outfits—blue jeans, sneakers, sports shirts with a collar, and nylon jackets with fire-breathing dragons embroidered on the back—we were on our way to the 105th Aviation Unit helipad. The chopper was already there when we arrived, engine whining, enormous metal blades swirling in an ever-accelerating gyre.

We climbed aboard.

The crew chief shouted something I couldn't hear, fitted headsets over our ears, and strapped us into the canvas seats. When he was satisfied that we were secure, he slid the large metal door shut and said something into the small mic in front of his mouth. The blades above revved faster, the chopper shuddered, and with a great, whooshing insult to gravity, the giant whirlybird lifted into an endless gray sky.

Seichō Matsumoto
(Japan)
Inspector Imanishi
Investigates

Magdalen Nabb
(Italy)
Death of an Englishman
Death of a Dutchman
Death in Springtime
Death in Autumn
The Marshal and
the Murderer
The Marshal and
the Madwoman
The Marshal's Own Case
The Marshal Makes
His Report
The Marshal
at the Villa Torrini
Property of Blood
Some Bitter Taste
The Innocent
Vita Nuova
The Monster of Florence

Fuminori Nakamura
(Japan)
The Thief
Evil and the Mask
Last Winter, We Parted
The Kingdom
The Boy in the Earth

Stuart Neville
(Northern Ireland)
The Ghosts of Belfast
Collusion
Stolen Souls
The Final Silence
Those We Left Behind
So Say the Fallen

(Dublin)
Ratlines

Rebecca Pawel
(1930s Spain)
Death of a Nationalist
Law of Return
The Watcher in the Pine
The Summer Snow

Kwei Quartey
(Ghana)
Murder at Cape
Three Points
Gold of Our Fathers
Death by His Grace

Qiu Xiaolong
(China)
Death of a Red Heroine
A Loyal Character Dancer
When Red Is Black

John Straley
(Alaska)
The Woman Who
Married a Bear
The Curious Eat Themselves
The Big Both Ways
Cold Storage, Alaska

Akimitsu Takagi
(Japan)
The Tattoo Murder Case
Honeymoon to Nowhere
The Informer

Helene Tursten
(Sweden)
Detective Inspector Huss
The Torso
The Glass Devil
Night Rounds
The Golden Calf
The Fire Dance
The Beige Man
The Treacherous Net
Who Watcheth
Protected by the Shadows

Janwillem van de
Wetering
(Holland)
Outsider in Amsterdam
Tumbleweed
The Corpse on the Dike
Death of a Hawker
The Japanese Corpse
The Blond Baboon
The Maine Massacre
The Mind-Murders
The Streetbird
The Rattle-Rat
Hard Rain
Just a Corpse at Twilight
Hollow-Eyed Angel
The Perfidious Parrot
The Sergeant's Cat:
Collected Stories

Timothy Williams
(Guadeloupe)
Another Sun
The Honest Folk
of Guadeloupe

(Italy)
Converging Parallels
The Puppeteer
Persona Non Grata
Black August
Big Italy
The Second Day
of the Renaissance

Jacqueline Winspear
(1920s England)
Maisie Dobbs
Birds of a Feather